T0194080

JOHN

John the Youngest—John the Oldest

JOHN MENCH

WESTBOW
PRESS®
A DIVISION OF THOMAS NELSON
& ZONDERVAN

WestBow Press books may be ordered through booksellers or by contacting:

WestBow Press
A Division of Thomas Nelson & Zondervan
1663 Liberty Drive
Bloomington, IN 47403
www.westbowpress.com
1 (866) 928-1240

ISBN: 978-1-9736-4073-8 (sc)
ISBN: 978-1-9736-4074-5 (hc)
ISBN: 978-1-9736-4075-2 (e)

Library of Congress Control Number: 2018911394

Print information available on the last page.

WestBow Press rev. date: 09/24/2018

DEDICATION

Dedicated to my wife, Rose, who for thirty-four years, focused our lives around Jesus' message and to my second wife, Ann, who encouraged me for the last twenty years. Her illness provided me with the time to write and her love of life encouraged me to tell my stories. God's grace to both of you.

CONTENTS

Acknowledgement

To my friends who after reading my book gave me critical guidance and loving care.

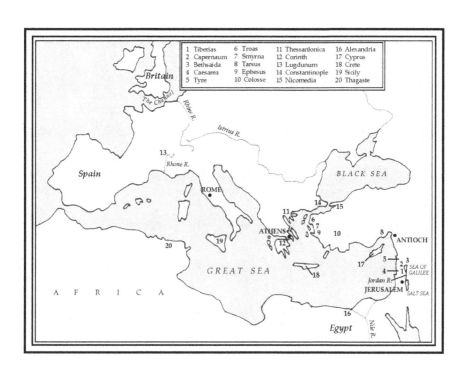

1 Tiberias	6 Troas	11 Thessanlonica	16 Alexandria
2 Capernaum	7 Smyrna	12 Corinth	17 Cyprus
3 Bethsaida	8 Tarsus	13 Lugdunum	18 Crete
4 Caesarea	9 Ephesus	14 Constantinople	19 Sicily
5 Tyre	10 Colosse	15 Nicomedia	20 Thagaste

Britain

The Channel

Rhine R.

Istrius R.

13

Rhone R.

Spain

BLACK SEA

ROME

11

14

15

6

7

ATHENS

9

10

8

ANTIOCH

12

17

5

3

SEA OF
GALILEE

20

19

2

4

1

GREAT SEA

18

Jordan R.

JERUSALEM

SALT SEA

A   F   R   I   C   A

16

Egypt

Nile R.

INTRODUCTION

The Foundation of Christianity

In an effort to stimulate your imagination, I have written a series of books concerning the formation of the Christian Church.

Our understanding of Christianity might have been formed when we attended Sunday school. Hopefully what we learned was based on the principles of the Bible. The Bible's New Testament provides us with a disjointed series of stories about Jesus. The stories are incomplete, and have caused me to be concerned about the incidents not preserved in history. Some will say they are a figment of my imagination.

After reading my books, I encourage you to form and record your imagination.

My series of books was written as fiction related to history. In my opinion, history concerning any specific topic of ancient times is fiction. The amount of written history that is accurate is pure speculation. The amount of fiction that is contained in written history is based on several items:

1. elapsed time (from event to now)
2. government influence (the winners of war write history)
3. greed (writing to make money)
4. perspective (being human)

When you read a history book, you are reading a written perspective that has been deemed acceptable by your generation and your environment. Most history books are the perspective of well rewarded victors.

JOHN THE YOUNGEST – JOHN THE OLDEST

When I joined the church, I had to recite a verse from the Bible. I chose John 3:16. I liked the message. When I was young, I probably liked John because my name is John. Now I like John because, as an old writer, he chose to deify Jesus.

John was a son of Zebedee. The family lived on the north shore of the Sea of Galilee. He and his brother James were friends of Jonah's sons Peter and Andrew. Both families made their livings as fishermen. Peter and his family worked as fishermen on someone else's boat. John and his family owned their own boats and employed people to help them fish. They owned a large piece of land and owned many servants. The families lived different lifestyles, but their sons became interested in the same itinerant preacher.

At a very young age, John, as a result of his brother's urging, decided to travel with the preacher. He didn't know anything about the preacher, but he knew he didn't want to work in the family business for the remainder of his life. He wanted to be involved with the Jewish religion like his brother James.

When John was twelve, he joined James and they traveled with John the Baptist and then with Jesus. He was Jesus' youngest disciple. After Jesus was killed, he and James became very involved with the early church. After the Jewish nation rebelled against the Romans, the Jewish nation and their temple in Jerusalem were destroyed. Many of Jesus' disciples were never heard from again. John was the exception; he was captured by the Romans. After many years in Rome, he was exiled to Patmos. Two years later, he was freed and spent the remainder of his life in Ephesus.

This is his story.

CHAPTER 1

IN THE BEGINNING

The north end of the Sea of Galilee was a beautiful area. It was home to many fishermen. Zebedee and Salome lived in Capernaum and recently moved to Bethsaida. They were happily married for many years. Zebedee decided to move because Capernaum became crowded with fishermen. They had two sons and a daughter, and their family was about to get larger. Zebedee was a successful fisherman and enjoyed his work. Salome missed the larger shops in Capernaum, but she loved their new home. She especially liked living close to the sea. They were close enough to Bethsaida to walk to town, which they did several times a week. It was early evening; the sun reflected as a red ball on the water. Zebedee, Salome, and the family finished dinner and walked outside. While they sat on the porch, they enjoyed the sea view and the breeze.

"Zebedee, it won't be long now," Salome said. "I think my time is approaching. Make certain Sara, my attendant, is ready to help me. I think I need her now."

Everything was prepared for her birthing. Zebedee took Salome by the hand and led her to the bedroom. He quickly found Sara and asked her to look after Salome. Then he started heating water. Zebedee and Sara were veterans of childbirth; they had helped Salome with the births of her other children. Sara just completed scrubbing, before it was time for the baby to arrive.

"It is a boy," Sara said. "I believe your husband was hoping for a boy."

"Yes, he wanted a boy," Salome said. "He plans to name him John."

"That is a good name," she said. "He is a little fellow."

Sara swaddled the baby, and she held him for Salome to see.

"This is it. I am finished, no more children for me," Salome said. "I hope Zebedee is happy with the size of our family. We are going to have to increase the size of our house."

They heard a loud crying voice. It was John, and they soon realized that they would hear a lot from him.

"Are you all right?" Zebedee asked. "We have a little baby boy. I was hoping for a boy. I can always use more help with the business."

"I am fine," Salome said. "Sara was a big help. Go look after your business. Sara will take care of us. If she needs help, she will use the servants."

Zebedee owned a large piece of property adjacent to the sea. After John's birth, he had several large rooms added to the house. Zebedee's family grew, and the family business grew. They enjoyed life.

A year elapsed. Zebedee, Salome, and the family sat in the living area of their home and discussed John.

"He sure is a loud one," Salome said. "I think we will hear a lot from him when he is older."

"I hear a lot of him now," Zebedee said. "My head hurts. I think I will go for a walk."

"He is more active and into more things than our other children," she said. "Zebedee, I think you should hire a helper for Sara."

"I couldn't hear you," he said. "I'm going for a walk."

"Listen to me," she said. "I need more help."

"I heard you," he said. "You want more help."

"I want more help, so we can do a better job for you," Salome said. "You and the children require many helpers."

"If you hire one that knows how to clean fish, I might use her when she isn't busy," Zebedee said.

"She will know how to clean fish," she said. "We always clean the fish you give us."

"You know that we clean the fish before you get them," Zebedee queried. "Why do you clean them again?"

"Because we all want them really clean before we cook them," Salome said. "Cleaning a fish to sell is different from cleaning a fish to eat."

He rubbed his hands together for a moment. He thought the fish were very clean when he gave them to Salome.

"Do you think our other customers clean the fish again before they eat it?" he asked. "Sometimes we grill fish at the lake before we bring the other fish to you."

"When you cook at the sea, you probably eat burned wood and sand," Salome said. "We just feed you fish."

"So, you want more help," Zebedee said. "I will have a few young women come to see you. You and Sara can pick the one you want to assist you."

"Thank you, dear," she said. "Are the servants' quarters large enough?"

Zebedee wondered how much Sara had been talking to Salome. He had an uneasy feeling. He sensed she had another request.

"I don't know. I will ask," he said and turned to her Sara. "Sara, do we have adequate quarters for another servant?"

"They need more rooms," she said. "They didn't want to complain."

Zebedee was thrilled about his new son and decided this wasn't the time to be difficult. Someday, he would probably want something.

He paused a moment and then he answered, "I will have another house built for us on the other side of the property. The builder will check with you about the size of house we need."

"We have plenty of room in the main house since the addition was completed," Salome said. "I'm certain the help will be very pleased with the additional space."

"I probably should have enlarged this house sooner," he said. "When you need something, you should tell me."

"We will be fine," Salome said. "I love the addition."

Zebedee took her hand, "Would you like to go for a walk? Come with me, and we will look at the land next to the house that is set aside for servants. It isn't very far."

"Don't go so fast," Salome said. "That land isn't going anywhere."

"I think I will make it larger than the existing house," he said. "We might hire another servant someday."

"That is fine with me," she said. "Let's go back to our house."

3

They joined hands and walked very slowly as they returned to the main house.

They sat on the porch and enjoyed the warm, gentle sea breeze.

"I will be busy fishing for the next few days," Zebedee said. "I will be glad when Hezekiah is finished at the university. He can run this business, and I will have more time to grow the business."

"I will miss you," Salome said. "Hezekiah should be home next week. He should be able to help you."

"I am anticipating him being home," he said. "I am thinking of purchasing another boat."

"He has been studying how to run a business and keep accurate books for several years," she said. "I am sure he will like doing it for us."

"I will depend on him. I prefer work that is more hands on."

He kissed Salome on the forehead and ran his fingers through her long black hair.

Salome thought about having her son home each evening. She missed him while he was away studying. She looked at Zebedee and smiled.

"It will certainly be nice to have everyone here with us," Salome said. "How is James doing with learning the fishing business?"

"Good," he said. "James is a good fisherman, but I'm not sure he wants to be a fisherman."

"You can always hire fishermen," she said. "James can read and write. He could do anything he wants to do."

Zebedee didn't need two bookkeepers, so he visualized James as a fisherman. He took a deep breath of the clean, fresh sea air.

"I'm concerned that he might want to go to the university," Zebedee said.

"That would be good," she said. "He is very smart."

"It seems that I teach them how to fish, and they want to do something else," he said. "My father taught me how to fish, and I am a fisherman. I think it is this younger generation."

"I think you are correct," Salome said. "They don't want to be like their parents. They want to be unique individuals."

4

As the sun went down, a breeze blew, and it became cooler. He put his arm around Salome to keep her warm. Soon, they retired.

The next morning, the sun reflected from the sea, and the air was hot. After breakfast, they would choose a new helper. Salome and Sara interviewed several women. They wanted to find someone who complemented them, and who would become part of the household.

"Didn't you like that woman?" Salome asked. "Don't you think she can help us?"

"No, I didn't feel quite right with her," Sara said. "Before we make a choice, I think we should talk to a few more women."

"That is fine with me," she said. "We have many more women that are interested in working with us."

"I would rather do a little more work than hire someone who doesn't fit into our group of helpers," Sara said. "We are a good team."

They relaxed for a few moments and drank a cup of tea. They agreed on the next woman, so Salome hired her.

Zebedee continued to be successful, and he had the first barn built next to the main house. Another house for servants was under construction. Zebedee purchased an old boat, and he had it put on blocks in an area near the sea. He planned on rebuilding it. Hezekiah finished at the university and returned home.

One evening as Salome, Zebedee, and the family relaxed in the living area of the house, the subject of another boat surfaced.

"What are you going to do with that boat?" Salome asked. "You can only fish one boat at a time."

She pointed a slender finger toward the boat by the sea.

"Hezekiah and I are going to repair it," Zebedee said. "Our mate is going to run the fishing boat."

"Can a mate manage a boat?" she asked. "I thought a captain managed a boat."

"Repairing boats is going to be our second business," he said. "Fishing is number one. After the additional boat is repaired, I might keep it, or I might sell it. It depends on Hezekiah and James."

"Why would you keep it?" Salome asked. "That boat is an eyesore situated in our backyard."

Zebedee sensed Salome's concern and carefully chose his words. He realized the boat might be an eyesore now, but the extra money it would generate wouldn't be a problem.

"Now that we have plenty of help with the house," he said. "I am having a few small houses built on the other side of our property. Our long time employees will be living in them."

Salome stared at Zebedee.

"A few houses?" she asked. "I hire one helper, and you build a few houses."

"I am planning to hire a few more servants," Zebedee said. "I want to be certain they will remain with us. The Romans are building everywhere and hiring everyone who doesn't have a permanent job. I want to keep our trusted employees."

Salome understood Zebedee's reasoning, and she understood why he agreed, so quickly, to build an additional house for the servants.

"Mother, I think we can grow our business in that manner," Hezekiah said. "We can fish, and we can repair boats."

"Repair boats?" she asked. "How many boats are you going to repair? I don't like looking at one old boat."

"I am certain I can purchase old boats at a very reasonable price," Hezekiah said. "I will have to determine the best sources for the repair materials. We have plenty of land and many opportunities."

"Is that what they taught you at the university?" she asked. "What else did they teach you besides how to make a business larger? Did they teach you about people?"

"They taught me how to make existing businesses more profitable," he said. "If everyone benefits from the increase in size, large is better."

"How large of a business do you want?" she asked. "I hope you know what you are doing."

"If this works out as well as planned, it might be difficult to determine what father and I might venture into next," Hezekiah said. "One never knows. Someday, I might have sons who would like to work with us."

Salome looked at Hezekiah. Her big brown eyes lit up and her faced exhibited a great smile.

"They would be my grandsons," she said. "I like that idea. I guess that university gave you some good ideas."

Little John toddled around, bumping into everything. Salome decided to have James play with his brother.

"James, take time to play with John," Salome instructed. "John waits all day for you to finish work, so you have time to spend with him. It probably won't be long before he will be able to do some of your work."

"Do I have to play with him?" James asked. "I am doing manly work for father."

"You can stop worrying about being a man," she said. "Your father always found time to play with you and Hezekiah."

"That is right, James," Hezekiah said. "Father even took us fishing."

"Hezekiah, I am glad you have so many great ideas," she said. I hope they all work for us. I especially like the idea of being a grandmother."

"I will play with him," James said. "All he does is play with the tools."

"Make him a small boat," she said. "That will get him interested."

"That is a good idea," he said. "I'll find some wood."

"He will like a boat," Hezekiah said. "We like boats."

"Making a boat will give me an excuse to arrange the tools," James said. "I can find them, clean them, and put them where John can't find them."

"Keep them in the boat being repaired," Zebedee said. "Then you will know where they are located."

James looked at John.

"I hope he matures rapidly," he said. "I could use some help."

"Just remember, you were just like John," she said. "You lost many of your father's tools."

James glanced at his mother. He didn't remember losing any of his father's tools.

The boat repair business expanded so rapidly that James worked with his father most of the time. Hezekiah sold boats and stayed busy locating new boats to repair.

"Tomorrow, we will all be going to the synagogue," Zebedee said

"Salome, I will take John, so you and Sara can have time with the women instead of having to care for him."

When morning arrived, the sun's reflection from the sea was beautiful. The family prepared to go to the synagogue.

"Hurry, John, put on your clothes," Salome said. "We are going to the synagogue. Your father and James are going to watch you today."

"Good," John said. "I like spending time with you, but James and I will have great fun. He explains a lot of religious things to me that you don't read to me."

"Make sure you understand the lessons," she said. "The message shouldn't change with the teller."

"When we get home, I am going to have James show me the boat that is being repaired," John said. "When we are finished, we will be ready for dinner."

"That is nice, John," she said. "You and your brother will need to listen for Sara. When dinner is ready, she will call for you. Sara decides when dinner is ready. You will have to wait for her to call you."

Every Sabbath, the family went to the synagogue and prayed. After services, they returned home to rest. The food was prepared by the servants the prior day, and no work was performed on the Sabbath. Sara always ensured a light meal was available. After everyone was satiated, they took time to relax and reflect.

"Father, may I show John the boat we are working on?" James asked. "He wants to see what we do all day."

"Yes, James," Zebedee said. "Remember, no work today. Take a short walk to the boat and then take a walk along the sea. It will be good for you and John. You might even see your mother and me."

James excused himself and took John to the boat repair area.

"When you repair a boat, you must be very careful," he said. "You can't hurry when repairing a boat."

"I will be careful," John said. "I won't hurry."

"If you do something incorrectly, the boat might sink," James said. "We will replace all the boards over there."

He pointed to a few rotten boards in the hull of the boat. John hadn't thought about a boat sinking. He looked at James.

"Where do you get the wood?" John asked. "I have seen some wood in the barn. What kind of wood do you use?"

"Hezekiah purchases everything we need," he said. "Enoch, one of father's helpers, makes certain the wood is stored properly. He ensures we have the proper wood."

"So, Hezekiah and Enoch help you," he said. "I like to watch Enoch. He can do almost anything."

"Father is a good businessman, and Hezekiah is a fast learner," James said. "We have a good business. To make money repairing boats, you must to do a lot of things correctly."

"When can I start working for you?" John asked. "Am I big enough?"

"You have to have father's permission. It can be dangerous working on these old boats. I am sure you could watch and start learning."

James was not looking forward to being responsible for John.

Zebedee and Salome walked to the boat. John looked at Zebedee.

"Father, can I work on the old boats?" he asked. "I want to learn like James."

"I will talk with your mother," he said. "Tomorrow, I will inform you of our decision."

Salome heard John's question, and she knew Zebedee didn't think John was ready to start working on the boats.

After they walked along the sea, Zebedee and Salome returned to the house. They sat on the porch, held hands, and watched the sun disappear.

"Salome, John asked me if I would allow him to work with his brother," Zebedee said. "I don't want him hurt, but I don't want to stifle his enthusiasm."

"I think he is too young," she said. "Tell him he can watch from the porch this year, and next year he will be old enough to do small chores for the repair crew."

Zebedee smiled at Salome.

"That is a good idea," he said. "I will speak with him."

"I think that will keep him happy," she said.

The next morning after a hearty breakfast, Zebedee talked with John.

"We want you to watch for a year," Zebedee said. "You can learn a lot in a year. I will tell James you are going to start doing small jobs next year."

A frown appeared on John's young face.

"A year?" he asked. "That is a long time; do I have to wait a year?"

"Yes, you are too small," he said. "I don't want you to get injured."

"I will watch every day," John said. "I will learn a lot, and I will be a good helper. I wish I didn't have to wait so long, did you have to wait a year?"

"When I was young, I didn't repair boats," he said. "I think a year of watching and learning will help you. After you grow up, we will get a boat for you to repair."

"Thank you, father," he mumbled. "Watch for a whole year!"

John went outside and walked up and down the porch. He looked at the boat being repaired and a tear appeared in his eye.

"That was a wonderful breakfast mother," John said. "I have found a perfect location on the porch to watch the boats being repaired."

"You did? Show it to me," Salome said.

He walked to the center of the porch and pointed down.

"Ok, this will be your spot," she said and gave him a hug.

"From here, I can see everything being repaired on the boat except the back of it," John said. "I didn't know we had to do so much shaping of the wood."

"They refer to that end of a boat as the stern," she said.

John looked at her.

"I didn't think about the boats not being shaped like a house," he said. "I guess it is more difficult to repair a boat than it is to repair a house."

James heard John's comment and replied, "Yes, John, it is definitely more difficult to build a boat than it is to build a house."

They discussed how many skills John would have to learn to be a skilled boat repairman. John listened intently. He began to smile.

"Your father is a good carpenter," she said. "Your sister is a good cook."

"We are nearing completion of this boat," James said. "Soon, we will get another boat to repair."

"Good," John said. "Put it where I can see it."

"It seems everyone wants to use boats, but no one wants to repair them," James said. "That is good for us."

"Mother, where is Chava?" John asked. "I want to thank her."

Salome gave John a hug. He shivered and made funny noises.

After only two months, John couldn't endure staying on the porch any longer. His father was nowhere in sight, so he decided to visit James at the boat repair area.

"Hi, James," he said. "What are you doing?"

James was concentrating on his work and hadn't noticed that John had left the porch. When he heard John's voice, he was startled.

"No, John," he said. "The question is what are you doing? If you don't go back to the porch, I will have to tell father."

"Why would you tell him?" John asked. "I didn't do anything."

"Father instructed me to keep an eye on you," James said. "If someone tells him you were at the boat repair area, I will be in trouble."

"I won't tell him," he said. "I'll be a good boy."

"You must go back to the porch," he said.

John looked at the ground, pouted, and slowly walked back to the porch.

James felt bad for John and decided to visit with John when he needed to rest. He hoped that if he spent time with John, he would remain on the porch. He explained to John what was going to be repaired next. John seemed interested and asked many questions. Late in the afternoon, Chava and Salome approached John.

"Did you learn anything today?" Chava asked. "Are you having a good day?"

"I sure did. One thing I learned is that I better stay on the porch."

"I thought you knew that," Salome said. "Father made that clear to all of us."

"He told everyone?" he asked. "I didn't know that."

"We all want you to learn," she said. "And we want you to be safe. After you watch for a year, you should have a better understanding."

John looked at his mother, raised his foot, and kicked at the air.

"Thank you," he said. "I think I am beginning to understand. James visited with me several times today. He is going to explain what is to be repaired. That way I will know what is happening."

A few months passed. It was early in the morning, and the sun shone on the sea. When James went to the boat repair area, it was already warm. He heard his mother call for John. Salome instructed John to have a seat. She wanted to talk with him. John sat down and took another piece of bread.

"Did you enjoy your breakfast?" she asked. "James went to the boat."

John thought, 'I must be in trouble.' He looked at his mother.

"John, your father and I are going to visit Jerusalem," Salome said. "We are going to meet the new high priest. We will be gone for several days."

John realized he wasn't going to be punished. He looked at his mother and smiled.

"That sounds like fun, do you know him?" he asked.

"No," she said. "He is not from this area."

"I will miss you," he said. "Hurry back."

"I will miss you," she said. "I want you to listen to your brothers and sister. Chava will make sure everyone has plenty to eat."

"We need lots of soup and bread," John said. "I like hot bread and hot soup. Working on the old boat is difficult. It makes me hungry."

"Chava, while we are in Jerusalem, I want you to stay with Sara. Learn as much as you can," Salome said.

"Yes, mother," she said. "She has already taught me how to cook some of the meals and how to work with the servants. Sara is a great attendant, and I like her very much. Hurry back. We will miss you."

"I want to go with you," John said. "I'm not very large. I will be quiet."

"I am sorry, John, but you will have to remain at home," Salome said. "This celebration is just for adults. You have to be invited."

"Who invited you?" he asked. "They should have invited the entire family."

"Your father was invited," she said. "I am going with him."

"Just for adults," he said. "Someday, I will be an adult. Then I can say, 'Listen to your sister. Don't touch the tools. Wait for a year. You are not an adult!' I can't wait until I grow up."

John went to the porch and sat down in his chair. He stared intently at the sea and contemplated being a grown man.

CHAPTER 2

A Grand Celebration

Zebedee and Salome traveled to Jerusalem for the great celebration. It was crowded, noisy, and joyous. The celebration was held to honor Joseph Caiaphas. Valerius Gratus had appointed him the new high priest. Hundreds of faithful Jews attended. It was customary for all those men who could trace their family to Aaron to have received an invitation. Zebedee not only could trace his family to Aaron, he was a relative of the former high priest Anenel. Zebedee and Salome were proud of his family roots, and they enjoyed being invited to these celebrations. Over the years, Zebedee and Salome only visited Jerusalem for Passover, so they looked forward to any additional special celebrations held at the great temple. The celebration was in the great reception hall attached to the temple. Each table was set for ten guests. Zebedee found a few of his friends and quickly took a seat at the table with them. He hadn't seen many of them during the last year.

"If we didn't get a new high priest almost every year, I would only get to visit with you once a year," Jude says. "Since Ananus died, a new priest has been appointed almost every year."

"It is always good to see you," Zebedee said. "You are correct. I hope Joseph keeps the position for a long time."

"Did you have a good journey?" he asked. "We live much closer to Jerusalem than you."

He looked at Zebedee and smiled.

"Yes, it was fine," Salome said. "If you like eating dust and smelling horses."

"It wasn't that bad," Zebedee said. "We have a nice carriage."

"It is still a long trip," Jude said. "I am glad we don't have to travel that far."

"I think we need some firm, positive direction within our religion," Zebedee said. "Religion has become too political."

"It has to be political," Jude said. "We have to keep the Romans happy."

"I suppose you are correct," he said. "Someday, that may not be necessary."

"How is the fishing business?" Jude asked. "I heard you are doing quite well."

"It keeps food on the table," Zebedee replied. "My oldest son, Hezekiah, is running the business. I occasionally give him some assistance; otherwise, I just fish for fun or go to the synagogue."

"That sounds like a good setup," he said. "We have a daughter who we are trying to get married. Do you have any young sons?"

"We have a son who just returned from the university," Salome said. "He is a good looking young man."

"He is working with me," Zebedee said. "I think he knows a young lady in town."

Zebedee paused, and then very intently stared at Salome.

"How is your family?" Zebedee asked. "I see your son, Job, at the temple on Holidays."

"We are doing well," Jude said. "My wife is looking forward to marrying off our only daughter."

"Mothers are always planning weddings," he said. "I am sure Salome is quietly planning for Chava's wedding."

"My wife has been planning our daughter's wedding for more than a year," Jude said. "All we need is someone willing to marry her. Our son is working for a land owner. He manages one of his vineyards. How are your younger sons doing?"

"James is doing well," Salome relied. "He studies very diligently and speaks and writes Greek."

"He writes Greek?" he asked. "I thought he was a fisherman."

"John is our youngest son," Zebedee said. "He is learning how to repair boats."

"James is our youngest adult son," Salome said. "John is a child."

"I keep James busy building and repairing boats," he said. "Our youngest son is a good student of our religion, but I can't get him interested in learning to write."

"He doesn't have to be able to write Greek," Jude said. "The fish won't know the difference."

He looked at Zebedee and laughed.

"He is not as focused as James," he said. "If you are ever in our neighborhood, stop and visit. I will have my wife cook some fish, and we can have a glass of wine. I hope to see you soon."

Zebedee turned to his wife. He put his finger up to his lips and signaled her to be quiet. He mumbled an unintelligible sound. Zebedee thought, 'I like living in Bethsaida, but I miss my old friends from Capernaum. I hope Jude will visit us, but I don't want any of my sons marrying his daughter.' Another friend and his wife took the last seats at the table. Those who arrived later would have to sit at a different table.

"Hello, Zebedee," Aaron said. "How well do you know Joseph Caiaphas?"

"I don't know him very well," he said. "I understand he is very devout and will provide strong leadership for our faith."

"I hope so," Aaron said. "We need direction."

"He will probably be conservative, and he might be opposed to many of the new ideas," Zebedee said. "I hope he will stand up for us and won't allow the Romans to continue to tax us into submission."

"Me too," Jude said. "I pay too many taxes."

"We all pay too many taxes," Aaron said. "Good and bad don't change significantly. They have been well defined for us. That sure is a nice carriage you have. Where did you get it? We are still walkers."

Zebedee and Salome had one of their servants drive them to Jerusalem in their carriage. Their horse and carriage were in the stable. The servant found lodging, and he cared for the horse and carriage.

"I purchased it from a man who owns a stable in Bethsaida," Zebedee said. "We purchase feed for the horses from him. One day, when I was at the stable, I saw the carriage. I asked about it, and he sold it to me."

"They sell carriages in Bethsaida?" Aaron asked. "I wasn't aware that Bethsaida was that large of a town."

"My carriage was originally built for a Roman Army officer," he said. "After a few years, it was sold to a company in Tyre. That company rebuilds used military carriages for family use and distributes them through stables located in remote towns. I am too old to walk, and I really don't like riding a horse, so I purchased the carriage."

"I thought it was new," he said. "They did a very nice job."

"With the carriage, we can make the trip home to Jerusalem in two days," he said. "The family appreciates the carriage as much as I do. I consider it a good investment."

"I think the new high priest is coming our way," Jude said. "We need to talk with him."

When Joseph Caiaphas and his escort make the rounds of the tables, he stopped and talked with all the men. He considered it important to meet each family.

"Congratulations on being appointed high priest," Zebedee said. "I am a relative of Anenel, and I'm a faithful member of the synagogue in Bethsaida. We made the trip, so we could meet you. We wish you great success, good health, and a long tenure."

"Thank you," Joseph said. "I understand it is beautiful living on the Sea of Galilee. I hope to spend more time at the sea. Do you get to Jerusalem often?"

"We come for Passover every year," he said. "We love the city, but it is a long journey."

"I too love the city," Joseph said. "I wish there weren't so many Roman military soldiers visible all the time."

"So do all of us," he said. "I guess they protect us with soldiers and taxes."

"I really don't believe they need as many soldiers as are here," Joseph said. "I think it might frighten some of the people. Let me move on. I am trying to talk to everyone. If I can ever help you, send me a message."

Joseph was polite and kept moving. The Rabbi, who escorted Joseph, was already at the next table. He took names and noted all who were related to previous high priests. When necessary, the Rabbi would politely remind Joseph they had many people to greet.

"Salome, he seems like a nice fellow, did you like him?" Zebedee asked.

"Yes," she said. "The women who know him say he will make a good high priest. He is very active at the temple."

"Are you ready to go home?" Zebedee asked.

"Not yet, I want to see a few more of my friends," Salome said. "Relax and talk with Jude."

"It is a long ride," he said. "I'll have a glass of wine with him."

"I don't get to see my friends very often," she said. "They tell me they still don't have a shop like the one in Caesarea where you can purchase items from everywhere. I won't be very long."

After a few glasses of wine, Zebedee found Salome and talked to her. She said she wasn't ready to go home.

"Ok, but I am ready to go," he said. "I will check and make certain the carriage is ready. Remember, it is two long days."

"If we leave now or in the morning, it is two long days," she said. "I'll be ready to leave in a few moments. I told you, I won't be long."

"Yes, dear," he said. "I will be waiting."

Zebedee excused himself and left the ceremony. He walked slowly to the stable. His servant had combed the horse. He told the servant to have the stable hand hitch the horse to the wagon; they would be leaving in a few moments.

"Is the carriage ready?" Zebedee's servant asked. "As soon as Zebedee's wife is ready, we are going to start home."

"Yes, sir, I will get everything ready for you," the stable hand said. "I hope you found everything you needed for your master's horse."

Zebedee had given his servant some extra money. The stable hand expected to be paid a little extra. That extra money ensured good service.

"Thank you for the good job," he said. "Put this in your pocket."

Eventually, Salome made her way to the stable.

"I am ready to travel," she said. "I think I talked to all my friends."

Zebedee had thought about the shops in Jerusalem.

"Yes, dear," he said. "I am surprised someone has not opened a shop with a better selection of goods. If someone can arrange for a better selection of goods, they will make a fortune."

"Now, you want to talk about a shop," she said. "Jerusalem has many people. They need a good shop."

"Jerusalem is not on the Great Sea, but it is near major trading highways," he said. "I think I have everything packed."

"Here, pack this for me," she said. "It is my present from the celebration."

Salome handed Zebedee a small package.

"You got a present?" he asked. "I didn't get a present."

"The high priest's assistant gave every lady a present," she said. "He is a nice man."

"He will be politically correct," Zebedee said. "I can see it all now."

Salome looked directly at Zebedee, and she gave him a polite smile.

They boarded the carriage and headed north.

"I plan to stop at the Inn in Sychar," he said. "I told Abraham we would be staying with him on our return trip."

"That is nice, dear," she said. "I like the Inn at Sychar. They have good food."

Their servant was a good driver. They stopped on schedule and allowed Salome to stretch and walk.

"Look, dear, do you see all those people walking?" she asked. "They are going our way. Why don't you give some of them a ride?"

"We can't do that," he replied. "With all the things you purchased, the carriage is loaded to the maximum."

"I didn't purchase that much," she said. "We can make room."

"Not now," he said. "We need to make good time."

"Why would they slow us down?" she asked. "I feel sorry for them."

"The horse only has a certain amount of power," he said. "The walkers will join a caravan. They will be fine."

"I hope they find a caravan," she said. "I didn't think about the horse's power."

"When I was young, father's family would visit Jerusalem," he said. "I remember we would walk or ride a horse with my father. Back then, very few families had a carriage. Today, some families have two carriages."

Salome gave him a big smile.

"Are we close to Sychar?" she asked. "I need a drink of water."

"No, we just have a good start," he said. "I have some water and a few things for us to eat on the way. Our servant purchased the food from the stable boy."

"See, I knew you purchased something," she said. "I wasn't the only one."

She looked at Zebedee.

"If we keep moving, we will reach the inn today," he said. "Tomorrow, we will need to get an early start. Here, have some water. If you want some figs, look in the other package."

"Thank you for the water," she said. "You think of everything."

"It saves time," he said. "I don't like too many stops."

"It is hot. I am dusty, and the horse smells," she said wearily. "I can't wait to get to the inn for a warm bath."

"Our room has a tub," he said. "I told Abraham you wanted a wash tub."

"Why are these highways so dusty?" she asked. "I hope the boys are doing as we instructed."

"They put dirt between the rocks," he said. "The dirt holds the rocks in place."

"What did you say?" she asked. "They put dirt between what?"

"You wanted to know why the road was dusty," he said. "It is the dirt between the rocks."

"I wish we could have brought them along," she said. "They always enjoy visiting Jerusalem. Do you think they missed us?"

"They are fine," he said. "Hezekiah is looking after the fishing business. I instructed the two younger ones to help the foreman and the workers clean one of the boats. I hope our daughter helped with the cooking and cleaning."

"I am sure she is fine," she said. "I told her to manage the kitchen while we were away."

"Salome, did you see the new coins?" I collected a few with the likeness of Tiberius on them," he said. "He looks a lot different than Augustus. He isn't as muscular. I guess he will be on all the new Roman coins."

"No, I didn't notice," she said. "Those Roman emperors all look alike to me. Are we getting close to Sychar?"

"It is not far," he replied. "Are you ready to stop for the evening?"

"I am past ready," she said. "The older I get, the longer this trip seems. Remember, I want to wash before dinner. Don't rush me."

"Yes, dear," he said. "I'll have our servant take the horse to the stable. I think I will visit with the stable keeper. The horse will need a good rest tonight. Then, I will have a glass of wine with Abraham."

They arrived at the inn.

"Stable keeper," Zebedee said. "We will be staying overnight. Clean, feed, and water the horse. Then bed him."

"I'll help him," Zebedee's servant said. "I have a comb for the horse."

"I would like you to clean the carriage," Zebedee said. "My wife doesn't like the dust."

"Your man can take care of the horse," the stable keeper said. "I will clean the carriage."

"When it gets light, I want to get on the road," Zebedee said. "Make certain you prepare for an early departure, and I'll have something for you. If you need anything, you can check with our servant."

"Yes, sir," he said. "We have a lot of guests staying with us tonight. I will be very busy with the horses, but I will do just as you asked. I will see you early in the morning."

Zebedee departed his servant and the stable hand. He found Abraham. Abraham poured two glasses of wine.

"Abraham, it looks like your business is doing well," Zebedee said. "I guess a lot of people are traveling."

"Yes, whenever they have an event in Jerusalem, I get busy," he said. "I hear we have a new high priest. I wish he would do something about all the Roman taxes."

"We all pay taxes," Zebedee said. "They tax my business."

"They tax my inn and my shop," he said. "I think I pay more taxes every year."

"That is income for the government," he said. "It keeps us all safe."

He tipped his glass toward Abraham. They both took a sip.

"I am thinking of changing the name of my inn to The Oasis in Samaria," Abraham said. "What do you think?"

Zebedee took a large gulp of wine. It went down the wrong pipe, and he coughed.

"I like the old name. Get me a glass of your good wine," Zebedee said.

"Pour yourself a glass. I am waiting for my wife. When she gets cleaned, we will have dinner. Have you got anything special tonight?"

"Yes, I do," he said. "I have some fresh game birds. I also have fresh fruit, bread, goat's milk, cheese, and nuts. I am sure we will have something you and your wife will like."

Salome entered the room. She was clean and nicely dressed. Her black hair reflected the candle light. She didn't look like she had spent most of her day in a carriage on a dusty road. She greeted Abraham and extended her hand to Zebedee. Abraham seated them.

"I am very hungry," Salome said. "I hope they have a good soup tonight."

"You can have more than soup," Zebedee said. "I have ordered fresh game birds with all the trimming. I will bless our food, and then we can relax. I am sure you will enjoy dinner."

The dinner was as good as Abraham had promised. Salome relaxed, and Zebedee became sleepy. A few glasses of wine always made Zebedee sleepy.

"Abraham, that was a great meal," Salome said. "I always like staying with you when we travel. I am always a little uneasy when we travel through Samaria, but I feel comfortable and at ease when we stay at your inn."

"I am glad you are comfortable," he said. "We work hard to please our good customers."

"We are going to turn in early," Zebedee said. "Make sure we get an early breakfast. I told the stable hand we want to leave early. We will need some water, and I want some dried fruit to take with us. Make sure our servant has plenty to eat."

"It is always my pleasure," he said. "I will personally cook breakfast for you."

The next morning everything was ready for them. The horse was rested, and Zebedee's servant had combed him. The stable hand loaded their packages and even helped Salome into the carriage. Zebedee paid him and then gave him one of the new coins. He placed the coin in his mouth and bit down on it.

The red sun was only slightly above the horizon, when they started for home.

"Did you bring any water?" she asked. "I am getting thirsty."

"Yes, dear," he said. "Abraham got everything ready for us. We have plenty of water, and we have a supply of dried fruit and nuts. If you relax, the trip will seem shorter."

"What is that noise, did you hear it?" she asked. "I hear something."

"It is only a stick caught in the wheel," their servant said. "I will stop and remove it."

"Please, relax dear, you will feel much better," Zebedee said. "Our driver will take care of everything."

"I will try," she said. "I miss the children. It sure is a nice day. How long do you think it will take to get home?"

"We will be home before sundown," he said. "We are making good time. I think the horse likes your chatter."

"What did you say?" she asked. "Are you making fun of me?"

"No dear, I would never do that," he said. "I said the wheels go *clickety clatter*. Relax and enjoy the ride."

About half way home, they stopped at a grove of trees. They drank some water and rested in the shade. Their servant gave the horse a drink of water. Zebedee took a short walk, and when he returned, they started back on the highway.

"I can see the sea," he said. "When I see the sea, I know that I am almost home. It will be several more hours, but we are close to Capernaum. You should recognize the area."

"I too like looking at the sea," she said. "The breeze is refreshing."

"When the horse smells the sea, I think he can sense that we are close to home," Zebedee said. "He seems to step more lively."

"Are we going to stop in Capernaum so I can purchase some supplies?" she asked. "I don't get to our old shop very often."

"No, dear," he said. "Not this evening. We need to get home. I will have James get whatever you need."

"I like to shop in Capernaum," she said. "I think we should stop."

Zebedee told the driver to continue home. Salome didn't like Zebedee's answer, but she didn't say anything. In fact, she didn't say anything for the remainder of the ride home.

"It certainly is quiet and peaceful along the sea," Zebedee said. "We will be home before sundown."

The calmness of the sea put Zebedee to sleep.

When they arrived at the house, the servant awakened Zebedee, and he helped Salome out of the carriage.

"That was a long ride," Salome said. "I am glad to get home. I need to stretch for a while."

"Watch your step," Zebedee said.

"I am sure Sara and the house servants will have everything ready for us," she said. "Let Nicia take care of the horse. Come in and rest. You must be tired. I am glad we didn't have to drive."

As she started to walk, her legs wobbled slightly. She looked at Zebedee.

"Yes, dear," he said. "I will be right there. I am going to look at the boat that James and John cleaned while we were gone."

Zebedee took Salome's hand and started towards the house. Then he walked straight to the boat. It looked much better than Zebedee remembered. James was still at work. Zebedee watched as he cleaned and put the tools away.

"James is the boat ready to be sailed?" he asked. "You know your friend Peter's father is going to purchase it. He has always been fishing for someone else, but he is going into business for himself."

"Yes, father," he said. "We helped the workers complete some of the repairs. It looks like a nice boat. I am sure Peter and Andrew will like having a boat."

"You boys get cleaned. Get your younger brother, and come into the house. Then you can talk with your mother and me," he said. "We missed you."

"Ok, I will tell Enoch that we are finished for the day," James said. "I am sure he and his helper will work for another hour."

Eventually, everyone was at the dinner table. Zebedee blessed the food, and they ate. It wasn't as fancy as at the inn, but somehow home cooking was always the best.

"Sara, that looks like a fine meal," Salome said. "Did you have any problems while we were away?"

"No, Miss Salome," she said. "I want you to know that your daughter made the bread. We were all busy working."

"That is good," Salome said. "Make sure Zebedee gets plenty of bread."

"We fed all the workers fruit, soup, and bread for lunch everyday while you were gone," she said. "We kept up the normal routine."

When Zebedee and Salome were not home, they always made certain there was plenty of food available for everyone. They left careful instructions for all their servants and their children.

"Zebedee, did you hear that?" she asked. "Your daughter made the bread for dinner."

"That is nice, dear," he said. "I am glad she can make bread. Chava, I ate an extra piece of bread, and I liked it very much."

"Thank you, father," she said. "When I have time, I will make more bread."

"Father, tell us about the celebration you attended," John said. "Did you have to get all dressed up?"

"Yes, we got all dressed up," Zebedee answered. "The new high priest was introduced, and then he spoke for about thirty minutes. When he finished talking, he came to each table. We were eating bread and drinking goat's milk."

"Did you talk to him?" John asked. "I thought you would have wine."

"Wine was available with dinner," he said. "The hall was lighted with many candles, and every priest in Jerusalem must have been there to honor Joseph. I saw Gamaliel, and he had a few of his student Rabbis with him."

"I can't wait until I am old enough to attend the temple ceremonies," John said. "When will we get another new high priest?"

"I hope it will be a long time," he answered. "We have to keep this one healthy and content. You don't want to wish your life away. You will soon be a young man."

"John, eat your dinner before it gets cold," Zebedee said. "Warm food is good for you. Make sure you try your sister's bread. Everyone else is almost finished."

"Do I have to eat bread?" he asked. "Chava really made the bread?"

Everyone ate an extra piece of bread. Chava smiled as she helped clean the table.

The sun was low in the sky, and the sea was red with its reflection. Zebedee and Salome were home with their family. Life was good.

CHAPTER 3

LIFE IN BETHSAIDA – FISHING & REPAIRING BOATS

Zebedee was an important man in the small town of Bethsaida. He was one of a few who owned their own fishing boat and employed people to fish for him on the Sea of Galilee. His crew fished six days a week. After they fished all day, they secured and cleaned the boat and the fish. They sold what they didn't consume to a market in town. When Zebedee began fishing, he employed a crew of two fishermen, and he, himself, handled the boat. Now, he worked part time, Samuel and his mate sailed the boat with three helpers. Zebedee also loved to look for and purchase old boats which his sons refurbished and resold for him. He employed two men who helped repair the boats. His three sons, Hezekiah, James, and John, all helped with the business. Hezekiah managed the daily operation of the enterprise for his father. James learned the boat repair business, and John tagged along with his older brother James. Zebedee's only daughter, Chava, learned how to manage the house and his wife, Salome, managed the family and large staff. They had several house servants and a stable hand. Salome's personal attendant was named Sara, and she was a faithful longtime employee. The house was situated, with easy access to the sea. The entire family enjoyed living at the sea.

As the family sat at the large dining room table, the food was served. Zebedee blessed the meal and then motioned to James.

"After dinner, I want to talk to you," he said. "I have an opportunity to purchase another boat."

Salome became accustomed to seeing a boat being repaired in her backyard. She had accepted the idea that boat repair was a good additional business for the family.

"Well, Sara, that was a mighty fine dinner," Zebedee said. "You have trained the staff well."

"Thank you," Sara said. "Chava was a big help."

"Salome, James and I are going to talk business," Zebedee said. "We might walk down by the sea."

He stood and stretched his legs. When he gained his balance, he and James walked outside.

"Careful, dear," Salome said. "Have a nice walk."

They walked to the sea.

"Today, when I was in town, a gentleman tried to sell me a boat," Zebedee said. When he approached me, I could tell he was quite old. His son stopped fishing and moved to a farm."

"How large is the boat?" James asked. "Is it in good shape?"

"Tomorrow, I will go to town and look at it," Zebedee said. "I hope you could go with me."

"Certainly, father," he said. "Do you know where the boat is located?"

"It is stored, under a tree, next to his house," he said. "If it is dry and rotten, it will require a considerable amount of work."

"I will have to inform the repair crew," James said. "They can work without me for one day."

"Just tell them I have given you another job for the day, and you will be absent," he said. "Once we see it, we may not want to purchase the boat."

"I will be ready in the morning," he said. "See you at breakfast."

Neither Zebedee nor James slept very well that night. The excitement of a new boat project kept them awake. Father and son projects united the family.

The next morning, while breakfast was being prepared, Zebedee walked to the stable and informed the stableman to prepare two horses.

As he returned to the house he noticed the sun's glimmer on the sea. The breeze felt good and smelled fresh.

"After I finish my breakfast, I will be ready to go," Zebedee said.

"Have you thought about how we are going to get the boat home?" James asked.

"Not yet," he said. "Before I make any plans, I want to see it."

They climbed up on to their horses and started to town. It was a short, enjoyable ride.

"I think that is his house," Zebedee said. "I see the boat. It is under a tree."

"Do you really think that is the boat?" James asked. "Let me secure the horses to the tree."

James walked around the boat. He pushed on a few of the boards in the hull and sniffed the wood.

"Father, this boat is in bad shape," he said. "You shouldn't have to pay very much for it."

If you can repair it, I will make him an offer," he said.

"It will take a lot of repairs," he said. "We will need to make some larger blocks to hold it."

"It is a large boat," he said. "It could make a fine fishing vessel."

"Good morning, Zebedee," Judah said. "I see you found my boat. I am willing to take almost any reasonable offer. It has been sitting under that tree for about a year."

Judah was an older, bald gentleman. He used a stick as a prop as he wobbled towards the boat. He turned to Zebedee.

"Make me an offer," he said.

Zebedee made Judah a low offer, and the boat was purchased. He paid him with silver coins. Judah never counted the money. He just went inside.

"Now you can determine the best way to get the boat home," Zebedee said.

James suddenly realized that getting the boat home was his problem.

"Father, I think we should take the boat and place it in the water," James said. "It will probably sink, but the boards will swell. Tomorrow, we can remove the water and tow it home with our other boat. I will bring extra oars, so we can row if it is necessary."

"Ok, let's get it into the water," he said. "I will see if we can get some help."

"I would help if I could," Judah hollered from his house. "If you need help, let me know."

Zebedee looked in the direction of the voice. He motioned at Judah. Judah found two neighbors who would work for pay. They helped push the boat to the water. Zebedee paid each of them a coin, and he thanked them for their assistance.

"It might sink," Judah said. "It hasn't been in the water for a while."

"We expect it to sink," James said. "I will bail the water out tomorrow."

"Ok, I hope you like it," he said. "It was a good boat for me."

Zebedee looked at James, and then they laughed. Zebedee wondered if he had made a mistake.

"Tomorrow, you, Samuel, and I will tow it home," he said. "Unfortunately, we will lose a day's catch of fish. I hope the boat is worth the investment."

Zebedee put his arm around James and hugged him. Then he pounded on the hull of the boat. He started walking toward the horses.

"This is already costing more than I planned," he said. "It is a good thing I like this boat."

When they returned home, Zebedee told Samuel and his helper that they wouldn't be fishing the next day. James knew it would be a major rebuild, but he was certain they were up to the task. When they sailed to where the boat was located, it was about half submerged and rested on the bottom. It took a while to bail the water from the boat. James tied the two boats together. As they headed home, they noticed water seeping into the old boat. The boat began to sink.

"I don't think we will make it all the way home," Samuel said. "Before we get the boat back to the house, we will have to stop several times to bail out the water."

"This is about what I expected," James said. "After we get her repaired, I think it will make a nice boat."

"I hope we can repair it," Samuel said. "This is going to be a major project."

James took off his sandals, climbed into the old boat, and bailed water. Soon, it began to float again. Samuel smiled at James.

"Good job," he said. "Put your sandals on, and let's go. Maybe we can make it home without any more stops."

They made two additional stops before they finally arrived home.

When they docked the boats at their home, they became excited. Samuel secured the fishing boat for the evening. James and the repair crew slid the new boat out of the water and secured it on the special large blocks they had built. James and his father didn't say anything. They just stared at the boat. Large smiles appeared on their faces. Zebedee put his arm around James' shoulders, and they walked toward the house. They lost a day of fishing, and an entire boat repair day with full crew, but they were certain the boat would be worth their sacrifices.

"We have to finish the boat for Jonas first," Zebedee said. "He and his sons are ready to start fishing with their own boat."

"We will finish it," James said. "It is almost complete."

"When do you think Jonas' boat will be ready for delivery?" Zebedee asked. "As soon as they take delivery of their boat, we will start working on the new boat."

"I think it will be ready in about three days," James replied. "You can send Jonas a message, and tell him to come and sail his boat home. You can tell him it will be ready next week."

"I think I will go and pick him up," Zebedee said. "I haven't been to Capernaum for a while. I may take your mother along. She likes to shop there."

A large smile appeared on James face as he said, "I heard her say something about wanting to stop on your way back from Jerusalem. I think she will be ready to do some shopping. She will probably fill the carriage with packages."

Zebedee looked at James, and they laughed.

"Yes, I am sure she will," Zebedee said. "The shops in Capernaum are nicer than those in Bethsaida."

"You might not have room for Jonas," he said. "Take some rope with you. You can tie her packages to the back of the carriage."

"Room for Jonas will be her limiting factor," he said.

Zebedee walked to the house and sat in his chair on the porch. He called for Salome, but she didn't appear. He called again.

"Yes, dear, what do you want?" Salome asked. "I heard you the first time you called."

"I am going to visit Jonas next week," Zebedee said. "I was wondering if you want to go along and do some shopping."

She stared at Zebedee, and then she shook her finger at him.

"You are going to allow me to shop in Capernaum!" she exclaimed. "I have made a very large list. Take a lot of money with you. You gave me plenty of time to create my shopping list. I have planned for this trip."

Zebedee realized he had made a costly mistake by not stopping on the way home from Jerusalem. The more he thought about it, the more he smiled.

"Yes, dear," he said. "You can shop while Jonas and I talk."

"You want to see Jonas, so I am allowed to shop," Salome said. "This is my lucky day."

She looked at Zebedee and tried not to laugh.

"I plan on bringing him home with us. He can get his boat and sail it back to Capernaum," he said. "He will stay with us over night. I hope the weather is good next week."

"I will go with you. You know I always like to shop," she said. "I will be ready to travel early in the morning."

Salome tried to think of everything she needed to purchase. She was familiar with the shops in Capernaum and knew many of the shopkeepers. She planned on having the carriage loaded with packages.

The next morning, Zebedee walked to the barn. He picked up a few pieces of the wood that were carefully stacked. He smelled the wood, and then he saw Nicia.

"Is the carriage ready?" he asked. "We will be finished with breakfast in a few moments."

"Yes, sir," he replied. "It is all ready for your trip."

31

Zebedee walked back to the house to tell Salome the carriage was ready.

"Zebedee, I love riding along the sea," she said. "It brings back many good memories. Just drop me off at the dry goods shop. When I am finished shopping, I will visit with my friends. We will be in the park."

"I haven't seen Jonas for a while," he said. "I hope everything is going well for him."

"When you are ready to return home," she said. "We can go to the shop and secure my packages to the carriage."

On their way to Capernaum, Zebedee and Salome enjoyed the ride along the sea. Salome moved closer to Zebedee. They traveled slowly, but time passed rapidly. He took Salome to the dry goods shop. Then he went to see Jonas.

The front door to Jonas' house was open. Zebedee entered the living area.

"Hello, Jonas," he called out. "Your boat is ready. If you aren't busy, you may return with us and sail it home."

Jonas exhibited a wrinkled forehead and slowly walked into the living room.

"I would like to do that, but when I told my boss that I was going to purchase my own boat, he told me he didn't need me and the boys any longer;" he said.

Zebedee was stunned. He hadn't anticipated any problems. He regained his composure and uttered, "He didn't give you any more work? That wasn't very nice of him."

"I didn't expect that," Jonas said. "We have been doing only day work for the last month. I don't have enough money to purchase the boat."

Zebedee was concerned about his friend and his family. Jonas looked at the floor.

"That is too bad," Zebedee said. "Are the boys working today?"

"Yes, they will be finished at noon," he replied. "They have steady work. It is only enough work for one person, so they go together and complete the job in half a day."

While they talked, Zebedee thought about what he should do. He decided that Jonas deserved the boat, and that he would catch plenty of fish to pay for it.

"When the boys get home, we will leave for Bethsaida," he said. "Other than only having day jobs, how are the boys doing?"

"Andrew is doing quite well," he said. "He can read, and he can write a little. Peter, on the other hand, can read, but he isn't interested in learning how to write.

He is quite good with his hands, and he is a great fisherman. Marriage is keeping him busy."

"Don't worry about paying for the boat," Zebedee says. "On days you catch a lot of fish, you can put some money away for me."

Jonas stopped looking at the floor. He looked at Zebedee and scratched his head.

"I don't know," he said. "I like to pay my bills."

"You can pay me something every month," he said. "You know I won't charge you interest. I want you to have a boat and be happy fishing."

Jonas was caught off guard by Zebedee's offer. He wanted to hug Zebedee but decided to verbally express his gratitude.

"That is very considerate of you," he said. "I will talk with my wife."

"Don't worry," he said. "You will catch plenty of fish."

Jonas found his wife in the kitchen. He explained Zebedee's offer. She was very pleased and told Jonas that Zebedee was just being a good friend. She wanted Jonas to have his own fishing boat. Jonas returned to Zebedee.

"Ok," he said. "Peter and I will return with you and your wife. My wife agrees that we will catch a lot of fish and pay for the boat within a year."

Jonas' sons returned home and saw Zebedee talking with their father.

"Peter, you remember Zebedee," he said. "We are going to go to Bethsaida with him to sail our boat home. Next week, we will be in the fishing business. Get some water, and we will get the carriage ready."

Peter surmised that his father had told Zebedee that they couldn't pay for the boat, but he was not certain what arrangements had been made. He didn't ask any questions.

They boarded Zebedee's carriage and went to the park. They didn't find Salome or her friends.

"I guess we should go to the shop," Zebedee said. "We have to pick up the packages. She is probably still shopping."

They looked in the park for Salome, one more time, and then returned to the shop. Zebedee entered the shop. He noticed a fishing knife that was for sale. He picked it up and felt the sharpness of the blade. The shopkeeper appeared.

"It is a fine knife," he said. "My brother made it."

"I probably don't have enough money to purchase it," he said. "I am certain my wife has spent all my money."

Zebedee smiled and greeted the shopkeeper.

"Is my wife here?" he asked. "She must have purchased everything you had in stock."

"No, she left some time ago," he said. "She said she was meeting her friends in the park. I will help you load her packages. You will need help."

Zebedee handed the shopkeeper some rope.

"I came prepared," he said. "We will tie a few of the large packages on the back of the carriage. Peter will have to hold the others."

After they loaded the packages, they returned to the park. Before they got to the park, they saw Salome and her friend. Zebedee called to her, and she walked toward the carriage.

"Hello, Salome," Jonas said. "This is, my son, Peter. He is a friend of James and John. He is going to help me sail our boat home."

"It is good to see you," she said. "I see you didn't forget my packages. I didn't think they would all fit into the carriage."

"We have already been to the park," Zebedee said. "We are ready to start home. Are you ready?"

Salome looked quietly at Zebedee.

"We became tired of waiting, so we went to the tea shop," she said. "He had several different types of very good tea."

On the way to Bethsaida, the four of them discussed old times. They talked about how much the boys had grown and that they liked to fish.

"I have to stand up," Jonas said. "The packages are digging into my leg."

They stopped for a few moments. After Jonas walked around, they boarded the carriage.

"Give me the packages," he said. "I needed to stretch my legs. I feel better. I am ready to travel."

Before they realized it, they arrived at Zebedee's house. Zebedee pointed at the boat repair area.

"Your boat is the one in the water next to our boat," he said. "The other one is a repair project. Go and check your boat. I will be with you in a few moments."

Zebedee took the horse and carriage to the barn. Hezekiah saw the carriage arrive, so he walked to the boat repair area.

"Hello, Peter," Hezekiah said. "I haven't seen you for a while. What do you think of your boat?"

"I don't know yet," he said. "I just arrived. I'll check her out."

"We have been working on it," he said. "It is ready for you to catch fish."

Jonas looked at Hezekiah.

"I love it," he said. "We will finally have a family business. I am eager to get it outfitted and start fishing."

"It can be a good business," Hezekiah said. "We like fishing."

"For whom are you repairing the boat on the blocks?" Jonas asked. "It is a large boat."

"Father purchased it last week," he said. "I don't think it is sold."

"It is a good looking boat," he said. "Our boat is just the proper size for us."

"It will take James and the repair crew quite a while to get it in ship-shape," Hezekiah said. "If father decides to sell it, he will find a buyer. He seems to really like that old boat."

Hezekiah had already decided that his father would probably keep the larger boat. Zebedee saw the men talking. He walked to the old boat and joined them.

"Zebedee, are you going to sell the large boat you are repairing?" Peter asked. "It will make a great dragnet fishing boat. You could catch a lot of fish with that boat."

"I haven't decided yet," he replied. "We could catch a lot of fish with her, but she will require a large crew."

"You will have to catch many, many fish to pay four men," Peter said. "I didn't think about that."

"If I don't find a buyer, maybe I will hire a mate," he said. "We could use day fisherman as helpers. I don't have to worry about that for a while. I want you to catch lots of fish with your new boat."

"We will, we will," Jonas said. "We will see you soon."

"Zebedee, before you get busy, you and the boys come in and eat," Salome said. "Sara has a nice meal ready for us. Did you have Nicia unpack the carriage?"

"Yes, dear," he said. "Your packages are in the sitting room."

Everyone enjoyed the meal. After they ate, they showed Peter and Jonas where they would be sleeping that night.

The next morning, they arose very early. The sun shone on the sea, and a gentle breeze provided some relief from the heat. Jonas greeted Chava and John. As soon as they finished eating breakfast, they went outside and looked at Peter's new boat. It took an hour to get everything prepared. Jonas and Peter pushed the boat away from the shore. When the wind caught the sail, the boat picked up speed. Peter turned toward the house and waved goodbye.

As they sailed out of sight, James turned to his father.

"Now, we can start work on the other boat," he said. "I have been looking at it, and I think I would like to make the repairs using cedar. Do you think that would be a good idea, father?"

Zebedee stroked his short black beard.

"Cedar," he said. "We don't have any cedar."

"You could purchase the cedar," John said.

"Yes, I suppose you're right," he said. "I want you to do an especially good job on this boat. There is something about this boat that I like."

The afternoon passed quickly. Zebedee, his sons, and helpers discussed the boat. They all agreed it was a great boat, and it would be a good boat for fishing.

Soon, they heard Chava call them to dinner. They had lost track of time.

"I think dinner is prepared," Zebedee said. "We better go inside and eat before your mother gets upset with us. Where is John?"

"I am right here," he said. "I have already washed my hands. I am hungry. I think Peter liked his new boat. I hope they catch lots of fish."

Fish was always available at Zebedee's house. Tonight, Chava, Sara, and the servants had prepared fresh fish. They took their seats at the table, and Zebedee thanked God for their many blessings, including Salome and Sara.

"Sara, the fish is delicious," he said. "I am glad you know so many different ways to prepare it. Did you give Jonas and Peter any food before they sailed?"

"Yes, I did," she replied. "I saw them preparing to leave, so I gave them some water and salted fish."

"Thank you, Sara," he said. "That was thoughtful of you."

"You get thirsty sailing a boat," she said. "I can tell that they really like their boat."

After they finished eating, the men slowly walked toward the sea. Zebedee looked at James.

"James, after the Sabbath is over, I want you to get a wagon load of cedar," he said. "Purchase wood that has been prepared for use on boats. I want to minimize our hand shaping the wood."

"You won't regret purchasing the cedar," John said. "And the boat will smell good."

"Take your brother, John, with you and teach him about choosing good wood," Zebedee said. "I think you can find what you need in Tyre."

"Yes, father," James said. "John, you heard father. We will travel the day after tomorrow. We will leave early that morning."

"I will smell the wood for you," John said. "Father always smells wood."

"Father, I am planning on replacing all of the wood in the hull and some of the supports," James said. "When we get finished, it will be a fine boat."

John jumped to his feet and ran toward the boat.

"That boat will smell like cedar, not like dead fish!" he yelled back to them.

John returned to the house and talked with James.

"Tomorrow we will all go to the synagogue," James said. "I will pray for our new boat. Before she is ready to sail, we will need all the help we can get."

"I will also pray for our new boat," John said. "I will do everything James tells me to do. We will make it into a boat you will be proud of, father."

"Thank you," Zebedee said. "I am proud of my family. The boat will be nice."

Salome smiled as she watched Zebedee and the boys enjoy the sea.

The Sabbath days were spent at the synagogue and at rest in the sea breeze. They enjoyed the Sabbath as a family. As they strolled along the sea, Salome and Zebedee held hands and thanked God for the good life they were allowed to earn.

When John and James rose the next morning, it was still dark. They ate breakfast, and the sun began to peek above the horizon. They started to Tyre. When they arrived, they located the largest saw mill.

"I need a wagon load of cedar wood," James said. "I want it hand-shaped to repair boats."

"I have some cedar," Boardus said. "Do you have any money?"

"I am sure I have enough money," he said. "My father gave me a bag of gold and silver coins."

"I will sell you all the cedar I have," he said. "If you purchase all the cedar from the Lebanon forest that is for sale in Tyre, I don't think it would fill your wagon."

"Do you know of another saw mill that might sell me cedar that can be used for a boat?" he asked. "If necessary, I will shape the wood myself."

"Yes, one other mill sells cedar," he said. "After I load my cedar on your wagon, I will escort you across town to the other mill."

Boardus wanted James to be a satisfied customer. He liked the large sale. James didn't find as much cedar as he wanted. He had to settle for some sycamore.

After the wagon was loaded, they started home. They didn't travel very fast. When it got dark, they stopped near a caravan and rested overnight.

"I will take care of the horses," James said. "Mother put some food in the wagon for us to eat."

"The wood sure smells good," John said. "Almost as good as mother's food."

The next morning, they ate salted fish, figs, and drank warm water. They hitched their horses to the wagon and started home. With the wagon loaded, the journey required all day. The boys remembered Zebedee's instructions not to hurry. They regularly rested and watered the horses. When they saw the sea, they were pleased.

"John, we are almost home," James said. "I hope father likes the wood. We weren't able to find as much cedar as I wanted. It isn't exactly what I told father we would purchase."

"You tell him," John said. "You can explain it better than I could."

John didn't want to give his father unwanted news.

When they arrive home, Zebedee stood at the barn. He walked to the wagon and inspected the wood.

"Hello, James," he said. "Why didn't you get all cedar?"

"I couldn't find a full load of cedar wood in Tyre," he replied. "I asked everyone, and this is all the cedar I could find."

"We looked all around," John said. "I guess everyone likes cedar."

"I have an idea how we can use this wood," James said. "I will use the cedar for the lower portion of the hull that will be below the water line when the boat is full of fish. The upper portion of the hull, above the water line, will be built with the sycamore."

Zebedee pondered James' idea.

"If you couldn't get cedar," he said. "I guess that is a good idea. Be sure to inform the foreman what you plan to do."

"I have some coins to return to you," he said. "I will put them on the table for you."

"Thank you," he said. "That is a fine looking load of wood. We will store it in the barn."

Throughout the next month, James, the foreman, and helpers worked six days a week on the boat. James was skilled at using a hand adz, and performed the final dimensional trim of the wood. John watched and built things from the wood scraps. Hezekiah stayed busy managing the fishing business and the boat repair business. He was a little concerned that Jonas and Peter took their boat without paying for it. He did the worrying for his father.

They were all working, when Zebedee saw Peter approaching.

"Hello, Zebedee," Peter said. "The boat is great, and we are catching a large amount of fish. Father told me to bring this money to you."

"I knew you would catch fish," Zebedee said. "I wasn't worried."

"Father said to tell you that I will bring you more money next month," he said. "I have to go. We are keeping the boat working as much as possible."

"Thank your father for me," he said. "Tell him I will send James and John to you next month. They can purchase supplies for Salome and visit with you. That way you can do more fishing."

Peter smiled as he started his journey home.

Zebedee gently tossed the money to Hezekiah. His smile covered his entire face.

"Hezekiah, here, you can stop worrying," Zebedee said. "I knew he would catch many fish. Take this money, and do with it whatever it is you do with our money."

Hezekiah caught the money. He was pleased Jonas was able to pay for the boat.

"I shouldn't have doubted them," he said. "You did a good thing, father."

"Friends do good things," Zebedee said. "Jonas is my friend."

"Lunch is served," Sara said. "Come and get it."

They were seated, and Zebedee prayed.

CHAPTER 4

MARRIAGE

Zebedee's fishing fleet and his boat repair businesses grew rapidly. His son, Hezekiah, returned from the university and managed both businesses. Zebedee and Salome enjoyed, a low stress life, living by the sea. Their daughter, Chava, had matured and started to manage the house. Zebedee allowed his friend, Jonas, to acquire a repaired fishing boat and pay for it as he and his sons earned extra money. A payment had just been made on the boat.

After Hezekiah put the money away, he returned to talk to his father.

"Father, I have something I want to discuss with you, do you remember the girl named Ruth?" he asked. "She lived near us in Capernaum."

"Many girls lived near us, which house was her father's house?" Zebedee asked.

"It was about four houses up the street," he said. "We want to get married."

Zebedee's face became red and he stroked his beard.

"You want to what?" he stammered. "You just returned from school."

Zebedee looked at Hezekiah with disbelief.

"I have been home quite a while," he said. "We are old enough to get married, and you know I have a good job."

He continued to look at Hezekiah.

"You really want to get married," he said. "I guess you've grown up."

"Yes, I have," he said. "I'm full grown."

Zebedee regained his composure and said, "Sure, I remember her. I think your mother will be very pleased. She liked Ruth and her family. Have you told her?"

"No, I wanted to talk with you first," he said. "I would like to continue managing our businesses."

"Are you certain you want the responsibility of a family?" he asked. "You are very young."

"I am certain, but I would like to remain with you and mother," he said.

"Good, I want you to continue to manage the businesses," he said. "I am sure your mother will want you close to us."

"I hope to build a house here on our land," he said. "We have a large area of land that we don't use. Is that acceptable to you?"

"It sounds like you have it all planned," Zebedee said. "We do have a large piece of property."

"You have to plan these things," Hezekiah said. "I am a planner."

"That you are," he said. "You and Ruth will have a visitor every day. You should go and talk with her."

Zebedee grinned broadly. He slowly walked toward the sea. He was already planning Hezekiah's new house. He and Salome decided the new house would be their wedding present to Hezekiah and Ruth.

The next morning, Zebedee went looking for Enoch.

"Enoch, do you know anyone who builds houses?" he asked. "I am going to have a house built for Hezekiah and his wife, Ruth."

Zebedee pointed east along the sea.

"I didn't know Hezekiah was getting married," he said. "Who is he going to marry?"

"A girl from Capernaum," he said. "We used to live near them."

"I guess your family knows her," he replied. "My brother and father build houses. I am certain they could build you a fine house. If you want to talk with them, I will have them come and visit with you."

"Good," Zebedee said. "I will be home tomorrow. I am looking forward to meeting your father. I think I know your brother."

"Yes, you know him," Enoch said. "When he is not busy with father, he works for us. I will talk with them this evening."

Zebedee knew he could trust Enoch to make the necessary arrangements. The next morning, Zebedee was seated on the porch.

"Hello, Zebedee," he said. "I am Enoch's father. My name is Solomon. Enoch told me you would like to talk with me about building a house for your son."

"Yes," he said. "My oldest son is getting married."

"I would be very interested in building a home for your son," he said. "I could start next week. We are just finishing with another house."

"That sounds good," he said. "Follow me. We can walk along the sea, and I will show you exactly where I would like it built. Hezekiah manages our business."

"You must own a lot of land," he said. "It is nice here on the sea."

"Yes, we own quite a large track of land," he said. "It is more than a quarter hour walk to the other end of our property, and it is about three times as deep as it is wide."

"That is a lot of land," he said. "You have room for many houses."

"When I purchased the land, it was being used to graze animals and grow fruit," he said. "It was a lot of grass and fruit trees. I liked it because it was on the sea. I want his house about here."

Zebedee stopped and pointed at the ground.

"How large of a house does he need?" he asked. "I will have to purchase the materials."

"You don't have to worry about the materials," he said. "My son, Hezekiah, purchases all of our materials. He knows all the merchants."

"I like to purchase my own materials," he said. "I make certain I have everything I need."

"Hezekiah will take care of it," Zebedee said. "I am sorry, but this is the way I do business."

Solomon sensed that if he wanted to build the house, he wasn't going to purchase the materials. He rubbed his hands together and then pulled on his stubbly beard. He looked at Zebedee and coughed.

"That way I won't have to spend days gathering the materials," Solomon said. "You can stack the wood where you want the house built."

"Just tell Hezekiah what you want, and it will be waiting for you," he said. "I think it should have about five rooms, an outside kitchen, and a barn. I want an extra bedroom for my grandsons."

"You will be proud of the house that I build for Hezekiah" he said. "Someday, you might need another house."

A month later, Zebedee and his family journeyed to Capernaum for Hezekiah's wedding. The ceremony was performed in the synagogue where he and Salome were once members. Ruth was welcomed into her new family. Their new house was under construction, and Salome planned to provide a servant to help with chores. Hezekiah rented a house for them until the new house was completed. Ruth spent a lot of time with Salome, Sarah, and Chava. Everyone tried to ensure Ruth felt like one of their family. They visited as often as possible.

Two months passed, James and John worked on the boat with Enoch and his laborers.

"Why did Hezekiah get married to Ruth?" John asked. "He has us, mother, and father."

"I guess he wants to have a family of his own," James answered. "When you decide you want to have children to teach, you get married. It is fine. He is going to live here. We haven't lost him; we gained a friend in Ruth."

John got a puzzled look on his face and then smiled.

"I didn't think about that," he said. "He is still here. I like Ruth."

"I have been checking loaded fishing boats," Enoch said. "If we replace the top three boards with sycamore, everything will be fine."

"Did I find enough cedar to do that?" James asked. "I can make another trip."

"We can also use sycamore for the new sail mast and the inner parts of the boat," Enoch said. "That way, we will have plenty of cedar for the entire hull that is in the water. Do you think your father is going to sell this boat?"

"I don't know," James replied. "He sure is showing a lot of interest in it, and he hasn't brought anyone here to look at it. He might just keep it."

Enoch looked at James and smiled.

Another month passed. Zebedee walked to Hezekiah's new house and found him at work on the business accounting records.

"Hezekiah, I have a question for you," Zebedee said. "If I keep the big boat, can we make more money?"

Hezekiah was ready for Zebedee's question. He was certain that it was just a matter of time before they owned a fleet of fishing boats.

"I think so," he replied. "The secret is having a good captain and mate. Samuel is great. He makes us a lot of money, and we can depend on him."

"Yes," he said. "Samuel is very good for us."

"Can you find another Samuel?" Hezekiah asked. "People in Bethsaida will always purchase all the fish we catch."

"That is true," Zebedee said. "Many days we don't have enough for everyone."

"Then they go to Capernaum to purchase salted fish," Hezekiah said. "If we provided more fresh and salted fish we would make more money."

"That is what I thought," Zebedee said. "I will look into it. I will start by talking with Samuel."

When Samuel returned with the day's catch of fish, Zebedee waited at the edge of the sea to talk with him.

"As soon as you and your crew take care of those fish, I want to see you," he said. After Samuel started the crew working on the chores of cleaning fish and salting the fish, he went to talk with Zebedee.

"Samuel, I have a question for you," he says. "Could any of your helpers be a mate?"

Samuel smiled and said, "I guess you are going to keep the other boat. It sure is a nice boat. Enoch, James, and the helpers are doing a fine job with that boat."

"I am considering keeping it," Zebedee said. "We will need help."

"Yes, I think two of my crew could be mates," Samuel said. "If we don't do something for them, they will probably be hired away by someone in Tiberias. That town is really growing."

"The Roman fortification brought many soldiers to the area," he said. "Others are moving there to provide services and sell items to the soldier's families."

"We need to retain our best employees," Samuel said. "I can always hire day labors to help us."

"Introduce me to the best one," Zebedee said. "I want to talk with him."

"You know Joel," he said. "He was part of your crew. He has been with you a long time."

"Yes, I know Joel," he said. "He was always dependable."

"If he had a good crew, he could be a first mate," he said. "I have an idea. You could make him first mate of this boat, and we will get him a new crewman."

"What are you going to do?" Zebedee asked. "That only solves one problem."

"I will be captain of the new boat, and the other helper could be my first mate," Samuel said. "I will find and train a new crew. I could also oversee the operations of both boats, and I could make certain all the fish are cleaned."

"I get it," Zebedee said. "Joel will work for you, and you will be captain of both boats."

"That way we won't have to have two captains," Samuel said. "It will save us some money."

"You make that work for us, and I will give you a nice increase in salary," he said. "I guess you should be the one to talk to Joel. I will tell Hezekiah what we are going to do."

That evening, after everyone finished working on the boat, the boys went to the house to wash and eat dinner. Zebedee sat on the porch in his favorite chair.

"Father, we just about have the boat ready to sell," James said. "Do you have a buyer?"

"No, James, I have decided to keep the boat. We will add it to our fishing fleet," he said. "Joel is going to be the first mate of the other boat, and Samuel is going to be captain of both boats. We will hire new crew members."

James smiled at his father.

"I thought you might keep it," he said. "Our business is growing."

"I did find another boat to be repaired," he said. "It will be a 'fix it' and 'sell it' project. No cedar in that one."

"I will tell Enoch," he said. "I think he will be glad. He is very pleased with this boat."

"Dinner is being served," Sara called.

Dinner that evening was interesting. Zebedee usually didn't talk shop at the dinner table. He usually waited until they had finished dinner and relaxed in the sitting room. Tonight, he was too excited he couldn't wait until after dinner.

"Salome, I am going to keep the boat," he said. "I am going to promote Samuel, and I will promote the two crewmen who have been with us a long time."

"I know Joel," she said. "He has been with us for years."

"When Chava can manage the house by herself, we will be able to do a little more traveling," Zebedee said. "Do you want to travel?"

"That is nice, Zebedee," she said. "I am sure they will appreciate making more money."

"They will make us more money, and I will share it with them," he said.

"Chava is doing very well," Salome said. "When you want to travel, I can be available. If Chava needs help, Sara will help her. Now, we have Ruth to help oversee things. She is a very smart woman."

Zebedee and Salome started traveling to Jerusalem at least three times a year. They also visited with their friends in Capernaum on a regular basis. Hezekiah managed a very prosperous enterprise. Ruth had an attendant, and they had many slaves.

After three years, Ruth had a baby boy. Hezekiah named him Jeremiah. Zebedee and Salome enjoyed every opportunity to tell people about their grandson. They sat in the living room and talked with the family.

"How was your trip to Jerusalem, mother?" Chava asked. "I have something I want to discuss with you."

Salome noted an anxious tone in her voice.

"Would you like to walk along the sea?" Salome asked. "I find it relaxes me."

She anticipated a mother and daughter discussion.

"That would be nice," she said. "I am sure you remember Ishmael. When we lived in Capernaum, you were very good friends with his mother."

"Yes, I remember him," she said. "He is a nice young man."

"He has asked me to marry him," she said. "I told him I would talk with you and father."

"The final decision is your father's," Salome said. "I will speak with him."

"Thank you," she said. "I am so excited."

"I am very happy for you," she said. "We need to tell your father, but I would wait until after dinner. He will be more relaxed. Watch for him to push his chair away from the table and sigh."

Zebedee was surprised at the wonderful dinner that was served. The dinner was so delicious; he worried about what Salome wanted to discuss that evening.

"I hope you enjoyed your dinner," Salome said. "Chava and I want to talk with you. Go and have a seat, and I will bring you a glass of wine."

Zebedee did as he was told. He got up, stretched his legs, and went to his favorite chair, just as he did every night after dinner. Tonight would be different. The women had planned the conservation.

"This is the good wine," he said. "You must have something important to tell me."

"Yes, it is important," Chava said. "Ishmael has asked me to marry him. I would like your blessings."

Zebedee refused to believe that his little girl had matured into a young lady.

"Ishmael, who?" he asked. "This is quite a surprise."

"It is time for me to have my own family," she said. "I know how to manage a house."

"Does he reside in Bethsaida?" he asked. "How did you meet him?"

"He lives in Capernaum," she said. "I met him when we lived there."

"Oh, that Ishmael," he said. "I know him; he was a good young fellow. I will want to talk with him. Does he have a good job? Can he support you?"

Salome motioned at Zebedee. She wanted him to slow down and relax.

"He has a steady job as a fisherman," Chava said. "He must think he can support me, or he wouldn't have asked me to marry him."

"Have James bring him to visit with me," he said. "I'll talk to him."

"Yes, father," she said. "I will talk to James."

"You know a marriage is the combining of two families," he said. "It is a big step."

"Yes, father, I know," she said. "I think you will like him."

"I do like his mother and father," he said. "I know them."

"I am going to tell James to get Ishmael," she said. "When he arrives, I'll let you know."

Chava walked to the boat repair area.

"James, I want to talk with you," she said. "Can you come here?"

"What do you want?" James asked. "Can't you see I am very busy?"

"I am going to get married," she said. "Father wants you to bring Ishmael, my future husband, here to speak with him."

"I will do that," he said. "First, I must complete this project."

"When will you be finished?" she asked. "I will tell father."

"In a few days," he said. "Probably about three days."

"Three days!" she exclaimed. "I tell you I want to get married, and you tell me to wait three days? My marriage is more important than that old boat."

"I have a job," he said. "My job makes money for this family. When I finish, I will help you."

"I am going to tell father," she said. "He will help me."

Chava returned to her father. She wasn't happy.

"James said he will be busy for three days," Chava said. "Tell him to go to Capernaum."

"Three days," he said. "That is not very long."

"What do you mean?" she asked. "My wedding is important to me."

"It is important to all of us," he said. "Having a business that makes money is also important."

"I'm going to talk with mother," she said. "She will help me."

Just then, Salome entered the room.

"Three days may seem like a long time," Salome said. "It is not very long."

"Patience is a virtue," Zebedee said. "Read the Bible and pray for three days."

Chava went outside and sat on the porch. Time passed slowly. Three days later, James went to bring Ishmael to see Zebedee. After James went for Ishmael, Chava became nervous. She hoped her father and Ishmael would have a pleasant meeting.

When James and Ishmael arrived at the house, it was afternoon. He and Ishmael went inside.

"Father, this is Ishmael," James said. "After you have talked with him, I will escort him to Capernaum."

"Thank you," Zebedee said. "Have a seat, Ishmael. You have grown quite a bit since I last saw you. How are your father and mother?"

"They are fine, sir," he said. "The reason I am here is that I want to ask your permission to marry your daughter. I will work very diligently and will be a good husband for her."

Ishmael was already making a good impression on Zebedee.

"Tell me about your job," he said. "Chava said you are a fisherman."

"Yes, that is correct," he said. "I am a fisherman. For the last two years, I have been working on a boat in Capernaum."

"Two years," he said. "They must like you."

"I think so," he said. "They have taught me all about fishing."

"Are you going to purchase your own boat?" he asked.

"I haven't thought about purchasing a boat," he said. "I make enough money to rent a place for us."

"Where would you live?" he asked. "We have a lot of land."

"I was considering Capernaum," he said. "We would live close to my job."

"That is good," he said. "How would you like to live in Bethsaida and fish for me?"

The question startled Ishmael. He hesitated for a few moments. He didn't know how to answer and just looked at the floor.

Finally, he said, "I would have to ask Chava. We only talked about living in Capernaum."

"Chava," Zebedee said. "Ishmael wants to talk with you. Maybe you need to take him for a walk. Your mother and I have taken a few walks along the sea."

Ishmael and Chava walked along the sea. They held hands and a peace came over them as they discussed Zebedee's offer.

Later, they returned to talk with Zebedee.

"I am getting ready to add a boat to our business, and I need a helper for my mate Samuel," Zebedee said. "Samuel is a good mate, and he has been with me for a long time."

Zebedee could see Ishmael was interested, but he didn't respond for a few moments.

"Chava and I have talked," he asked. "We want to start by making important decisions as a team."

Zebedee was impressed with his concern for Chava.

"What did you decide?" he asked. "This is a good opportunity."

Ishmael looked at Chava. They smiled at each other.

"I would like to give it a try, sir," he replied. "We are very excited."

"You can be married, and I'll hire you to fish for us," he said. "That should make everyone happy, except your current employer."

Zebedee thought for a moment.

"You need to give him notice," he said. "He has been good to you."

Zebedee stood, took Chava by the hand, and addressed Ishmael, "When you get home, tell your mother to contact my wife about planning the wedding. I am certain that will keep them busy for a while."

Zebedee and Salome walked along the sea that evening.

The next day, Zebedee announced to his family and workers that he was going to add another fishing boat and that his new son-in-law was going to work on the boat.

A few weeks passed, Zebedee sat on the porch of the house with Salome.

"Zebedee, I have been busy. I have the wedding all planned," she said. "It will be here at our local synagogue."

"Good," he said. "I thought we might have to go to Capernaum."

"The priest will see you about the details," she said. "Afterwards, we can have the celebration here at our house on the sea. I think those who attend would like that. Maybe, James and John could take the smaller children for boat rides."

"I have also been busy," he said. "I have found a house for them. Before they move in, it will be refurbished. It is close enough that Ishmael can walk to work. I hope they have it finished before they are married."

Salome looked at Zebedee.

"Take me to see their house," she asked. "Did you rent it or purchase it for them?"

"I purchased it for them," he said. "I thought it would be a good wedding present. It is a good starter house for them."

"When we were married, we couldn't afford a house," she said. "You are a good father."

"If they have several children and need a larger house, maybe we can build them a house on our property," Zebedee said. "Come. I will show it to you."

"I will remember that promise, built next to Hezekiah's house" she said.

Zebedee took Salome by the hand, and they walked to town. They talked about their family and getting older. They hoped for many grandchildren. When they arrived at the house, Salome sensed Zebedee was upset.

"The house doesn't look like it will be ready," Zebedee said. "Foreman, you told me you would have the house ready for me by next week. What is the problem?"

"My helper only comes to work about half the time," he said. "I am sorry it won't be ready for about three weeks."

Zebedee turned to Salome. He had a disappointed look on his face.

"Well, Salome, I guess we will have a newly married couple living with us for a few weeks," he said. "I hope they don't mind."

Salome stared at Zebedee. She pointed her finger at him.

"That will not work, Zebedee," she said. "You will have to come up with another plan. I am not going to expect my daughter to spend her wedding night with you and me."

"The house won't be ready," he said. "What do you want me to do?"

"Rent them a room at the inn until the house is ready," she said. "Rent them a very nice room."

"Rent them a room," he said. "We have plenty of rooms."

"How would you liked to have stayed with your father and mother the night after we were married?" she asked. "You get my point?"

Zebedee was no longer jovial. He thought about the cost of a nice room at the inn. He said something derogatory about the carpenter.

On the wedding day, Chava looked stunning. Her white head cover and dress contrasted with her dark hair and eyes. She looked very mature, and Ishmael looked very young. The celebration on the sea was completed with boat rides for everyone. Ishmael and Chava spent the first week of married life at the inn. When their new house was completed, Zebedee was a happy man. Ishmael and Chava couldn't believe they had their own house. Chava became pregnant.

CHAPTER 5

JAMES AND JOHN

Life in Bethsaida was quiet and profitable for Zebedee and his family. The fishing business was strong as the market for fresh fish was not being satisfied. Zebedee had three boats in the water and his crews fished six day each week. His boat repair crew rebuilt a boat every three months. Zebedee and his wife enjoyed living the life of the employer class. James and John were good fishermen, and they both possessed good carpentry skills. James was an accomplished scholar, and John could read Greek and Latin. They studied their Jewish religion faithfully.

James and John walked to the boat repair area. They hoped for a sea breeze that would cool the hot air.

"I see father has a new boat for us to repair," James said. "I wish he would purchase something exciting like another large boat."

John looked at the new project that was secured on blocks.

"This one should be fun," John said. "Show me what you want me to do first. It looks like this boat is not too old."

"All we have to do to this one is replace the mast," Enoch said. "I have located a sycamore pole. It is being delivered today. Be careful with the old mast. I want to salvage as much as possible. I am certain we will find a use for the wood."

James wiped the sweat from his brow and looked at John.

"When you were at the synagogue last Sabbath, did you hear anything about a itinerate teacher?" he asked. "I heard that large crowds attend his lessons."

"No, I didn't hear anything," John replied. "Was he in Bethsaida?"

"No, I think he was south of Capernaum, near the sea," he said. "Maybe someday, he will visit Bethsaida."

"I guess we had better help get this old mast off the boat," John said. "Enoch and his helper will soon be ready to start fitting the new pole."

"I will remove the accessories," James said. "Then we can remove the mast."

"I'll get a horse," John said. "After we remove it, we'll clean it. Then, Nicia and I will drag it up alongside the barn."

"Don't forget, Enoch wants to reuse the wood," James said.

"Sure thing," he said. "I will make certain it is protected."

Zebedee watched his sons as they removed the mast and hauled it to the barn. He left the shade of the porch and walked to them. He sensed they were laboring in the heat and planned to give everyone a break. He motioned to the boys. They carefully set the old mast down and joined their father.

"James, after this boat is refurbished, I don't have another project," he said. "Take your brother, and go visit with Peter and his family."

"Why don't you have a boat lined up for us to repair?" he asked. "I am sure you could find one."

"I thought we might rest for a few days," he said. "It's too hot."

James and John looked at the sky, and they rubbed their eyes. The sweat rolled down their backs.

"I enjoy visiting with Peter," James said. "I am sure John will enjoy the trip."

"They will probably give you some money to bring home with you," Zebedee said. "Take good care of it. When you get home, give the money to Hezekiah."

James smiled at his father.

"In the meantime, I will be looking for another boat project for us," he said. "If I don't find one, you can repair nets."

"I hope you find us a boat," James said. "If necessary, I could teach John how to repair nets."

"Tell Nicia to get the carriage ready," Zebedee said. "You might as well learn to drive the carriage. Someday, I might be too old to handle the horses."

"Yes, father," James said. "After breakfast tomorrow morning, John and I will go to see Peter. I will tell Enoch we won't be at work tomorrow."

The following day, James and John arose early and walked to the barn. They were excited about taking the carriage. They watched Nicia prepare the horse.

"Did you have breakfast?" Nicia asked. "The carriage is ready. Take good care of it. Your father really likes it."

"Yes, we ate salted fish and dates," James said. "We will be careful. I have only driven the wagon a few times. I have never driven the carriage."

The brothers climbed aboard the carriage.

"Easy boy," James said. "Follow the lane to the larger road."

When they arrived at the road, the horse turned and headed toward Capernaum. The horse seemed to know the way and wasn't difficult to control.

"This is fun," John said, smiling. "Can we go faster?"

"No, remember what Nicia told us. We must be careful," James said.

The air quickly turned cool, and the wind started to whip. James encouraged the horse to trot at a quicker pace. The horse raised its head and the reins flexed in James' hands. He held on tightly. Suddenly, a streak of lightning danced across the sky. Then, they heard a loud clap of thunder. The horse reared. James struggled with the rein.

"Look at that black cloud," James said, pointing to a dark mass in the sky. "I think we are going to get some rain. Easy boy, it was only thunder. Easy, easy."

The sky turned dark. Only a small slice of sun shone through the dark clouds. It was an eerie scene. James looked at his brother and saw fear in his face.

"Hold on John," he said. "The horse is scared. The carriage is wobbling."

"I am scared," John cried out. "Do something! We might overturn."

The carriage swayed from side to side. A loud crack was heard.

"I think that last pothole in the road must have broken something," James said. "Hold on. We have a problem."

"Stop the horse!" John hollered. "Stop the horse!"

James tugged on the rein. He talked to the horse. The horse slowed.

"I think I got it," he said. "We've stopped."

John was so afraid, he started to cry. He didn't know what they would do.

"Are you ok?" James asked. "It looks like one of the wheels is broken."

The carriage leaned precariously, but it had stopped. The horse was nervous and pranced around. John's face turned pale. He thought the carriage was going to turn over. James stepped out of the carriage and stood beside it. He was scared, and his legs wobbled. He surveyed the situation. The sky started to clear, and the sun peaked from behind the dark clouds. The horse stopped his nervous behavior. John climbed out of the carriage and grabbed James. He looked at the carriage.

"Now, we have done it," he said. "Father is going to be really angry with us."

"Come on," James said. "Help me unhitch the horse, and we will ride him back to the house."

"We don't have a saddle," he said. "I might fall off."

"You can hold on to me," he said. "I have ridden this horse bareback."

Sobbing, John looked at James.

"Don't go too fast," he said.

They both climbed aboard the horse. James gave the horse a nudge, and it started for home. John held on to James very tightly. James felt him trembling.

"Nicia will know what to do," James said. "He always knows what to do. This isn't the first wheel that has needed to be repaired. Maybe, we should start repairing carriages and wagons."

"Are you going to abandon father's carriage?" John asked. "Someone might steal it."

"If they don't have a wheel and a horse, they aren't going to steal it," he said. "Just hold on to me. Everything is under control."

"I guess I am just scared," he said.

By the time they arrived home, John felt better and had stopped trembling.

"I hope you can explain our problem," John said. "I wouldn't know how."

"I will do the talking," James said. "Our problem was caused by the storm."

"I hope father agrees with you," he said.

They went directly into the house, and James found his father.

"Father, we encountered a problem with the carriage on the way to Peter's," he said. "I was having trouble handling the horse during the thunder storm, and we hit a hole in the road. A wheel broke. John and I rode the horse back."

"You broke a wheel?" Zebedee asked. "Are you sure it was a wheel?"

"Well, the wagon was sitting at a strange angle," he said. "I think it is the wheel."

"Where is the carriage?" he asked. "Will we be able to find it?"

"Yes, it is not far," James said. "I can take you to it."

"We will find it. James, go inside and get dry," he said. "Get some food for yourself, and feed your brother."

"After we are dry, we will feel better," he said to John.

"I will tell Nicia to take the wagon, rope, and some helpers. I will have him bring the carriage home," Zebedee said. "Then, we can replace the wheel."

"Can you get a wheel in Bethsaida?" John asked.

"We keep a few extra wheels and an extra axel and hub," Zebedee said. "I hope you learned something from this experience. When it thunders, you should stop immediately and steady the horse."

"Yes, father, I will remember that," he said. "Stop at the first sound of thunder and steady the horse."

Salome saw Zebedee talking with the boys and walked in their direction. She could sense they were frightened.

"John, what are you doing home?" she asked. "Your father told me you and James would be visiting with Peter today."

"There was a thunder storm, and we broke a wheel on the carriage," John said, anxiously. "Father is going to have Nicia fix it."

"Don't be afraid, John, calm down. Your father has broken several wheels," she said. "Have some fruit and goat's milk."

James looked at John. A small smile appeared on John's face.

"Father broke a wheel?" James asked. "I didn't know that."

"Keeping the carriage running is part of Nicia's job," she said. "Your father will have him fix it."

When James and John arose the following morning, the carriage was in the barn being repaired. They decided to stay away from Nicia until he was finished.

Sara prepared a hot breakfast. They were relieved that she never mentioned the carriage. After breakfast, Zebedee talked with his two sons.

"Boys, when Nicia has the carriage repaired, I want you to try again to visit Peter," he said. "Remember, at the first sound of thunder, stop and steady the horse."

The day before, James and John were surprised their father handled the broken carriage wheel without showing any anger. Today, they wondered why they expected him to get angry. A worried look appeared on their faces. He was never a hostile father, but he was occasionally quite firm.

After the carriage was repaired, they thanked Nicia and headed to Capernaum. This time the trip was uneventful. They spent the day talking with Peter and Andrew. Later that day, they drove home very slowly. When they returned, they gave Hezekiah the sack of coins Peter had given them. They received a special welcome.

"Hi, boys," Enoch said. "No broken wheel today?"

"Very funny," James said. "Today, I can see your humor. Yesterday, it would have been a different story. I guess dealing with conflicts is all part of growing up."

The next week, Zebedee sat on the porch and enjoyed the sun. It shone brightly and reflected beautiful reddish-yellow colors on the sea. He saw Hezekiah and waved to him. Hezekiah headed in his direction.

"I am thinking of having you purchase a larger carriage for us,"

Zebedee said. "That way, we could all travel at the same time, what do you think?"

"We have a carriage and a wagon," Hezekiah said. "Do you we need another carriage?"

"Yes, I do," he said. "When the carriage is broken, we are stranded."

"It only takes a day to fix it," he said. "We keep spare parts."

"We could keep a spare carriage," Zebedee said. "It would be a really nice carriage."

"I have an idea," Hezekiah said. "When you purchase a new carriage, you should require that they train one of your employees to repair wheels and carriages."

Zebedee hadn't thought about a business repairing carriages and wagons. Hezekiah's idea intrigued him.

"Repair carriages," he said. "I think that might be a good idea."

"When the wheel on our carriage was broken, a few weeks ago, we took it to Bethsaida to be repaired, do you remember?" Hezekiah asked. "The stable in Bethsaida was busy repairing military wagons. The one person who repairs wheels couldn't schedule our repair, so he sent it to Tyre."

"That is why I keep a few spare parts," Zebedee said. "Nicia can replace the broken part. Sometimes it takes a long time for a repair."

"I think I could make a deal where we repair the non-military carriages and wagons. Then the stable in Bethsaida would repair only military units," Hezekiah said. "That is more than enough work for him."

"You know he is going to keep the military happy," Zebedee said. "I would do the same."

"When we aren't busy, we could even agree to help him repair military wagons," Hezekiah said. "How would you like to expand your business? I think this is better than adding another fishing boat."

Zebedee stood and paced the floor. He stroked his gray/black beard.

"I am a fisherman," he said. "Let me think about this. It might be a good idea."

Zebedee was aware that many people had purchased carriages and that it took a long time to get a wheel repaired. He thought about it for a while, and then he found James seated on the porch.

"James, if I were to expand our business to include repairing carriages and wagons, would you like to manage that part of the business for the family?" Zebedee asked. "We could hire a helper for you."

James didn't answer immediately.

"Father, I don't want to disappoint you, but I think I would like to be a teacher," James said. "I have been thinking about studying to become a Rabbi."

Zebedee wasn't certain he had heard James correctly. He paused for a moment and reviewed the conversation in his mind. He looked at James.

"That is a surprise to me," he said. "Have you told your mother this?"

"No," he said. "I guess I should."

Zebedee regained his composure.

"I think it might be nice to have a Rabbi in the family again," he said. "You know we are related to the former high priest, Anenel?"

Zebedee was shocked at James' statement. He and Salome had discussed the possibility that James might not stay in the family business.

"Yes, I know," James said. "I was hoping you would understand. Talk to Enoch, I think he would be interested in learning new skills."

"Enoch, do you think he could repair carriages and wagons?" Zebedee asked.

"I am sure he could repair almost anything," he said. "He is very good with his hand and with tools."

"I will consider him," he said. "Before I talk with him, I will think about it."

"You could allow him to manage all repairs," James said. "You could promote the helper to boat repair foreman and hire a new helper for him."

A smile appeared on Zebedee's face.

"That might work," he said. "Do you know where Enoch is?

Enoch mostly worked with boats, so Zebedee walked to the repair area and found him. Enoch sensed he wanted to talk with him, so he stopped working and looked at Zebedee. Zebedee made small talk and then discussed the new opportunity.

"Enoch, you have been with me for a long time, and you have been my foreman for many years," Zebedee said. "I am thinking of expanding our business to include repairing carriages and wagons. I would like you to manage that part of the business."

"Repair carriages and wagons," Enoch said. "I am a boat repairman."

"You have worked on boats for a long time," he said. "Now, you can manage the repair of all our equipment."

"Boats don't have wheels," he said. "A wagon isn't like a boat."

"If it is wood, you can repair it," he said. "You can learn how to make a wheel."

"I like my job," Enoch said. "I am comfortable repairing boats, what if I can't make a wheel?"

"I will send you to Tyre for a week to learn about repairing wheels, axels, and hubs," he said. "Then, you can bring our new larger carriage home with you."

Enoch paused for a moment. He stared at Zebedee.

"You are going to purchase another carriage?" he asked. "Where will we keep it?"

Zebedee decided his questions were rhetorical and didn't answer him.

"We will promote your helper to foreman," he said. "He has been with us for a long time, what do you think?"

"It scares me," he said. "You could hire someone to repair carriages."

"I want to promote you," Zebedee said. "I want to hire a helper."

Enoch picked up a rag and wiped the sweat from his forehead.

"I guess I can learn how to repair and build wheels," he said. "I have never been to Tyre."

"I will find you a new helper," he said. "Hezekiah will purchase the new carriage and make the arrangements for you to be trained."

"We will need to purchase a few more horses," Enoch said. "We could use two strong, young horses."

"We should have an extra horse," Zebedee said. "I will purchase a black horse."

Zebedee had just learned that James didn't plan to stay in the family business. He had a new large carriage, and he had three more horses. Enoch knew how to repair carriages and wagons, and Hezekiah taught him management techniques. Hezekiah told his mother that she was going to be a grandmother. Everyone was very excited for Ruth. Salome walked to Ruth's house and talked with her.

When Enoch returned from Tyre, Zebedee spoke with him.

"Enoch, now that you have a business to manage, you should have a shop built," Zebedee said. "Next to the barn would be a good location."

"Yes, sir," Enoch said. "I will leave enough room to store our outside wood."

"You will be close to the barn and the boat repair yard," he said. "You may have your brother build it. He did a good job on Hezekiah's house and barn."

"He is very busy," he said. "I will talk with him."

"Make sure it is large enough," he said. "It should hold at least three carriages. While your brother is here, tell him to build another barn behind the existing one. We need more space to store our equipment."

"I will see him tomorrow," he said. "I hope he is able work for you."

"You can get with Hezekiah and give him a list of materials we will need," he said. "It will take a few days to have the material delivered."

Zebedee was so busy talking; he didn't hear what Enoch had said.

That evening after dinner, everyone sat in their favorite chair and watched a beautiful sunset. Zebedee explained his building plans to the family.

Salome looked at him and said, "Yes, dear."

Enoch talked with his brother Thomas, "Zebedee has several building projects, when will you be available?"

"You know I am very busy," Thomas said. "I have promised my client that before I take another job, I will finish his house."

"Will you talk with Zebedee?" Enoch asked. "Do that for me."

"Just tell him I am busy," he said. "He will understand."

"He has always been fair with you," he said. "He is my boss. Please, you have got to help me."

The next day, Enoch and his brother talked with Zebedee.

"I am sorry, but first, I must finish the house I am working on," Thomas said. "After that, I can build whatever you need."

"When will you be finished?" Zebedee asked. "I want to start a new business."

"It will be at least two weeks," he said. "The weather has been good, and I think it will continue to be good."

"Two weeks," he said. "Build Enoch's shop first."

"I can't do that," he said. "I gave my word that this house would be my only project."

"I am disappointed," Zebedee said. "I give you a lot of work."

"I promise you that your shop will be my only project, when I work on it," Thomas said. "You can count on me. So can my other clients."

Zebedee appreciated Thomas' honesty and work ethic. He smiled at him.

"I will tell Hezekiah, you will be here in two weeks," he said. "He will have all the necessary materials waiting for you."

Zebedee found James and told him it was time for him to go to Capernaum. He was quite clear, that they should ride horses. He also told them to check with their mother for her shopping list.

"You don't want me to drive the new carriage?" James asked. "I have never driven a large carriage."

Zebedee scratched his head and smiled at James.

"Both of the carriages are being used," he said. "I don't know how we survived so many years with only one carriage and a wagon. I am certain Peter will have some money for us."

"Yes, father," he said. "I will take John along. He likes visiting with Peter. Before we come home, we will eat at the inn."

"Do you need any money?" Zebedee asked. "Get meal money from Hezekiah."

"I usually pay for our meals," James said. "If Hezekiah pays for our meals, I would be very pleased."

"Why don't you eat at Jonas' or Peter's house?" he asked. "Peter's wife is a good cook."

"Peter's wife is busy taking care of her mother, so when she asks we will tell her we can't stay and eat," he said. "We will tell her we must pick up mother's packages and get back to work."

"You could eat with Jonas," he said. "They would feed you."

"They are old like you and mother," John said. "I like eating at the Inn."

Zebedee grabbed John's arm. He was startled.

"Old like me and mother?" he asked. "James what do you think about that?"

"John likes to eat at the inn," he said. "I'll take him there."

Zebedee turned him loose and gave him a pat on the head. Then he walked away.

John looked at James.

"I said the wrong thing, didn't I?" he asked. "I didn't mean any harm."

"You have to be careful what you say," James said. "Some old people are sensitive about their age."

He hugged John, and they laughed.

When the boys went to see Peter, it was a beautiful day. James was glad that they rode the horses. He thought they only had a few small items to pick up for their mother, but they put the large saddle bags on the horses.

"John, I am going to stop at this shop," James said. "Mother gave me a list for the shopkeeper. Before we go home, we must stop and get the items she wants. If you want to look at the knives or hats, you can come into the shop."

"I'll just wait with the horses," John replied. "I am ready to visit with Peter. I hope he is home."

James talked to the shopkeeper for a few moments, and then he and John were on their way.

"Hi, Peter," John said. "I am glad you are home."

"I have been waiting for you," Peter said. "My father told me you would be visiting today."

"It is our monthly trip to Capernaum," James said. "We visit you, and we pick up supplies for mother."

"I think my father has an agreement with your father," Peter said. "Here, put this sack of coins in your saddle bag. Then we can talk for a while."

"I am ready to walk," John said. "Riding the horse is tiring."

Peter told them he had chores to complete after they departed. They went for a short walk. When Peter explained his interesting news, he seemed excited.

"The other day, Andrew and I went and listened to a traveling teacher," he said. "He was talking about the coming Messiah."

John expressed interest in a new Messiah.

"His message was a lot different from the message at the synagogue," Peter said. "He spoke directly against the Romans. He said that they are not treating us fairly."

"That is true," James said. "Father said he pays too many taxes."

"The people liked his message," Peter said. "When I told my father what he said, he told me that the teacher would get into trouble for saying that type of thing. He warned me not to repeat it."

"Was he in Capernaum?" John asked. "Is he staying here?"

"No, he was south of town," he replied. "If you were old and wanted to hear him speak, you probably would have taken a carriage. We just walked along the sea."

"I would like to hear his message," James said. "It sounds controversial."

"There were a lot of people listening to him," Peter said. "He doesn't stay anywhere very long. I think he moves to a new place almost every day."

"I wish we could have heard him," James said.

"Did you know Enoch is now repairing carriages?" John asked, changing the subject. "Father is having a shop built next to the barn where we will repair carriages and wagons. James and I mostly still work on boats."

"No, I didn't know you could repair carriages," he said. "I see a lot of them around town. I guess someone has to fix them."

"By the way, how is your boat?" James asked. "I hope you are catching a lot of fish."

"It has been great," Peter said. "Father is like a new person. We are catching a lot of fish, and we always have plenty to sell. He likes the boat so much, he helps us clean it."

"We are working on a very challenging project. You should see it," James said. "It needs a lot of repair work. When we are finished, it will be as good as new."

"Have a safe ride home," Peter said. "Thanks for coming. It saves me having to ride to your house."

"How is your wife's mother? John asked. "I hope she is better."

"My mother-in-law isn't much better," he said. "Most of the time, my wife is with her."

"I am sorry," James said. "Tell her we will say a prayer for her. We must go now. Mother always needs something from the store. When we stop on our way out of town, they will have her goods packaged for us to pick up. See you next month."

Leaving Peter's house, the two brothers couldn't stop talking about the traveling teacher. They couldn't believe a teacher spoke against the Romans. Their minds were busy. When they were about three quarters of the way home, James realized that they hadn't picked up their mother's packages.

"John, we forgot the packages," James said, frantically. "Take this sack of coins and put it in your saddle bag. Go straight home. Give the sack to Hezekiah and tell mother I am fine, but I will be a little late."

John became worried. James turned his horse around and rode out of sight.

"You had better hurry, James" John mumbled. "You need to be home before dark."

James didn't hear John, and he didn't see him wave. He steadied the horse at a brisk pace. He picked up the packages and started home. He was concerned that his father was going to be upset. He knew he had to be home before dark. He had become an accomplished rider and kept his horse at a steady pace.

When John arrived home, he was greeted by Enoch.

"Hello, John, where is James?" he asked. "I want to talk to him about our next boat project."

"He will be along," John said. "We forgot mother's packages, and he went back for them. He will be home before dark. I have to go. I have to see Hezekiah."

John walked to Hezekiah's house.

"Hi, John, where is James?" Hezekiah asked. "He usually brings me money."

"The money is from Jonas as payment for his boat, isn't it?" John asked. "I have a sack of money for you."

"Yes, it is," he said. "Did you visit with Jonas or with Peter today?"

"Jonas gave the money to Peter," he said. "We visited with Peter."

After visiting with Hezekiah for a few moments, John walked to their house and sat on the porch. As he waited, he thought about all the bad things that might happen to his brother. The sun was low in the sky, and the late afternoon air was cooler. John shivered and looked down the lane for his brother. It wouldn't be long before it would be dark. His mother saw John and sat in the chair next to him.

"Hi, John, where is your brother?" she asked. "I don't see him."

"He isn't home yet," John replied. "We were talking and forgot your packages. He went back to the shop to get them for you."

"I hope he gets home before dark," she said. "You both know your father's rules. Until James comes home, I would stay away from your father. Go and work on the boat."

John walked to the boat, but he didn't pick up a tool. He watched for his brother.

After what seemed like a long time, he saw a horse coming down the lane.

"Hi, John," James said. "I just made it. It is getting dark."

"I am glad you are here," John said. "Mother and I were both worried."

"Take my horse, and tell Nicia to give him extra water and freshening," James said. "The horse was great, he didn't complain at all. I am going to see mother and deliver her packages."

He placed the packages under his arm and walked to the house.

"Hi, mother," he said. "I have all your packages."

"It is good to see you," she said. "I was worried you wouldn't make it before dark."

"I made it with time to spare." He said.

"It was too close," she said. "Thank you for bringing my packages. Dinner is ready. I will call your father."

"You sure purchase a lot of items when we go to Capernaum," he said. "We have all of it. If you need any more than today, we will need to take a carriage."

"Yes, they have a lot of things I can't locate in Bethsaida," Salome said.

"I shop about every other day in Bethsaida, and you go to Capernaum once a month. That way I can keep our kitchen stocked for the servants."

"I am late," he said. "Before I eat, do you want me to take the food to the blind man? He will be worried that we forgot him."

"He doesn't worry," she said. "I have been feeding him once a week for many years. I have never forgotten him."

"I will have John take him some food," James said. "The blind man's faith is very strong."

"One of us could be blind," she said. "Yes, send food to him and tell your brother to hurry back. We will be eating."

The family enjoyed a hot dinner. Zebedee told James he was glad that he got home before dark. He suggested leaving Capernaum a little earlier next time. That way, he would get home earlier. He explained that both he and the horse would appreciate it.

"The boat that is waiting for repair is not a rush job," Zebedee said. "I want you to work on it for the next two weeks. After that, I want you to help Enoch, his father, and his brothers build a new shop and another barn."

"I have never built a barn," John said. "Will Enoch teach me?"

"When you are finished constructing the two buildings, we can finish up with the boat," he said. "I might end up purchasing that boat. We will fix it up for the owner so he can sell it."

"That is a little different," James said. "A job is a job."

"The sack of coins you gave Hezekiah this evening contained a message to me," Zebedee said. "Andrew wrote that one of their friends might want to purchase a boat. He is going to have him come and inspect it. If he likes the boat, I will purchase it and outfit it for him."

The next day, the weather was hot. Salome decided she would be cooler if she took a walk along the sea. She hoped a breeze would be blowing. When she passed the shop, she saw Enoch.

"Enoch, if you see Zebedee, tell him I have walked over to see Ruth," she said. "I didn't see him in the house."

"Yes, Miss Salome," Enoch said. "I think he is down at the boat giving instructions to Jonah."

"Who is Jonah?" she asked. "Do I know him?"

"Yes, you know him," he said. "He used to be my helper. He has worked for Zebedee for many years. When I went to Tyre to learn how to repair carriages, he took over running the boat repairs. I still oversee him."

"I never knew his name. I have seen him working with you for a long time. Our business is getting so large that I don't know everyone's name anymore. I am on my way to see Ruth," she said.

Salome thought Zebedee had built a very nice business. She wondered how they could afford a second carriage and a new boat. A smile appeared on her face as she walked very slowly, daydreamed, and enjoyed the breeze.

Eventually, she arrived at Hezekiah's house.

"Hello, Ruth," Salome said. "I thought I would check on you. How are you doing? Have you seen you mother lately?"

"I am fine," Ruth said. "I am getting a little bigger. I haven't seen my mother for several months. I miss her, but I really like living with you and being at the sea."

"Do you think she would like to visit?" she asked. "She could stay with you for a few days. If I remember correctly, you have a younger sister at home."

"I think she would love it," she said. "Father doesn't have a carriage. She would have to ride a horse, but father doesn't have an extra horse."

"The next time, John and James go to Capernaum, I will instruct them to bring her back to visit with you," she said. "Maybe, they won't forget her."

"That would be nice," she said. "I will tell Hezekiah we are going to have a visitor."

"Do you want to walk down to the sea?" she asked. "Zebedee and I often walk by the sea. It is very relaxing."

"Don't go too fast," she said. "I'll take a walking stick. I don't want to fall."

"When we decided to move, we thought Capernaum had become too large for us," Salome said. "We looked and looked for a large piece of land at the sea. This was the largest piece of land that we could afford."

"You were lucky to find it," Ruth said. "It is beautiful."

"I am very happy. I wasn't certain Zebedee would purchase it," she said. "I had to convince him the sea would have fish here in Bethsaida for him to catch."

Salome and Ruth had a short, slow walk along the sea.

When Salome returned home, she saw Zebedee on the porch. They talked about the wonderful sea breeze, and then she told him about inviting Ruth's mother to stay with her. Zebedee thought it was a good idea. He hoped Hezekiah would agree.

CHAPTER 6

JAMES STUDIES TO BE A RABBI

Zebedee's family was closely bound and many evening they sat on the porch and talked. James hoped that this evening would be a good time to discuss his future with his father.

"Father, I spoke with the Rabbi at our synagogue," he said. "I would like to start working and studying with him two days a week. Is that acceptable to you?"

Zebedee stared at James.

"No," he said. "I need you here."

"I don't plan on being a fisherman," he said. "This is a good opportunity for me. Our family is ready for another Rabbi."

Zebedee knew he wasn't going to prevail. He realized James was going to become a Rabbi no matter what he said. His main concern was the effect it would have on John.

"When do you plan to start studying with our Rabbi?" Zebedee asked. "We have a boat to repair."

"I was hoping to start soon," he said. "I wouldn't be away much, just two days a week."

Zebedee shook his head and looked at James.

"If it is that important to you, I guess we can survive without you," he said.

"John has become a good worker," James said. "You can count on him."

"I guess I could hire a day worker," he said. "Someone would like to be paid for working two days a week."

"You don't have to hire a day worker," he said. "When I am at home, I will work longer days."

"We can try it," Zebedee said. "If that is what you really want to do."

"I would really like to get started," he said. "I will tell the Rabbi that I have your approval."

"James, you are a young man. You must make and then live with your decisions," Zebedee said. "I will help you as much as possible. What does John think about you leaving him?"

"He wanted to go with me," he said. "I told him he was too young and needed to remain at home with you."

"I was afraid of that," Zebedee said. "John wants to do everything you do. He needs to know that I am counting on him."

"You should talk with him," James said. "He will listen to you."

"Tell Jonah which days you won't be at work," he said. "On those days, Hezekiah will have to pay day laborers."

"Are you certain you want day workers?" James asked. "If you are, I will tell him."

"Today, it is two days per week," he said. "Soon, it will be three. We need to locate the best day workers available."

"That is true," he said. "Someday, you will have to replace me."

"I hate to plan for that eventuality, but I have to face facts," he said

"I will make you proud of me," he said. "Maybe someday, you and mother will visit me in Jerusalem."

James planned to leave home as soon as he could make a living as a Rabbi. He hoped to go to Jerusalem. Zebedee considered how he would tell Salome and their friends.

After dinner, the family was seated in the living area. Salome started a conversation with Zebedee.

"It is time for the monthly trip to Capernaum," she said. "I have a very long list of items that I need. Ruth's mother is also coming for a visit. Who do you plan on sending with John?"

"I haven't thought about it," Zebedee said. "I guess I will ask Nicia to go with him. He can take the larger carriage, and he can teach John how to drive."

Early the next morning after breakfast, the sun peeked above the horizon. It was already quite warm. As he walked to the barn, Zebedee tried not to look directly at the sun. He covered his suntanned forehead with his hand.

"Nicia, I want you to take the large carriage and make a trip to Capernaum," he said. "John will go with you. You can take John to visit with Peter while you pick up this list of things for Salome."

Zebedee handed Nicia a list of household supplies. Nicia looked over the list.

"This is quite a list of items," he said. "I will start getting ready. It will take me about an hour."

"Before you start back, you will pick up Ruth's mother and bring her home," he said. "She is going to stay with Ruth for a while."

"Yes, sir," Nicia said. "Sir, you might want to consider hiring another servant."

"Hire another servant?" he asked. "How many do we have?"

"We have more work than we have servants," he said. "If you had another small house built next to mine, I am sure I could find a good family to help us."

"Do we really need another servant?" he asked. "Our business is getting very large. What makes you think the servants are overworked?" he asked. "Things are getting completed."

"Yes, sir," he said. "But we don't have any time to spend with our families."

Zebedee became concerned. He paused before he answered.

"I will have to talk with Hezekiah," he said. "I will get back to you."

Zebedee walked to Hezekiah's house. They discussed the need for an additional servant family. Hezekiah agreed with Nicia. They both agreed that happy employees do better work than disgruntled employees. Zebedee returned to Nicia.

"Hezekiah said you are correct," Zebedee said. "I will tell Enoch's brother to build another small house. He has just finished my new barn."

Zebedee told Salome they were going to have two more servants, a man and a woman.

"It is about time," she said.

She enlightened him by telling him it wouldn't be long before Chava would have children of her own, and she wouldn't be available to help any longer. They took a short walk along the sea. Salome explained how she planned to spend more time with her children and grandchildren. As they enjoyed the beautiful morning sky, Zebedee took her hand and kissed it.

After an hour when Nicia was ready to travel, he found John at the boat.

"Good morning," he said. "Your father told me to teach you how to drive the carriage. We can start by hitching up the horses."

"Are we going to Capernaum?" John asked. "Those trips seem to be when we learn how to drive."

"I guess you know where we are supposed to go?" Nicia asked.

"Yes, I know where to go," he said. "After you drop me off at Peter's, go to the shop and purchase whatever mother needs."

"She must need a lot," he said. "We are taking the large carriage."

"She always prepares a long list of items," John said. "You can give the list to the shopkeeper. When you are finished at the shop, you can come back and get me." "Then we will pick up Ruth's mother," Nicia said.

John climbed aboard the carriage. Nicia explained that the secret of driving the large carriage was not to get in a hurry or make any quick movements. About half an hour out of town, he allowed John to drive. When John took the reins, he remembered James and the thunderstorm. John thought driving was fun, but he gladly returned the reins to Nicia.

"Two horses are much more difficult than one horse," he said. "I have very little experience with driving a carriage."

"You will get used to the feeling of the reins," he said. "It takes practice."

"I will try it again another day," he said. "We have several chores today."

"I hear your brother is studying to be a Rabbi," Nicia said. "Have you decided what you want to do?"

John looked at Nicia.

"Yes, he is going to be a Rabbi," John said. "I think I will also be a Rabbi. I don't want to repair boats all my life. I think being a teacher would be satisfying. Turn down the second street. I think it is about the fourth house."

"After I have purchased all the supplies for your mother, I will return," he said. "Have a good visit with Peter."

John climbed out of the carriage. Peter saw him approach.

"Hello, John," he said. "Where is James?"

"He is not with me today," John said. "He is spending a lot of time studying to be a Rabbi. He only works with me about three days a week."

"I didn't know he wasn't at home. Is your father concerned?" he asked

"He is not very happy," he said. "He misses him, but must face the fact he isn't going to be a fisherman."

A concerned looked appeared on Peter's face.

"Where is James studying?" he asked. "He only works three days a week?"

"Our Rabbi is working with him," he said. "He goes to our synagogue."

"What about the boats?" he asked. "I know you must miss him."

"We are using a day worker," he said. "He is good and is pleased to work for us."

"I am glad you found a good worker," Peter said. "Many day workers aren't dependable."

"He isn't the first day worker we have tried," John said. "I don't think it will be long before James moves to Jerusalem, and the day worker will be full-time."

"Here, let me give you this money," he said. "Father said to tell your father that this is the last payment."

Peter handed John a sack of coins.

"You must be catching a lot of fish," John said. "We knew you would be successful."

"He also said to thank him very much," Peter said. "Without your father's help, we wouldn't have been able to purchase a boat. It is hard to believe we've had our own boat for a year now."

"It seems longer than that to me," John said. "I remember many trips to Capernaum."

"You come to see me once a month," Peter said. "Jonas tries to set money aside every week to pay for the boat."

"You have a nice boat," John said. "I remember getting it ready for you. We have repaired several boats since then."

"Where is your horse?" he asked. "I didn't see it."

"Nicia brought me in the new carriage," he said. "He was teaching me how to drive a large carriage."

"You were driving a large carriage?" he asked. "I thought you only had a small carriage."

"We do," he said. "Father has two carriages and a wagon now. I think he also has three fishing boats. His business has become quite large. We are building another house, and he is hiring two more servants."

"That is quite a business," Peter said. "How many people do you employ?"

"It can be confusing," John said. "We have employees as fisherman, mates, captains, and attendants for mother and Ruth. We also own many slaves."

"I will have to tell father," he said. "He will be happy for your family."

After they talked for about two hours, Nicia came for John.

"I have to go now," John said. "It has been good talking with you. I guess I won't see you for a while."

John climbed aboard the carriage.

"Your mother purchased a lot of supplies," Nicia said. "No wonder your father told me to bring the large carriage. Let's go and get Ruth's mother."

They waved goodbye to Peter and started to the other side of Capernaum.

John had a little problem recognizing Ruth's home. They drove down several streets looking for the house. When he recognized the house, he motioned at Nicia. He climbed out of the carriage and went to the front door.

"Hello, my name is John. I am here for Ruth's mother," he said. "Is she ready? We will load her bags."

"Come in," she said. "My name is Ester. I am Ruth's younger sister."

"Where is your mother?" he asked. "I will help her get into the carriage."

"Unfortunately, my father will not allow mother to leave home and visit with Ruth," she said. "He is sending me. He told me that I don't need to come home until after the baby is born."

John wasn't certain what he should do. He looked at the young lady.

"I was told to bring your mother. Can I talk with her?" John asked.

"Don't you believe me?" Ester asked. "Mother is embarrassed."

"I am sorry, but I need to tell my parents that I tried to bring her back," John said.

"Yes, you can talk with her," she said. "I will get her."

Soon, Ester returned with her mother.

"Hello," John said. "I am here to take you to visit Ruth."

"I appreciate you coming for me," she said. "You will have to take Ester."

"Ruth has planned for you to visit with her," he said. "I have been instructed to bring you home with me."

"I won't be going," she said. "I have to care for my husband. Please take Ester."

John was confused. He looked at Nicia. Nicia nodded. John looked at Ruth's mother. He understood that she wanted to visit with her daughter, but she was required to stay at home and take care of her husband.

"I am sorry you can't visit with your daughter," he said. "Mother was looking forward to visiting with you."

"Tell her I am fine and will visit her," she said. "Maybe someday, we will have a carriage."

"Ester, where is your bag?" John asked. "I will put it in the carriage for you."

"This is all I have," Ester said. "I can carry it. Is that your carriage?"

They boarded the carriage and started for Bethsaida.

"Yes, this is my father's carriage," he said. "This is Nicia. He will be driving us home."

"You have a large carriage and a driver?" she asked. "It must be nice."

"They aren't mine," he said. "I work for my father repairing boats."

"You repair boats too?" she asked. "Mother said your father was a fisherman."

"My father owns several different businesses," he said. "Ruth's husband, my oldest brother, runs the businesses for him. Father no longer does much work. Nicia has worked for him for a long time. You will like living with your sister."

Ester considered everything John had said.

"I will like being away from my father," she said. "I need to find a job."

"Your sister has a large house near the sea and has servants," he said. "She even has an attendant to help with the chores. Her house is located on the same land as our house. We will be able to visit."

On the way home, Nicia didn't have a chance to teach John anything about driving. John and Ester remained busy talking and learning about each other and their families.

"When we get home, take us to Hezekiah's house," John says. "Ester will be staying with Hezekiah's wife."

"Yes, Mr. John," Nicia said. "I will drive straight to Hezekiah's house." Nicia looked at John and smiled.

Salome watched as the carriage arrived. It passed her and stopped at Hezekiah's house. Salome waved and walked toward the carriage.

"I see you are back from Capernaum," Salome said. "Did you purchase my supplies and bring Ruth's mother back with you?" She looked in the carriage and was surprised to find a young woman, not Ruth's mother.

"I have some money from Peter's father, and we did get all your supplies,' John said. "Nicia will bring them in for you. Ruth's mother wasn't allowed to come with me. This is Ruth's sister, Ester, who will be staying with Ruth until after the baby is born. She only has one small bag of belongings."

Salome looked at John.

"Thank you," she said. "I will check with Ruth and make sure everything is well with her family."

That evening during a large dinner, the topic of discussion was, not surprisingly, Ester. Everyone expected Ruth's mother, so they were quite curious about the arrival of her sister. James informed his father and mother that he had been given a job as a Rabbi- in-training in Jerusalem, and that he would relocate.

Tears appeared in his mother's eyes. She looked worried and concerned.

"We are pleased for you," Zebedee said. "I hope you like living in Jerusalem. I am certain you will have more opportunities to learn about our religion."

"I knew I would have to move," James said. "Now that the time is here, I am sad."

"That is normal," Zebedee said. "You have lived with us your entire life."

"I will miss you all," James said. "Thank you, father, for allowing me this opportunity. Come visit me in Jerusalem."

"We will miss you," he said. "We also knew this day was coming, but we weren't looking forward to you leaving home."

"I will be with you in spirit," James said. "I will come home to visit when I can."

"Your mother and I will visit you," he said. "We love Jerusalem."

John was very quiet at dinner. After dinner, he and James took a long walk along the sea. It was obvious to everyone that John was upset about his brother leaving home. When they returned, it was late. The sun had gone below the horizon. They didn't speak to anyone and went straight to bed.

The next morning, Salome arose early.

"For those lucky enough to live by the sea, it is the start of another beautiful day," she said. "We have a wonderful breakfast. Take your places in the dining room."

Zebedee wasn't sure why Salome was so happy. He, James, and John sat at the table.

"What is the special occasion?" Zebedee asked. "Breakfast sure smells good."

"James won't be with us much longer," she said. "I decided we should enjoy a large breakfast."

Zebedee saw tears in her eyes. After breakfast, Salome went outside and walked to Ruth's house. She visited with her and Ester.

"Hello, Ruth," Salome said. "I understand you have a house guest."

"Yes, come in, Salome, this is my sister Ester," Ruth said. "Father is quite conservative. He wouldn't allow mother to leave home. He wanted me to have a helper, so he sent Ester."

"I looked forward to seeing your mother," Salome said. "Ester, I am glad you came to stay with Ruth."

"I am sure Ester will be a great help to me," Ruth said. "We have always been very close."

"Welcome to our home," she said. "We might just want you to stay."

"Thank you, Miss Salome," she said. "I have never seen such a beautiful home. We have a small house in town."

"Years ago, we lived close to your mother," she said. "I know her very well. I visited her often."

"I have been sharing a room with at least one sister all my life," Ester said. "I am the youngest."

"We didn't always have a large house," Salome said. "I remember our first house."

"I am glad to be with Ruth and you," Ester said. "Everyone here is so busy. At home it is hard to find work. Does your husband work on the boats?"

"No, not any longer," she said. "He owns all the businesses, and Hezekiah manages them for him."

"You have many houses," she said. "Do all those people work for you?"

"Yes, dear," she said. "I am sure Ruth will introduce you to all the servants and the employees."

Ester remembered everything John had told her.

"I hope you like fish," Ester said. "Today, we are having fish."

Salome smiled at Ester.

"Some of the workers have been with us for many years," she said. "I have only one attendant. Her name is Sara."

"It must be nice to have a steady job," she said. "I would like a steady job."

"We like it here. I hope you will be comfortable living with us." she said. "Come and visit with me."

"I will," she said. "I love it here."

"Ruth, did you hear about James?" Salome asked. "He is moving to Jerusalem."

"Yes, Hezekiah told me," she said. "We will all miss him."

That evening after dinner, Salome announced to Zebedee that they were going to be grandparents. Both Chava and Ruth were expecting. Zebedee didn't understand why that was such a big deal or why it should influence his life.

"Zebedee, it is time to build another house," Salome said. "You built a house for Hezekiah and Ruth. I think you should build a house for Ishmael and Chava."

"Hezekiah is my son," Zebedee said. "Chava is my daughter. I have already given them a house."

"You promised that you would build them a larger house when they had children," she said. "Now, they are going to have a child."

"Did I say that?" he asked. "I don't remember."

"You are not the only one who can forget. I can also forget things," she said. "If I were you, I would try very hard to remember."

She stared at Zebedee. He knew she was adamant about another house.

"Our family is really going to grow," Zebedee said. "Someday, it might be a large family."

"I had three boys and a girl," Salome said. "If they each have four children, we would have sixteen grandchildren. I get tired just thinking about it."

"It is good we have plenty of land," Zebedee said. "So, I promised her a house when she had children?"

"Yes, dear," she said. "It will be nice to have her living closer to us."

"If we are blessed with sixteen grandchildren, we will need many houses," he said.

"I know you and Enoch like to plan to build houses and barns," Salome said. "Have him build a house next to Hezekiah's for Chava."

Zebedee was still thinking about sixteen grandchildren. He smiled at Salome.

"I will talk to Hezekiah about it," he said. "You know it costs money to build."

Zebedee took a walk. He found Hezekiah and they talked.

"Hezekiah, your mother wants me to have a house built next to your house for Chava and her husband. What do you think?" he asked.

"I like the idea," Hezekiah said. "That way, the women could help each other. Ishmael is a very good worker. Someday, maybe he will be a mate for you. We could rent his house. The rent would be additional income for us."

"Oh," he said. "We could rent the house to generate extra income? And you would take care of all of that?"

"Certainly, father," he said. "I have been looking after our houses for several years. I could manage a few more properties."

"A few more properties, I guess you are correct," he said. "I am glad we talked."

Zebedee walked home to see Salome. He told her he had changed his mind. He didn't mention renting the old house.

"Salome, I decided to grant your wish. I will have a house built for Chava," he said. "You can invite them over for dinner and tell them the news."

"Will the house be next to Ruth's house?" she asked.

"Yes," he said. Hezekiah thought the women could help one another if they lived as neighbors."

"I agree," she said. "Thank you."

After he informed Salome, he found Enoch.

"Enoch, tell your brother I need another house," Zebedee said. "I want him to build a house for Chava next to Hezekiah's house. Tell him to leave room for an addition. She might have more children."

"I thought they have a house," he said. "Do they want another house?"

"She is going to have a baby," he said. "I decided it would be better if they lived here with us."

"Sure, boss," he said. "I think you are my brother's best customer."

Life changed again for Zebedee and Salome. Their second son had moved to Jerusalem. The reality that their son moved from home was a big adjustment for them. It was also a great adjustment for John. He seemed to have lost a certain enthusiasm he had always exhibited. This was offset somewhat with the addition of two grandsons to the growing family. Ruth's son was a large baby with a full head of black hair. Chava's baby was small and bald. Zebedee and Salome loved both of them.

CHAPTER 7

JAMES, JOHN, AND JOHN THE BAPTIST

Life was very different for John, now that his brother James no longer lived at home. He felt like he was constantly being scrutinized. He worked diligently for his father, but he wished he was with his brother. Zebedee and Salome thought for several years that James would eventually relocate to Jerusalem and study to become a Rabbi. They missed James, but they moved forward with their lives. Things were also very different for James, now that he wasn't at home. He gained significantly more control over his life, but with control came responsibility. Every morning, he arose and performed his assigned duties in the temple. His duties ranged from the mundane to the more spiritual. He often led a special prayer group. After noon prayers, he met with the Rabbi who mentored him. They reviewed James' assignments, and then he studied.

When the students met with the head teaching Rabbi that evening, he seemed a little unsettled.

"You are going to take a break from your normal studies," he said. "You are to collect specific information that will be given to the high priest, Joseph. He asked me to have you infiltrate the ranks of those who are following John the Baptist. He expects you to determine why John became so popular."

James raised his hand.

"Do you know where he is teaching?" he asked. "It sounds like this assignment is going to take us away from our studies for a long time."

"If the high priest is going to change our program of study, he must be very concerned," a student Rabbi responded. "This might be interesting for all of us."

"I will tell you everything you need to know," the Rabbi said. "Students, you will visit an itinerant Jewish teacher. He teaches in the area along the Jordan River."

James visualized the Sea of Galilee.

"I am going to be close to home," he said. "The Jordan River flows out of the Sea of Galilee, and I lived by that sea."

"Please pay attention," the Rabbi said. "One of you will be with him each week. We are interested in what John the Baptist says and how many people listen to his teaching."

James thought, 'this must be the teacher Peter talked about. When I find John the Baptist, maybe, I will see Peter.'

"Immediately, after you return from your week with John the Baptist, you will document your observations by preparing a written scroll," the Rabbi said. "After six weeks, the priest will read and study all the scrolls. If more information is needed, each of you will make a second trip."

"Will you discuss the scrolls with the students?" James asked. "I am interested in what John the Baptist says."

"This is a very important assignment," he said. "James, you will be the first to travel. I believe the teacher goes by the name of just John, not John the Baptist."

"Thank you," James said. "I will pack a bag. Do you know where he is teaching?"

"The last I heard he was at the fortification near Tiberias and headed north," he said. "It will take you about three days to find him. After you locate him, spend a week with him. After seven days, I will send the next student to travel with him. It is very important that we listen to his message and record it accurately."

James planned to tell his brother John about his experiences. It took him three long days to locate John the Baptist. When he found the teacher, he was greeted by a friend.

"Hello, my name is Philip," he said. "I know you are from Bethsaida. I haven't seen you recently. How are your brothers and father?"

Philip was small and appeared timid. James tried to remember him.

"They are fine," he said. "I remember you. You were a good friend of my younger brother. John is still at home working for father. He repairs boats."

"So, he is still at home," Philip said. "Is he planning to stay with your father?"

"I think he will eventually leave home," James said. "I left home a while ago and work in Jerusalem. I have heard about John the Baptist and decided to come and listen to him. Have you heard him teach?"

"Yes, I have been traveling with him for a few weeks," Philip said. "I have lost track of time. I also have left home. I worked in Capernaum. You will like John. He has a very interesting message."

"I am looking forward to hearing what he has to say, how many people travel with him? Will he stay here for a while?" James asked.

"You sure have a lot of questions," Philip said. "We never know when he will move to the next location."

"I will be with you for a week," James said. "I want to learn as much as I can."

"I think we will be here for at least a few more days," he said. "A lot of people, including the soldiers, attend his meetings. They enjoy listening to John."

"If you like Roman soldiers, being near a fortification is where you should be" he said.

"I guess about twenty of us travel with him," he said. "His next message will be early in the morning. Do you know how to fish? I have a small net, but I don't seem to be able to catch many fish."

The sun settled low in the sky as Philip and James walked to the river. They continued to talk about their boyhood homes. James was delighted that he had found a friend.

"Sure, I know how to fish," he said. "Give me your net, and I will show you how to use it."

"Good, I like fish," Philip said. "Now, I will be able to catch my meals."

"I am surprised you don't know how to net fish," James said. "My father taught me how."

"My father was not a fisherman," he said. "We bought our fish at the market."

"The secret is not to cast a shadow in the area where the fish are located," he said. "So, keep the sun at your face and cast the net as high and as far as you can throw it."

"Let me try," he said. "I think I can do it. Oh, that didn't work. Help me get this net off of me."

James looked at Philip and grinned. He struggled to get free from the net.

"Relax," he said. "Don't rip the net."

"It isn't as easy as I thought it would be," Philip said. "I need some help."

"Wait, I'll free you," James said. "Then just watch me cast the net. After I catch our meal, you can try again."

On his second cast, James netted several fish. Then he handed the net to Philip. He cautioned him not to hurt himself. Philip frowned and grabbed the net.

"Remember, keep the sun at your face," he said. "Throw the net up and out away from you. In the meantime, I will clean and cook the fish."

"I'll give it another try," Phillip said.

The smell of fresh fish being cooked filled the air. A few of John's followers smelled the fish and joined Philip and James. James successfully cast the net a few more times. Everyone ate fish and enjoyed an evening of fellowship. The smell of the fire lingered in the air and the dark of night overcame the men.

The next morning was beautiful. The sun reflected off of John as he taught about the coming Messiah. Later in the day, he taught a second lesson concerning how the Roman officials had taken control of people's lives through taxation and military presence. On other days, he expanded his teachings to include the need for everyone to repent. On James' last day, John performed the ceremonial cleansing called 'baptism.' James wasn't exactly sure what was happening.

"Philip, do you understand what John is doing?" James asked. "It seems to be more than just a ceremonial cleansing."

"Yes, at least once a week, he performs this baptismal ceremony," he said. "When John places people's heads under the water, all of their sins are forgiven (washed away). For the cleansing to be effective, those baptized have agreed to repent and start a new life."

"Does baptism work?" he asked. "It seems very spiritual."

"It depends on the resolve of those being baptized," he said. "It points them in the proper spiritual direction, but they must make changes in their lives."

"I have never seen anything like that," he said. "I will leave tomorrow. I hope I will be able to visit with you again."

"If we go north, I might be able to visit home," Philip said. "I haven't been home for quite a while. It would be good to see my mother and father."

"I hope you get to visit home," he said.

"When we visit Capernaum, I hope to meet with Peter and Andrew," Philip said. "They spent a day or two with us and seemed very interested. Have a safe journey."

James returned to Jerusalem, and another student Rabbi left to join those traveling with John. James wasn't quite certain what to think about John's message. He anticipated a lively discussion after the scrolls were prepared and the students and teachers had read them. He walked for two and a half days before he arrived in Jerusalem.

"Welcome home," the Rabbi said. "Write down what you saw and heard."

"I will do that in the morning," James said. "I am tired. It was a hot, long, difficult walk. The wind really blew along the lake."

The teacher looked sternly at James. He noted he was tired and dirty.

"No, I explained that I wanted you to write your findings as soon as you returned," he said. "I don't want you to forget anything."

"I don't know if I can stay awake," he said. "I will try."

James wanted to sleep. He wasn't interested in writing a report.

"You can clean and rest tomorrow," the teacher said. "I won't assign you any temple duties. Go into the library. I will bring you a scroll and writing material."

"Yes, sir," he said. "I will be in the library."

Before going to the library, James washed his hands and face. When he entered the library, he found the scroll and writing instruments. He worked diligently and recorded everything he could remember. Soon, his tiredness caught up with him, and he fell asleep.

"James, wake up," the Rabbi bellowed. "I instructed you to write about your experience. You must learn to follow my instructions. The longer you wait to write the report the more details you will forget."

James became startled. He rubbed his sleepy eyes and turned towards the voice that interrupted his sleep. He saw the Rabbi's mouth still moving.

"You aren't going to write much while you are asleep," he said. "Let me see how much you have accomplished."

He took the scroll and read it. He pointed at him.

"I am disappointed in your effort, James," he said.

"I attempted to stay awake," he said.

"If you can't stay awake while you are seated, stand up and write," he said. "It is much more difficult to fall asleep while you are standing. Now, finish writing what you witnessed."

"Hand me the scroll," James said.

"It is important to us that we can depend on you to do what we tell you to do. Not what you would like to do. Have I made myself clear?" he asked.

James immediately stood up. He was surprised by the Rabbi's attitude and sensed the Rabbi was very disturbed.

"I'll give standing up a try," he said. "Thanks for the suggestion."

James stood as he wrote, and that seemed to work. When he started to fall asleep, his knees buckled, and then he wobbled. The wobbling woke him, and he started writing again. After he finished writing about his journey, he gave his scroll to the student standing night watch. Then he went to his cot in the student sleeping quarters and immediately fell asleep. When he woke the following morning, he was told that he was excused from his morning duties in the temple, but was still assigned duties during the afternoon and evening.

James felt homesick. He worried about how his instructor treated him. He thought about the peaceful sea and his brother, John.

After Zebedee, Salome, and John finished their dinner, they sat in the living room and relaxed.

"Mother, have you heard from James?" John asked. "I miss him. Working on the boats is no longer fun. When can I go to Jerusalem and become a Rabbi?"

"I haven't heard from James, but I talked to Philip's mother," Salome said. "He recently visited his family. Philip is traveling with a teacher named John."

"Peter told us about a traveling teacher who he and his brother visited," John said. "They listened to him teach a lesson. It is probably the same teacher."

"Philip informed his mother that James spent a week with John the Baptist," she said. "I guess listening to new teachers is part of his training."

That evening, Salome told Zebedee she was worried that John missed his brother very much. Later, Zebedee found John. They sat by the fire and talked.

"John, your mother tells me you aren't happy in your job," Zebedee said. "Let's discuss want you don't like about it."

"Well father, I miss James," he said. "When he was here, repairing boats was fun. Now that he is gone, repairing boats is just a job."

Zebedee looked directly at John.

"What would you like to do?" Zebedee asked. "Would you like to be a mate of your own fishing boat?"

"No, I don't want to fish," he said. "I want to be with James in Jerusalem."

"I think you need to stay here with us," he said. "I don't think you can be a student like your brother."

"Why not?" he asked.

"Before he was allowed to study with the Rabbi in Bethsaida, James had to know how to write," Zebedee said. "Before he went to Jerusalem, he had to learn how to perform many of the temple duties. Being a Rabbi takes a great amount of discipline and work. You are probably too young."

"I am always too young to do what I want to do," he said. "Someday, I will be old enough."

"Don't wish your life away," he said. "Before you realize it, you will be old,"

"James was always a better student," John said. "I don't know what I want to do."

"You have plenty of time to think about it," Zebedee said. "Don't be in a hurry."

"I will think about it," John said. "Enoch has taught me many skills. I guess I will repair boats for a little while longer. Thank you for talking with me, father. I feel better."

The next day, Enoch told all those working on the boats that they had a new project. It was a boat that had capsized in a storm. It would be necessary for them to make the boat more stable and change its color.

"John, we have never had a project like this," Enoch said. "It will be a challenge."

"Have you decided what you want us to do first?" John asked. "I guess we can start by cleaning the hull."

"I am going to talk with your father," Enoch said. "Getting the boat cleaned is necessary and independent of what changes we make."

Enoch walked to the house and found Zebedee seated on the porch. They had a long, involved discussion about the boat. Later, Enoch returned to those working on the boat and explained what needed to be accomplished.

"We decided to make major modifications," he said. "We are going to reshape the hull. We will make it wider and more stable in the water. We will rebuild the keel and make it nearly flat. We are also going to increase the size of the underwater fin. It won't be very fast, but it will not capsize again."

"That might work," John said. "We need to make the underwater fin counterbalance the force of the wind in the sail."

"I don't want this to be a rush job," Enoch said. "We must plan our work and work our plan."

Neither brother, James or John, was completely satisfied with his job. After James left home, many things had changed for both of them. Late one afternoon while James studied, a Rabbi approached him.

"James, I want you to make another trip to listen to John" he said.

"This will probably be your last visit. It is obvious to us that he isn't going to be teaching very long."

"Do you think he is going to quit?" he asked. "Many people are with him."

"No, we don't think he will quit," he said. "We have informed the Roman officials about him. They aren't happy about his criticism of the government, and they plan to put him in jail."

James looked at the Rabbi in disbelief.

"They are going to put him in jail?" James asked.

"If you see any Roman military troops attending the gatherings, be very careful," he said. "John might be correct, but he is too aggressive. You must be careful. You mustn't make any statement or retaliation against the Romans."

"I will leave tomorrow morning," he said.

James remembered how he had been treated by the Rabbi when he returned from his last trip. He thought about his brother and Philip. He packed his few belongings into a bag. He planned a visit with his family and to leave most of his belongs with them. He would only carry what was essential for his existence. He decided not to return to Jerusalem. John the Baptist was near Capernaum. It required James four days to find and join the teacher. He was greeted by Philip, Andrew, and Peter. The number of those following John had grown.

"Hello," James said. "How long have you and Andrew been with Philip? Are you planning to stay with Philip and the teacher?"

"Yes, we told our father to hire day workers. We explained that we were going to travel with John," Peter said. "He was not happy with us."

"I think his exact words were 'have you two gone crazy?'" Andrew said. "He told us to get the boat ready and go fishing."

"He paid a lot of money for the boat," James said. "I'm not surprised he was disappointed."

Eventually, he said we could go to John," Peter said. "I think he gave up on us. He kept reminding me that I was married."

"He told us we could always come home if things didn't work out for us," Andrew said. "How long do you plan to be with us?"

"I have decided to join John and the three of you," he said. "I plan to travel home first and see my brother. I will see you in about two or three days."

"If you are planning on bringing John back with you, good luck," Peter said. "You won't be seeing us in two days."

"Good luck and safe journey," Andrew said. "I hope your father will understand."

James returned home and asked his brother if he would like to become part of those traveling with John the Baptist. John immediately said yes. John was pleasantly surprised to learn that Philip, Andrew, and Peter were among those that traveled with John the Baptist. James explained that he would need their father's approval. When James talked with Zebedee, he was disappointed and didn't understand.

"He is not like you," Zebedee said. "He is young and playful. He can't leave us."

"He is not happy working at home. He would be happy with me," James said

"Have you discussed this with your mother?" he asked. "She will never allow him to leave."

"John and I both discussed it with her," he said. "Mother said that she will be disappointed, but she wants John to be happy."

"I am going to talk with her," Zebedee said.

He walked away to find Salome. Zebedee didn't understand what was deficient with the life he provided for John. Fathers expected their sons to work in the family business. Hezekiah did very well. Even after he talked with Salome, he wasn't appeased. He returned to James and instructed him to take good care of his little brother. Zebedee asked James and John to remain at home for a week before they left. He hoped they might change their minds.

"We do want both of you to be happy," Zebedee said. "Stay with us for a week and make us happy."

"I told Peter I would return in two or three days," James said. "If I stay with you for a week, I guess he will understand."

Zebedee was shocked. He paused for a few moments.

"Peter isn't home with his wife? He isn't fishing with his father?" Zebedee asked. "When did this happen?"

"Peter and Andrew have both left home. They joined Philip to follow John the Baptist," James said. "Jonas finally understood, I guess."

"What about the boat?" he asked. "Who is fishing with that nice boat?"

"Jonas is using day workers," he said. "Peter said they are successful."

After a week, James and John departed their home and walked to Capernaum to join their friends.

"Hello, Peter," James says. "I have my brother John with me. He is excited about hearing John the Baptist."

Peter stood next to James. He towered over him.

"That was a long two days," he said. "I was worried about the two of you."

"My father asked us to stay a week with mother before we returned," he said. "They are disappointed, but want us to be happy."

"I think my father was just mad," Peter said. "Maybe someday, he will understand."

"When will we hear John the Baptist?" John asked. "James has told me about a few of his lessons."

"I am sure he will have a good lesson for us in the morning," Peter said. "Today was a day of prayer and fasting."

"Fasting? I'm too young to fast," John said. "I don't like to fast. Mother says it is not good for youngsters who are still growing. I like to eat."

As they talked, John the Baptist approached them. He noticed little John.

"Hello, my name is John," he said. "Many people call me John the Baptist. Who is this child you have with you?"

"He is my brother, John," James said. "He is not a child. He just looks very young. He is a man. He has worked longer and harder than many of those who are here."

"Looking young can be a good thing," John said. "Does he understand our religion?"

"He is a faithful member of our synagogue, and he knows the laws and practices them," James said. "He will be with me, and he will not disturb anyone. I am responsible for helping him."

"I am glad he is with you," John the Baptist said. "Welcome John, it is nice of you to join our gathering. I like your name."

John the Baptist turned and walked away. John looked at James.

"I think he likes me," he said.

"I am certain he likes you," James said. "He likes all of us."

The next morning, John the Baptist spoke to a gathering of about sixty people. His message was about the Messiah. He stated the Messiah would arrive soon. He stressed how important it was for everyone to prepare for the Messiah's arrival. John listened very carefully. Then he and Peter asked James many questions.

"Do you think the Messiah is actually coming soon?" Peter asked. "How does he know? Does John talk directly with God?"

"I have read that we will receive a Messiah," James said. "It is predicted in the writings of several of our prophets, including Jeremiah and Ezekiel. I don't think they predicted what John is talking about. I will need to hear many more of his lessons."

"We are going to start traveling again in the morning," Philip said. "We attract new followers when we move around."

John the Baptist and his disciples headed south traveling along the sea. The sea was beautiful, but they didn't notice it. They thought about John's last lesson.

When they reached the south end of the sea, they traveled along the Jordan River. Each day after the lesson, Philip, Peter, Andrew, James, and John reviewed the lesson and discussed it. They all had read many of the writings available at the synagogues, and they enjoyed discussing what they had heard. They spent hours trying to reconcile John's lessons with what they had been taught to believe. The young men each matured in their own manner. James was pleased he had returned home and brought his brother with him.

"John, are you glad you joined us?" James asked. "Do you like living with us better than being at home?"

"Yes, I know the verses where Jeremiah predicted a Messiah," John said. "The days are coming, declares the Lord, "When I will raise up to David a righteous Branch, a King who will reign wisely and do what is just and right in the land." (Je, 23, 5, NIV) I am pleased that you came for me."

John smiled and looked at Philip.

"Philip, what do you know about John the Baptist?" he asked. "How does he know so much?"

"His father is a priest," he replied. "I think he learned from him."

"I didn't know his father was a priest," John said. "I am sure he taught John all about God."

"John also lived in the pastures with the shepherds, and he spent some time with the Essenes," Philip said. "He seems to be a man of Great Spirit. When he was growing up, I know he and his father studied and prayed."

Soon, several Roman troops began to attend the lessons. Philip informed John the Baptist, but he was not interested. He explained they were probably from one of the military fortifications near the Jordan River. James remembered what he was told by the Rabbi in Jerusalem, but surprisingly, nothing unusual happened. John's teachings continued.

Many followers explained to John that they had repented and wanted to start a new life. During the next day's gathering, John baptized a large group of people. James saw Philip and asked about the crowd.

"How are we going to handle so many people?" James asked. "How many will he baptize?"

"Whoever wants to be baptized," Philip answered. "Sometimes it takes all day. Wait, what was that? Did you see a bright light?"

"No, I didn't see anything," James said.

"I saw it," John said. "James, you didn't see the light or hear a voice?"

"No, I didn't see or hear anything," James said. "What did you hear?"

"I heard a voice," John said. "It sounded like it came from the sky."

After many were baptized that day, John and his disciples rested. Philip inquired about the light he saw. John the Baptist replied that he had baptized a man named Jesus. God told him Jesus was the Messiah. John explained that Jesus would be much greater and of more importance than he. They wanted to meet Jesus. John the Baptist informed them that Jesus had departed. He agreed to introduce him to them the next time he attended a meeting. Word of the great light and Jesus' baptism was discussed by all of John's followers. Soon, a group of Pharisees and Rabbis from Jerusalem came to hear John the Baptist. They wanted to ask him a few questions. They wanted to hear John's explanation of Jesus.

"Are you the Messiah?" the Rabbi asked. "Are you sent from God?"

"I am not the Christ," (John, 1, 20, NIV) John said. "If you saw him, you would not know the Messiah because he is among you. I have been sent to prepare a way for him. I speak the words of a man weeping in the wilderness."

John's remarks caused great concern among the group from Jerusalem, and they went home. The Rabbis reread their testament trying to learn more about the Messiah. They concluded that Jesus couldn't be the Messiah. They went about their normal routines.

After several days, Jesus attended one of John the Baptist's lessons. After the lesson, Jesus talked with John. It was apparent to John's followers that John and Jesus knew one another. John introduced Jesus to his disciples.

"Look, the Lamb of God who takes away the sin of the world," (John, 1, 29, NIV) John the Baptist said. "This is the one I told you about."

"Which one do you mean?" John asked. "Is he the one you baptized?"

"Yes, I baptized him," John the Baptist, said. "I have known him as a friend for many years. Now, I know him as our Messiah."

"How do you know him from before?" James asked.

"His mother and my mother are related," John the Baptist said. "We lived in the same area and studied scripture together at the synagogue. He has several brothers and a sister."

"Some of our followers are going with Jesus," Peter said. "But, I am going to stay with you."

"You will follow him one day," John said. "He is the way to the future and our link to the past."

Many of John's disciples were confused. A few followed Jesus to ask him questions. Philip, Peter, Andrew, James, and John stayed with John the Baptist. They talked all evening about what they had witnessed. They recalled how John the Baptist said, "He is much greater than I am." They decided that if Jesus returned, they would ask him several questions.

After a few days, Jesus did return.

"Come on, John," James said. "I am going to go with Jesus and hear what he has to say. John the Baptist thinks he is our future."

"We will see you soon," Peter said. "We are going to talk more with John the Baptist, before we join you."

John the Baptist continued to teach. He didn't change his message. Roman soldiers attended many of his lessons. When they reported John's attack on morality, the soldiers were told to arrest him. He was charged with speaking against the Roman government and taken to prison. He offered no defense. It was almost impossible for his friends to find out any information about him.

Most of John's followers found Jesus and stayed with him. Jesus told them he would start his teaching soon, but first he had to do a lot of praying. He also explained that he planned to attend a wedding for the sister of one of his and John the Baptist's good friends. He invited all his closest disciples to attend the wedding. He advised them that, after the wedding, they would go to Capernaum for a few days and then to Jerusalem for the Passover. After the religious holidays, they planned to decide where and to whom they would teach. Before going to the wedding, each of the disciples returned home.

CHAPTER 8

THE WEDDING

Jesus walked to Cana to attend the wedding of the sister of a childhood friend. The wedding was performed in the synagogue. It was planned as the greatest wedding ever performed in Cana. The ceremony and first feast lasted an entire day. Many planned to extend the festivities for several days. Jesus attended the wedding with his mother and his siblings and invited the disciples of John the Baptist. Afterwards, Jesus planned to go to Capernaum. He hadn't explicitly told his followers why he was going there. There were some who didn't want to attend the wedding and went directly to Capernaum.

Before they traveled to Cana for the wedding, James and John visited with their parents. It was hot, and the breeze that blew across the sea made them all feel more comfortable. They sat on the porch with their mother and father..

"Mother, that was the best meal I have had in a long time," John said. "When you move around several times a week, you don't take time to cook good meals."

"I thought you might not be eating properly," Salome said. "Have some more goats' milk. It is very good for you."

"I will have a little more," he said. "Thank you. I don't want you to worry about us eating."

She looked at him.

"I do worry about you," she said. "It is my job. I am your mother. You need good food, so you can work hard."

"When the people come to hear the lessons, they bring food," John said. "Some days, we have food left over and distribute it to the poor."

"That is nice of you," she said. "We always have the poor with us."

"We can always eat fresh fish," John said. "James has taught several of our friends how to cast fishing net."

John and James enjoyed being at home, but they looked forward to going to Cana.

"You and James can come home anytime. We will make sure you have good meals," she said. "Sara, be certain they have some dried fruit to take with them."

"James and I leave tomorrow morning to go to the wedding," John said. "It is great that you are allowing us to follow our chosen path. We love you and father very much."

Zebedee and Salome decided not to complain about their sons leaving home.

"You have been a good son," he said. "We will miss you and James. We hope you will visit us when you are in the area. Would you like to see the boat we're working on?

"No," John said. "When I was small, all I wanted to do was be with my brother and work on boats. James and the boats were the focus of my life. After working on the boats became a job, I lost interest."

He waved at the boats.

"Life isn't all fun," Zebedee said. "Having a good job is important to most people."

"Most of my days are fun," John said. "Helping people learn about God is fun."

John looked at his father.

"We will visit, occasionally, when we are in this area," James said.

"John, I want you to know, if your brother had not promised to look after you, I wouldn't have allowed you to go," Zebedee said. "If you need any help, I want you to count on your brother."

John looked directly at his father and then gave him a hug.

The family spent an enjoyable evening talking. They watched the stars' reflection glimmer on the Sea of Galilee and occasionally heard a fish splash.

The next morning, they arose early and ate breakfast. Then James and John gathered their packs and headed out the door.

"Goodbye mother," John said. "We are walking into town to meet Phillip, and then we will be on our way."

"Say hello to Phillip's mother for me," Salome said. "I haven't seen her this week. You boys be careful."

They waved goodbye as they headed into town. Their bags were heavy, because Sara had insisted that they take several packs of dried fruit.

While the two brothers walked, they discussed boats, their family, and traveling with John. When they arrived in Bethsaida, they went to Phillip's house. They didn't see him and knocked on the door.

"Hello, we have stopped for Phillip," John said. "Is he ready to travel?"

"He isn't ready," Phillips mother said. "He is in a melancholy mood."

"He is just being lazy," John said. "Tell him I am here."

Phillip came to the door. He was not wearing sandals.

"Come in, John," he said. "I'm not feeling very well. I think I will stay home another day or two, and then I will meet you in Capernaum.

"You will miss the celebration," John said. "They will have a lot of food."

"I will be fine. I should be ready to travel in a few days," Phillip said.

"You don't look sick to me," John said. "Get your bag, and let's go to the wedding."

"No, I am staying here for a few days," he said. "I will see you in Capernaum."

"We will all miss you," he said. "You will miss the chance to be with Jesus He will be there with us."

"Tell him I am ill," he said.

"I will tell him you wanted to stay home with your mother for a few more days," John said. "We will look for you in Capernaum. James and I are excited about going to the wedding."

"We will tell Peter and Andrew that you will meet us in a few days," James said.

They didn't know what to think about Phillip refusing to go with them to the wedding.

John and James stopped in Capernaum and joined Peter and Andrew. The four of them continued on to Cana. It wasn't a long journey. They talked about their new teacher and questioned each other about marriage.

"Peter, is your wife religious?" John asked. "I don't know her."

"She isn't very religious," he said. "She is always taking care of her mother. Her mother is very ill."

"That is too bad," John said. "Andrew, are you going to get married?"

"Not now," Andrew said. "I am too busy traveling and trying to learn about our Messiah. At some point, maybe, I'll get married."

"Are you going to get married some day?" Andrew asked. "I mean when you grow up."

"Probably not," John said. "I want to teach. I don't think I'll have time for a wife. Our brother, Hezekiah, is married and has two children."

"Our sister is also married," James said. "They have one child."

When they reached Cana, they found that tents were provided for out of town guests. They were relieved that they didn't have to sleep outside or pay for a room. They joined several other disciples and made their way to the tents.

The next morning they arose early. John rubbed his eyes and sniffed the air.

"I smell food, do you?" he asked. "I am hungry. Let's get up and see what is cooking."

"Yes John, that is food," James said. "I think it is coming from the synagogue. They must be preparing breakfast for us."

John rubbed his stomach. As they got ready, a stranger approached them.

"Hello, my name is Paul," he said. "I am glad all of you could make it to the wedding. Are you friends of Solomon, the groom?"

John decided to speak for the group.

"No, we are friends of Jesus," he said. "You must be the brother of the lady who is getting married. Your father certainly has been nice to his guests. We appreciate the tents."

"I know Jesus. When we were younger, he, John, and I were good friends," Paul said. "You must be traveling with your brother, a disciple of Jesus."

John pointed to James.

"He is my older brother, James," he said. "Father made him promise to protect me."

"You have a good brother," Paul said. "Have a good time."

"I am a young man and have been working for many years," he said. "I am also very lucky to have an older brother to help me."

"You are lucky," Paul said. "I, too, have an older brother. He has often given me good advice."

"I guess we have a lot in common," he said. "I also have a sister."

Paul looked at John and smiled.

"This wedding is a big deal for my father," Paul said. "Yona is his only daughter. He enjoys making a big fuss over all of us."

"Fathers can be like that," John said. "My father worries about me."

"It is my father's way of compensating for always being at work," Paul said. "I must go to the house now and meet the other guests. Be sure to have a big breakfast. It will have to satisfy your hunger until after the ceremony."

Paul turned and walked to the next group of guests.

"He was a nice fellow," James said. "He sounds proud of his father."

"I don't think much of him," John said. "He is a little too nice for me. I'll bet he has never done a day's work."

They walked towards the odor of breakfast. They were joined by another man with long, brown hair.

"Hello," James said. "We planned to meet you in Capernaum."

John looked at Jesus and asked, "Tell us more about John the Baptist, did you know his father?"

James looked at John.

"We are hungry," he said. "After the wedding, we will have plenty of time to get to know each other."

The groom was handsome, the bride was beautiful, and the ceremony was long. When the wedding ceremony was over, everyone was invited to change clothes and attend the celebration party at the synagogue. Table after table of food and drinks were provided for the guests. The wine was used for toasts, and everyone had a toast for the bride and groom.

John wiped food from his face.

"James, I feel a little out of place," he said. "I hope no one minds us enjoying ourselves."

"No, not at all," James said. "Let's get another plate of food, and then we'll sit with Peter and Andrew. I think they have found some other disciples."

"Have you ever seen so much food?" Peter asked. "I plan to try a little of each dish. I even like the fish."

"Our father had a nice wedding for Chava, but not this nice," John said. "He did build her a nice house."

"I have been told that Paul's father is providing everything," James said. "See, John, I told you he was a nice fellow. He even provided tents for us. One of his businesses is making tents."

"He is like father," John said. "He has more than one business."

"There are two other sons. Each runs a tent-making plant. Paul is a student and a Rabbi in Jerusalem," James said. "I don't think I met him before today, but I have met his tutor Gamaliel. He is a very well-known scholar and Rabbi."

"You know Paul's tutor?" he asked. "Then, I am surprised you haven't met Paul."

"There are many students learning how to become a Rabbi," James said. "Many of the buildings on the temple grounds are for housing and for teaching students."

"Did you see the look on the groom's face at the ceremony?" John asked. "He looked like he was about to fall over. I think he was in shock."

"He did look a little pale," James said. "I asked Paul about him."

"What did he tell you?" he asked. "Does he like him?"

"His name is Solomon, and he works for Paul's brother at the plant in Tyre," James said. "He must help make tents,"

"I wonder how he got the job," John said. "Cana is not near Tyre."

"He was raised on a farm near Cana," he said. "While working on the farm, he learned how to handle tools."

"I guess he didn't want to be a farmer," John said. "So he went to Tyre."

"Paul really likes him," James said. "He said he is a good worker and very good with his hands."

"I wonder if Solomon has brothers and sisters," John asked. "I see many people I don't know."

"He has two brothers," he said. "I think he has one sister."

"You sure know a lot about him," John said. "I hope he will be happy."

"I asked Paul a great number of questions," James said. "I wanted to learn to know Paul, and that gave me an opportunity."

"Are you still hungry?" John asked. "I think I could eat another plate of food."

"Let's get a glass of wine before it is gone," Peter said. "Everyone seems to be enjoying the wine."

A few hours passed when the disciples saw Paul approach. They wondered why he wasn't with the others enjoying the party.

"I'm frightened we are running low on wine. Do any of you know the merchants in Cana?" Paul asked. "Can you help us find more wine?"

The disciples didn't know much about Cana, but most of them went into town to try to find additional wine. They instructed young John that he was to stay at the wedding. After walking many blocks looking for wine, they realized that all of the shops were closed because the merchants were attending the wedding. John wanted to talk with Jesus, so he walked and looked for him. After several tries, John found him, but Jesus was busy with some of the servants. John overheard what was being said. He didn't approach Jesus until he was finished instructing them.

"Hello, Jesus," he said. "I guess we are running low on wine. My brother and the others have gone to find more wine. I wanted to stay here to talk with you."

Jesus was surprised the men had gone into town. He smiled at John.

"You found wine?" John asked. "Paul will be pleased."

Jesus explained that the servants had found wine in the jars they thought were full of water. Jesus took a glass and sampled the wine. He held it up so the servants could see it. The servants still disagreed with him.

"Fill the jars with water," (John, 2, 7, NIV) Jesus said.

"The jars are full of water," a servant insisted. "I know because I don't enjoy wine, so I have been drinking the water. My friend has also done the same."

Jesus suggested they sample the wine.

"Ok, I will try it." The servant took a sip.

"This isn't water!" he shouted. "Something has happened. I know that jar was full of water."

"Here, try this," the servant said to his friend. "Let me give you some water."

He handed him a glass of wine.

"It tastes like wine," his friend said. "But the last time you gave me a drink from this jar, it was water."

"It must have been a different jar," the servant said, confused.

"Now draw some out and take it to the master of the banquet," (John, 2, 8, NIV) Jesus said.

"Yes," the servant said. "But how did you do that?"

His friend looked at him and said, "I guess the jars are magic. I may just take them and sell them for a lot of money."

Then he laughed.

"It tasted like water to me," the servant said. "I must have been wrong. I am sorry for the inconvenience."

John smiled at Jesus and consoled the confused and scared servants. He walked away as the servants moved the jars of wine.

"The wine jars aren't magic," one servant said, pointing to Jesus. "He is magic."

"No wonder he is popular," another servant said. "If I could turn water into wine, I would be popular."

Jesus joined John, and they walked toward the guests.

"I think the servants were actually trying to keep the wine," John said. "They probably have been drinking it all along. You exposed their plot."

Jesus looked at John, and he understood the servants were doing a good job and were honest hard working men.

Jesus excused himself and went to his mother. She asked about his discussion with the servants. He told her the servers were confused, and he had found wine. He ensured her all was well. Jesus explained to Paul's father that he should not worry. In fact, his son-in-law would be remembered for keeping the finest wine until last. No one was aware of what happened. When the disciples returned, the celebration was quite lively. They weren't really interested in John's story at that time.

When James returned, he went to Paul.

"Paul, we looked throughout the town," he said. "All of the merchants are here, so every shop is closed. We will be able to get more wine in the morning."

"Everything is fine," Paul said. "Enjoy yourselves. Jesus found more wine for us. I'm not sure where he got it, but it is very good."

"I will take a small glass," James said.

He tasted it and held it up so Paul could see it.

"This is fine wine," James said.

They each found a new plate, filled it with food and continued to enjoy the celebration. That evening, the tent area was a joyous place. Many unbelievable stories were told.

The next morning, James overheard the servants talking about the mysterious jars of wine. They insisted the jars were full of water, and that, all of a sudden, they were full of wine. They didn't know what happened. No one believed them except John. The others guests thought they had sampled too much of the fine wine. The celebration continued for another day.

Jesus and his disciples walked to Capernaum. It was a short walk, and the weather was mild. When they approached the town, they saw many fishing boats on the sea. Jesus watched intently. Peter approached him.

"Jesus, this is our home," he said. "Andrew and I grew up in this area. Our father owns a boat, and we are both very good fisherman. We know the people of Capernaum. It is a nice town."

Jesus put his arm around him. He was pleased and indicated that he intended to speak to the people.

"My brother and I are very familiar with the synagogue," he said. "We know most of the people who attend the lessons. We will show you the way."

Jesus spent the day with the people at the synagogue. They seemed very interested in what Jesus had to say. When night approached, Jesus and his disciples rested at the Sea of Galilee. Many of the townspeople went with them. They started a fire and cooked fish that was provided by Peter's father. They all enjoyed the meal and Jesus' stories.

After a few hours, James and John found a place to sleep under a tree. Peter spoke with Jesus.

"Would you like to go out on the boat tomorrow morning?" Peter asked.

Jesus agreed, because he had never sailed on a fishing boat.

"It is a really nice boat," Peter said. "James and John rebuilt it for my father."

Jesus was surprised that little John could help build a boat.

"Yes, they fish and repair boats," Peter said. "Their father is a very good man, and he is very successful."

Peter told Jesus all about Zebedee's large piece of land near Bethsaida on the Sea of Galilee. He explained how his father's boat sat on large blocks while James and John rebuilt it. He also told Jesus about the other members of their family and about their businesses. Jesus smiled at Peter. Peter sensed that Jesus knew something about the financial arrangement. He ended the conversation and went to bed.

The next day, Jonas, Peter, James, and John took Jesus fishing. They caught a boat load of fish and returned before noon. They showed Jesus how they cleaned and salted the fish. That evening, the disciples decided to rest by the sea.

When Peter approached Jesus the next morning, the sun shone brightly. Peter informed Jesus about his sick mother-in-law.

"My wife's mother is very sick," he said. "She has been sick for a long time. My wife has devoted her life to caring for her. She rarely has any time for me."

Peter noted Jesus' interest in his mother-in-law.

"She is a lady of strong faith," he said. "The Rabbi knows her very well. She used to be a regular at the synagogue."

Jesus and Peter went to the synagogue and spoke to the Rabbi. "Jesus left the synagogue and went to the home of Simon. Now Simon's mother-in-law was suffering from a high fever, and they asked Jesus to help her. So he bent over her and rebuked the fever, and it left her. She got up at once and began to wait on them. (Luke, 4, 38-39, NIV)

John looked at his brother.

"James, did you hear him address God as father?" John asked. "If God is his father, then he, himself, must be a God."

"Yes, I heard him," James said. "He thinks of God like we think of our father."

"It is a father-son relationship," he said. "I wonder if God has any other sons."

James looked at him.

"I don't think so," he said.

The few disciples who were not present during Jesus' feat in Cana now believed in him.

They discussed Peter's mother-in-law.

"I know her very well," Phillip said. "I have visited with Peter and her many times. I thought she was going to die."

"Now, she is well and walking," John said. "She no longer is controlled by a demon."

"Jesus can do miracles," he said. "Without him, she would have died."

"Actually, his father performed the miracles," John said. "Jesus just asked for his help to strengthen her faith. Now do you believe me about the wine?"

"I believe you," Phillip said. "I should have attended the wedding."

Soon after Jesus healed Peter's mother-in-law, Mary, Jesus' mother, returned to Nazareth.

The local Rabbi sent a message to the head Rabbi in Jerusalem. He wrote about the teacher who talked at his synagogue and became extremely popular. After his lesson, the teacher visited with a member of the synagogue at her home. The Rabbi explained that he, himself, had been praying with the lady for two years. He claimed Jesus said only one prayer, and she was healed. She even got out of bed. The teacher was so influential, that the Rabbi was afraid the members of his synagogue would leave and follow him.

Jesus and his disciples stayed in Capernaum for a few days. Many learned of his message. They marveled at Jesus' words. Stories, about his ability to heal the sick, spread quickly throughout Galilee.

Thanks to Peter's mother-in-law and a shortage of wine, Jesus began his ministry.

CHAPTER 9

JOHN AND JAMES TRAVEL WITH JESUS

Tiberius, the emperor of Rome, was not a powerful leader. The senate and his advisors managed the empire. Tiberius wanted to be known for his willingness to serve his people. He enjoyed traveling, so he spent very little time in Rome. He was aware of John the Baptist, but viewed him as a local problem in Galilee. He knew less about Jesus and wasn't concerned about him.

As Jesus approached, James and John sat in the shade under a tree.

"It is good to see you. We met in Cana," James said. "I imagine that you have been very busy recently."

Jesus sat down with them.

"The wedding was wonderful," James said. "It is a pleasure to finally have some time to talk with you. Many of us are from this general area, north of the sea. We are from Bethsaida. I think you've met my younger brother."

James stood up and pointed to John. John smiled at Jesus.

"I remember seeing Jesus at Cana," John said. "I was with him when we had a small problem with the wine. He eventually convinced the servants the jars were full of wine."

"I had gone into town to look for more wine," James said. "Your mother, Mary, agreed to care for the young children."

"My mother, Salome, tries to care for all of us," John said. "I am certain your mother looked after you."

"John and I have spent a little time with John the Baptist," James said. "When we listened to him talk of you, we decided to follow you."

"I heard John say he prepared the path for you," John said. "Now, it is your time. We must go forth and proclaim the word of God."

"Before we started spending time with John the Baptist, I was in Jerusalem studying to be a Rabbi," James said. "On one of my trips to hear John, I started to understand his message of repentance."

Jesus looked at James and John. Paul had told James about Jesus' family.

"Our older brother and our sister live with mother and father," James said. "We come from a very hard-working family. We were fishermen and also repaired boats. Peter and Andrew are our friends. Our parents know each other."

Jesus patted John on the head as he departed. John looked up and smiled.

He spoke to his brother, "I could sense that Jesus is pleased that we decided to travel with him and help spread the good news about God. I think he especially likes me, because it is very obvious I am his youngest disciple."

The time of Passover approached and Jesus with his disciples made the journey to Jerusalem. When they arrived, the city was crowded with the faithful who had traveled to visit the temple. John and James were surprised to see Roman soldiers posted at the intersection of every street. Jesus and his disciples planned to spend a quiet Passover praying and meditating. As they approached the Sheep Gate, they saw many disabled people including a lame man.

"When Jesus saw him lying there and learned that he had been in this condition for a long time, he asked him, "Do you want to get well?"

""Sir," the invalid replied, "I have no one to help me into the pool when the water is stirred. While I am trying to get in, someone else goes down ahead of me."

Then Jesus said to him, "Get up! Pick up your mat and walk."

At once the man was cured." (John, 5, 6-9, NIV)

Soon, the Pharisees heard that a man had been healed. They were not happy with Jesus' actions. About twenty of them convened in a room at the temple to discuss the incident.

"He healed a lame man," a Pharisee said. "He and his disciples prayed for the man, and the man stood up and walked."

The leader of the discussion stroked his long, black beard.

"Are you certain the man was lame?" another Pharisee asked. "Was he healed, or did it just look like he was healed."

"That man has been sitting by the city gate for many years," another said. "He wasn't there today."

The Pharisees were perplexed.

"When did this happen?" he asked. "Was it on the Sabbath?"

The head Pharisee smiled at the group.

"Yes, it was," he said. "This teacher should know that there is no work on the Sabbath. We are expected to rest and honor God, but he is teaching his followers to be unfaithful."

"What was the teacher's name?" he asked.

"His name is Jesus," a Pharisee said. "He is the one John the Baptist talked about. John said that Jesus is the Messiah who is prophesied about in our scripture."

One afternoon, the disciples saw Jesus make his way through the crowd toward the temple. They followed him.

"It is Passover," John said. "I am looking forward to the celebration."

Jesus noticed that several other disciples had joined him.

"We have a friend who is involved with the Jewish mint, but I am not certain how," James said. "Some of you might have met Paul at the wedding."

At the temple, John saw the money changers and asked James what they were doing. John's father always took care of the Passover offerings, so he was not familiar with the money changers.

"The faithful will make a sacrifice to God," James said. "If they have a large sum of money, they will purchase a lamb to be sacrificed. If they have a modest amount of money, they will purchase a dove."

John looked at his brother.

"James, do you know what father purchased when we were here for Passover?" John asked. "Did he purchase a lamb?"

"No, I think he purchased a dove," James said. "It cost father a lot of money for all of us to travel to Jerusalem."

James looked at John.

"To purchase a temple animal you must use Jewish coins," James continued. "The Roman coins bear a likeness to the emperor and are considered unclean. They must be exchanged for Jewish coins. The Jewish coins are engraved with a Jewish symbol on one side and a required Roman engraving on the other side. It looks to me like these money changers are charging a fee to exchange the coins."

Jesus was insulted by the money changers' actions against the faithful. He was furious that they wronged God in His temple. Before anyone realized what was happening, he walked directly to the money changers and abruptly overturned their tables.

"Get these out of here! How dare you turn my Father's house into a market?" (John, 2, 16, NIV) Jesus asked.

This caused a loud commotion. Many people hurried to gather the coins that were dropped on the floor. The money changers were frightened and fled.

Confused, the disciples fled the temple and regrouped a short distance north of the city. James had John by the hand and did his best to protect him. John was having trouble keeping up. He began to struggle free from James. James gripped his hand more tightly.

"John, stay with me," James said. "Things are a very confusing. I'm not sure what upset Jesus so much, but I am sure the temple priests will be looking for him."

John stopped to catch his breath.

"Jesus was upset that the money changers were charging an unfair amount," John said. "If the temple priests knew that, maybe they would understand why he was upset. What will they do to him?"

"I'm not sure, but if they're looking for him, they will be looking for us," James said. "We must hold hands and remain a unit."

"You lead the way," John said.

After the disciples thought they were safe, they stopped and prepared dinner. The red sun disappeared below the horizon. The disciples relaxed and discussed Jesus' actions. It was a serious debate. John watched as a man joined them.

"I have come to talk with Jesus," he said. "My name is Nicodemus, is he with you?"

John stood and walked to Nicodemus.

"Hello, sir," he said. "My name is John. I will find Jesus for you. Have a seat by the fire."

John stretched his legs and then disappeared. He was gone for quite some time. He finally returned with Jesus and introduced him. Jesus stepped forward and welcomed Nicodemus.

Nichodemus was surprised he knew of his position.

"I listened to John the Baptist," he said. "He recognized you as our Messiah."

"I am sorry it took me so long to see you. We had a little trouble with the money changers at the temple this afternoon," John said. "We are probably in trouble with the temple Rabbis."

"Rabbi, we know you are a teacher who has come from God. For no one could perform the miraculous signs you are doing if God were not with him," (John, 3, 2, NIV) Nicodemus said.

Jesus looked directly at Nichodemus.

"I tell you the truth, no one can see the kingdom of God unless he is born again," (John, 3, 3, NIV) Jesus replied.

Nicodemus didn't understand how a man could be born again. Jesus and Nicodemus talked for a long time.

The disciples heard Jesus say "I tell you the truth; no one can enter the kingdom of God unless he is born of water and the Spirit." (John, 3, 5, NIV)

Nicodemus didn't fully understand Jesus' message, but he was pleased that he had spoken with him. He thanked the disciples for their hospitality and returned to Jerusalem, where he resumed his position as a Pharisee.

Jesus took his disciples into the Judean country side, and he taught them how to baptize followers. John looked at James and smiled.

"I have seen John the Baptist, baptize people," John said. "He baptized many people."

"He baptized Jesus," James said. "Now, we will baptize those who follow and hope to start a new life."

Early the next morning after the sun eased above the horizon, they walked along the Jordan River and searched for an appropriate location. The sky was blue, and the weather was warm. James looked at John.

"Baptism is an outward expression of one's faith," he began. "When you put a person completely under water, this person is ceremonial cleansed and born anew."

John smiled at his brother.

"You need to be clean to worship," John said. "We always clean before going into the synagogue. It shows respect for God."

The disciples spent the day practicing baptizing the followers. As he walked into the river, the sun shone on his beard, causing it to appear red. He waved his arms.

"I think baptism is important to God and to those who want to help themselves," James said.

Many people were converted and baptized that day.

Jesus and his disciples remained north of Jerusalem a short while. Soon, they walked north to an area where Jacob had given his son a well many years earlier. It was situated on a great piece of ground. One of the disciples talked about the Inn at Sychar to his friends.

"I have heard of this area," James said. "One of the Rabbis in the temple, Paul, always stayed at the inn. His family knew the inn keeper to be a faithful man."

"Are we staying at the inn?" John asked. "I don't have any money."

"No," James said. "The innkeeper will provide food and a place to stay near his stable."

"Jesus, do you know that the women of Sychar come to the well each evening?" John asked. "I've seen them fill their jars with water and return to the city before dark."

"Jesus, tired as he was from the journey, sat down by the well." (John, 4, part of verse 6, NIV)

Then a woman from Sychar arrived. Jesus told this woman about her entire life. She was frightened at first, but she came to understand that only a Messiah could have known so much about her. She was confused, but decided to talk with Jesus.

"I don't know you," she said. "How do you know about me?"

She looked at Jesus. She thought Jesus was a prophet. She filled her water jars, and then she returned to the city. She told everyone that she had met a man who knew her entire life. She was certain that he was the Messiah. Her changed spirit was evident to the men of the town, and the next day, they visited with Jesus.

The following day was warm and sunny. The disciples rested. They cleaned their clothes, and they spent several hours praying.

"Peter, did you see Jesus with that woman?" John asked. "She was a Samaritan. I wasn't sure if Jesus would talk to a Samaritan woman."

"Yes, John, I saw him," he said. "He is trying to help everyone understand the idea of one God for all."

The men of Samaria spent the next few days listening to Jesus. They understood his message and believed he was a man of God. Soon after, the disciples helped form a church in Sychar.

Jesus' stories became very popular, and many people came to hear him. Jesus walked north and stayed in his home town. When Jesus spoke at the synagogue, he was rejected and turned away.

"I tell you the truth," he continued, "No prophet is accepted in his hometown." (Luke, 4, 24, NIV)

The next town they visited was Cana. The memory of the wedding was fresh in his mind. Jesus went to the synagogue and spoke to the people. A servant who worked in the synagogue recognized him and told the other servants about the wine incident.

"He is the one who turned the water into wine," the servant said. "I am sure he is the man."

Many people came to listen to Jesus' message. After the lesson, Jesus and his disciples were approached by a distinguished looking man.

"The people of Cana have told me much of you," he said. "I have a son who is very sick. Will you pray for him? He is in Capernaum. I have traveled to Cana to talk with you."

James took the man's hand.

"What is wrong with your son?" he asked. "How do you know he is sick?"

"He doesn't make sense," he said. "He speaks in a very loud voice. People are afraid of him."

"We are traveling to Capernaum," he said.

Jesus looked at the man and said "You may go. Your son will live." (John, 4, 50, NIV)

Jesus and his disciples went to Capernaum and performed many other miracles. A demon that possessed the young man was cast out, and he was returned to normal.

"Thank you for healing my son," the father said. "How much money do I owe you?"

"We didn't make your son well," John said. "His faith in God healed him. Your debt is to God."

"I give thanks to God twice every day," he said. "I will go to the synagogue every Sabbath."

"That is a good start," John said. "Feed the poor, visit with those in prison, and bring your friends to hear our message about God."

Many were baptized by the disciples, and the converts started a new life. All those with diver's disease were healed and went back to the sea. The people of Capernaum loved Jesus and large crowds attended his lessons.

At the end of a very long day, Jesus and his disciples rested. John found them and brought them a leper. To many it appeared that Jesus did nothing, but the leper was healed. John, however had noted a smile on Jesus face and saw him gesture with his hand. As scales fell from his arms, new flesh seemed to appear. The leper fell to the ground and gave thanks. He then thanked Jesus and departed.

James looked at his brother.

"It has been a long Sabbath," he said. "Doing God's work is very rewarding."

A puzzled look appeared on John's face.

"Should we work so hard on the Sabbath?" he asked. "Many won't like what we are doing. The Sabbath is a day of rest."

"You are correct. Many will not understand," James said. "We are doing God's work and being a servant of God is a never ending job. Stay with me and help me serve God. Jesus won't lead us astray."

After some time had passed, the disciples walked through a field and ate some grain to satisfy their hunger. When the Pharisees learned of their actions, they questioned Jesus about working on the Sabbath.

"Look! Your disciples are doing what is unlawful on the Sabbath."

He answered, "Haven't you read what David did when he and his companions were hungry?" (Matthew, 12, 2 & 3, NIV)

The Pharisees didn't answer. A discouraged look appeared on their faces and they departed. As they walked back to Jerusalem, they planned other methods to discredit Jesus actions and message.

"Being close to nature and doing God's work is invigorating me," John said. "I don't understand why the Pharisees are so worried about us."

"We are doing God's work, but we aren't always popular with the Jewish priests," James said.

That evening, the disciples and Jesus met and prayed together. They asked God to bless them and they took his message to the people of the area.

John looked at his brother.

"I love you and I know you love God," he said.

Traveling with Jesus is totally different than what I was taught at the temple," James said. "Jesus stresses love and caring for each other. When I was in Jerusalem, I had to learn laws and recite them every day."

One Sabbath while they were teaching in a synagogue, a man with a withered hand came forward. He was healed because he had faith. Jesus explained it is right to do God's work on the Sabbath. Because of the many people who were being healed, the crowds continued to get larger. Many didn't understand Jesus' message, but they witnessed his miracles. John sat with James and shared a loaf of bread.

"I don't think I have ever seen such a large crowd," he said. "These people have come from as far away as Tyre and Sidon. Are we going to help all of them? Many of them are women."

"Yes, John," James said. "They will help themselves through their faith. They will all be healed."

"We will be very busy," John said. "Jesus and all of his disciples will help us. I will help you prepare them to talk with Jesus."

"Before they return home, he will talk with each of them," James said.

John remembered a sermon Jesus taught and he turned to those waiting and told them, "Blessed be the poor, for yours is the kingdom of God."

The disciples and crowd didn't understand all of Jesus' words, but they were humbled by his great sermons.

After, they rested, Peter was humbled by all that had been accomplished, and he went to James and John.

"James, do you have to be present to heal a man?" Peter asked. "Does being present have a lot to do with healing?"

"Yes, I think you must be present," James said. "If you were not present, how would you be healed?"

"You are healed by faith in God," John said. "Not by your actions, therefore, you don't need to be present."

"The infirm are healed because of their faith," Peter said. "I am beginning to understand."

"Remember once Jesus asked God to heal the servant of a centurion, and he was healed because those around him had great faith," John said. "It is important you understand. God heals through your faith in him."

Peter's tan forehead was wrinkled. After a few moments, a smile appeared on his face.

As Jesus and his disciples walked a short way to the town of Nain, the sun shone brightly and a gentle wind blew. John noted a number of people followed them. As they looked upward into the distance, they marveled at the snow on the peaks of the mountain. The white snow reminded them of God's cleansing power. They approached the town's gate where a dead boy was being carried away. His mother, a widow, followed, and a large crowd followed her.

When the Lord saw her, his heart went to her and he said, "Don't cry." Then he went up and touched the coffin, and those carrying it stood still.

He said, "Young men, I say to you, get up!" The dead man sat up and began to talk and Jesus gave him back to his mother. (Luke, 7, 13 – 15, NIV)

Many found God that day. It wasn't uncommon for the Pharisees to attend Jesus' healings. One of them approached Jesus.

"Hello, Rabbi," Simon said. "Will you and some of your disciples have dinner with me? I am a Pharisee and have watched you heal people."

Jesus paused for a moment and talked with John. Then John spoke with the Pharisee.

"Yes, he will be glad to dine with you," he said. "The others will be busy preparing for tomorrow."

After Jesus returned from his dinner with the Pharisee, he spoke with John concerning the meeting. John became excited and immediately located to his brother.

"The Pharisee wanted to know how Jesus heals people," he said.

"I believe God can do anything," James said. "The people who are healed have great faith in God."

"The Pharisee explained, 'many of my members have always been faithful, but before you were with them, they weren't healed. Your presence was important to them. What did you said to God?'" John exclaimed.

"Jesus prays for God to be with them, and they ask God to heal them," James said. "It is their faith and God's will."

"I also ask God to be with the sick, the Pharisee explained," John told his brother.

John then excitedly told James an astounding story. This is what the Pharisee said,

"Jesus, there is a girl here to see you," he said. "I don't think we know her."

Jesus didn't respond.

John continued, "Simon asked her to come in. The woman hoped to gain forgiveness. After she anointed Jesus with oil, she wiped his feet with her hair. Jesus didn't interrupt her, and he allowed her to be with him for a few moments. The Pharisee was troubled by her actions,"

"When the Pharisee who had invited him saw this, he said to himself, "If this man were a prophet, he would know who is touching him and what kind of women she is – that she is a sinner." (Luke, 7, 39, NIV)

"He asked Jesus about her. Jesus answered by telling Simon a story, and then Jesus forgave the women of her sins," John said

He looked at James. They discussed the incident for several houses.

The next morning, the inner group gathered and planned their short term itinerary. They planned to move to the next town. As more women became followers, the group increased in size almost every day. James and John were instrumental in planning the new itinerary and discussed logistics.

"The large crowd doesn't move easily," John said. "It will take some time."

James wondered what Jesus' next story would be about. He asked John his opinion.

"Maybe, it will tell a story to make a point," he said. "Many people can relate to a story better than they can listen to a lecture."

Jesus' story about a farmer who planted his seeds in different types of soil made a large impression on John. He explained it to James.

"I love that story. It took me some time to understand it," John said. "Jesus meant the increase in the number of plants will depend on the quality of the soil. Do you think that our followers understood the story?"

John was pleased that he was able to interpret Jesus' story. James was very pleased and hugged him.

"Not everyone will understand at first," he said. "They will remember the story for a long time. Eventually, they will understand it."

They found a place under a tree and knelt for prayer. When John arose he saw Jesus' mother. He called to Jesus.

"Your mother and brothers are here to see you," John said. "They walked from Nazareth."

Mary ran to Jesus and hugged him.

"The crowd is so large, I was afraid I wouldn't get to see you," she said. "I have brought James and Thomas. Salome is home helping to care for your younger brothers."

The family enjoyed their time together. They joked about Thomas always taking notes when he listened to Jesus.

"You may be joking, but I did take notes," Thomas said. "I really enjoy your stories. Someday, I hope I will be able to tell your stories to those who never had the chance to listen to you. Not everyone can visit Jerusalem."

The family spoke to each disciple before they departed.

One day, they brought a man who was blind and mute to Jesus. He healed the man, and the Pharisees soon learned of the miracle. They warned the people against Jesus.

"It is only by Beelzebub, the price of demons, that this fellow drives out demons," (Matt, 12, 24, NIV) the Pharisee said. "He is an evil person."

The Pharisees carefully planned their attack against Jesus.

"We want you to stay away from him," another Pharisee said. "Come and pray with us at the synagogue."

When James heard of the actions of the Pharisees, he was perplexed by their actions. He knew they were strong members of their Jewish faith. He went to his brother, and they prayed for the Pharisees' understanding of Jesus' good works.

Jesus and his followers continued to visit many towns, where they healed many people. They stayed close to the Sea of Galilee, and John obtained a boat for their use.

"Jesus would you like to take a boat to the other side of the sea?" he asked. "It is very calming."

Jesus looked at the boat and agreed. They stepped aboard the boat. John raised the sail, and Jesus was seated. After a short time, the rocking motion of the boat put Jesus to sleep. John sensed that Jesus was asleep and the waves became quite large. He tugged on Jesus arm.

"Wake-up, wake-up!" he hollered, "The wind is very strong, and the waves are quite large. I am afraid we might be in trouble."

Jesus looked at the waves.

"Quiet! Be still," (Mark, 4, part of verse 30, NIV) he said.

John held the rudder and sail rope very tightly. The waves subsided. He smiled at Jesus, and they sailed back to shore. Jesus and John had formed a strong friendship that continued to grow.

"The local Roman ruler, Herod, isn't willing to learn from your message," James said. "I wish he would listen and respond by repenting and accepting God."

John joined the conversation.

"The Roman senate is busy," John said. "It is concerned with growing the empire. They work at controlling people's lives. They don't take time to think about what you are saying. Emperor Tiberius doesn't care about the senate or you."

The twelve gathered, so Jesus could give them direction.

"When Jesus had called the Twelve together, he gave them power and authority to drive out demons and to cure diseases, and he sent them out to preach the kingdom of God and to heal the sick." ((Luke, 9, 1-2, NIV)

Peter wiped the dirt from his brow and looked at Jesus.

"I will do more of God's work," Peter said. "We will help you."

James looked at Peter and they discussed the proper use of their new powers.

Soon, the large crowd found Jesus, and he and the disciples realized that it would be necessary to feed a very large group of people. James and John pondered how Jesus would accomplish the feat, but they knew Jesus could make it possible. He started with a few fish and loaves of bread. The disciples distributed fish and bread for hours; somehow, the baskets were never empty. The crowd didn't believe everyone was fed. Moreover, the disciples then gathered up the remaining food and gave it to the poor.

That evening, John and James talked with Jesus. They discussed, Mary of Magdala, a recent convert who had joined their followers.

"She has acknowledged God and your words," John said. "She is a new woman. I am glad I took the opportunity to talk with her."

"Mary is a fine woman," James said.

He motioned for John to be quiet. John was not completely satisfied with the situation. He didn't understand the meaning of what James said. He thought about Jesus and Mary several times but decided not to ask additional questions.

The disciples did as Jesus requested, they sailed toward Capernaum. Early in the evening, the sky and the lake provided many beautiful moments. The sun was low in the sky, and it looked like it was attached to the horizon. The disciples approached Capernaum.

"Look, James, it is Jesus," John said. "He is walking on the water. He said he would join us. Make room in the boat for him."

They were all amazed that Jesus could walk on water.

"Jesus, join us in the boat," James said. "We have plenty of room."

Jesus joined the disciples and told them a story about how God had prepared room for everyone, and that God's mansion is never full.

Soon, they were in Capernaum.

Another large crowd joined them the following day. Jesus taught that his message was the bread of life. He explained if they believed in his message, they would have eternal life. They asked for a sign so they could believe him.

"He is your sign," John said. "All you have to do is believe in him. The miracles are the work of God, and they bring good news to his people. You must have faith in God."

'I am sure they have faith in God,' John said to himself. 'As they come to know you, Jesus, their faith will continue to grow.'

James explained to John that he had become Jesus' most beloved disciple.

"Jesus likes me because I am young and have Great Spirit," he said.

"It is not your age," James said, "It is your faith and Great Spirit."

John hoped his brother was keeping good records of Jesus' message.

"James, did you write about this?" he asked. "I wish I had paid attention to you and learned how to write."

"Yes, John," James said. "I have made note of everything. Jesus is an amazing man."

"He is beyond amazing," John said. "He is divine."

James looked at John.

"When I was in Jerusalem, the Rabbi sent me to listen to John the Baptist, and that is how I first met Jesus," James said. "I knew you had to be with him. That is why I returned home for you."

"Where do you think we will go next?" John asked. "Do you think we will stay here for a while? Is there any chance of us going home for a few days?"

"I will ask Jesus if we may go home to visit," James said. "Our parents would be surprised to see us."

The next day, John planned for five of the disciples to go home for short visits. It was a joyous event.

"Andrew, get Peter and let's go home for a few days," John said. "I have arranged this with Jesus. We must be back in a week. I will get James and Philip."

"Peter and I won't be going with you," Andrew said. "We have been visiting with our family on a regular basis."

James was surprised.

"I didn't know you were going home to visit," James said. "I guess I never really thought about Capernaum being your home. We will see you in a week."

"Get your packs, and let's get moving," John said to James. "We haven't seen our parents for a long time. I hope mother has hot food for us."

"I am sure she will have plenty of food for us," James said. "Philip, we will be back for you in about a week. We will expect you to be ready to return."

Philip smiled at James.

"James, I am glad you brought me along," John said. "I really like Jesus. I had no idea so many women traveled with him. I guess they like the message of one God for everyone."

"Everyone should understand that message," he said. "It could bring comfort to many people."

"When I met the woman named Mary, she thought I was a child," John said. "I told her I was your brother, and that you looked after me. Do you know her?"

"Yes, I told you she was a fine lady," he said. "Jesus has many followers. It is our job to help convert everyone."

The brothers walked quietly toward their house. They could smell the sea breeze. They remembered the days when they repaired boats. Finally, they saw their mother and father on the porch. Zebedee and Salome had fallen asleep while looking out at the peaceful sea.

Suddenly, their mother woke up and saw them. She stood and started running toward them. She had tears in her eyes.

"Hello, boys," Salome said. "I want a hug. Tell us about your adventures. Are you going to stay for a while?"

"We can stay for six days," James said. "Then, we will stop for Philip, and return to Jesus in Capernaum."

"Only six days," she said. "I've missed you so much."

"Is father repairing many boats these days?" James asked. "I see a boat on blocks."

"Yes, he is," she said. "We have never been busier. We have several new workers. I know he will be glad to see you. I will tell your sister that you are home. We will all have a meal together."

"Hello, father," John says. "It is great to see you. James and I are here to visit for a short while."

"Hello, John," he said. "Have you met Jesus? Are you traveling with him?"

"Yes, father," he said. "We travel with him."

"We hear of him on occasion," Zebedee said. "The local Rabbi keeps us informed. He says Jesus is attracting very large crowds."

"That is true," John said. "We rarely get to meet everyone. We are busy helping Jesus and the followers. We have a lot of converts and have started many churches. We formed one in Capernaum."

"I heard Jesus healed Peter's mother-in-law. Is that true?" Salome asked.

"Yes, it is true," John said. "She is fine. Peter is a firm believer. He is firm like a rock."

"You should ask Jesus to heal your friend," she said. "Then you could start a church in Bethsaida."

"I am a little afraid to ask," he said. "Jesus always says people are healed due to their faith."

"I am not afraid," James said. "When we return, I will ask Jesus to heal him."

"James, how has John been?" Zebedee asked. "Are you looking after him as you promised?"

"He is doing great," he said. "Jesus likes him very much. I think he is Jesus' favorite disciple. His faith is so pure."

"Take good care of our little boy," he said. "Did you see the boat we are repairing?"

"I will visit it tomorrow," James said. "Tonight, we just want to visit with you and mother."

They sat peacefully on the porch and enjoyed one another.

The next day, the boys visited the boat repair area and met the new employees.

"Hello," he said. "My name is John, and this is my brother James."

"We have been told about you," he said. "It is good to make your acquaintance."

They noticed several new houses had been built for the employees. James and John rejoiced in the company of all their family. They dinned and enjoyed a large home cooked dinner each evening. The week passed quickly.

Six days later, after they enjoyed breakfast with their mother and father, it was time for them to leave. John looked up the lane that led to town. James noted a tear in his eye.

"We can stop for Philip and meet Jesus and the disciples in Capernaum this evening," John said.

As they walked up the lane to the main road, they waved goodbye to Zebedee and Salome. They stopped for Philip, who was waiting for them. They laughed about the last time. They pick up their packs and started to Capernaum.

When they found Jesus' group, Peter saw them.

"How was your family?" he asked. "Can I help with anything?"

John looked at Jesus.

"Jesus, you can help," he said. "I have a friend who is a blind man."

Jesus listened to John's story and sensed his great love for the man.

"Our family has been taking him food for a long time," John said. "He knows mother and me. He lives in Bethsaida. I would like you to talk to him and see if he can be healed."

Jesus agreed to visit John's friend.

The next day, Philip, James, John, and Jesus went to Bethsaida to visit the blind man. Jesus took him by the hand, and he began to walk. After a short walk, the man's sight was restored. He was astounded and profusely thankful. Jesus told him that he didn't heal him, but that his faith in God's help had healed him. Jesus asked Philip, James, John, and the man not to tell anyone about the healing miracle.

"Don't go into the village," Jesus said. (Mark, 8, 26, NIV)

"I think he will be a great fisherman," James said. "I am sure father will hire him."

"Father is always looking for good fisherman," John said. "He will give him a good job."

They pointed the man in the direction of the boat that was being repaired, and they returned to Capernaum that evening.

CHAPTER 10

THOSE ON THEIR KNEES SEE JESUS CLEARLY

John and many of the fishermen, who lived on the north end of the Sea of Galilee, traveled toward the wilderness with Jesus. They were going to the great temple in Jerusalem. As the traveled just west of the Sea of Galilee, they were relaxed by the majesty of the water. John was troubled because Jesus seemed upset that his disciples didn't understand his message. On occasion, Jesus would ask the disciples specific questions and provide them specific experiences. John understood that He was the Son of God, but many of the disciples still didn't understand Jesus.

"When Jesus came to the region of Caesarea Philippi, he asked his disciples, "Who do people say the Son of Man is? They replied, "Some say John the Baptist, others say Elijah; and still others, Jeremiah or one of the prophets. "But what about you?" he asked. "Who do you say I am? Simon Peter answered; "You are the Christ, the Son of the living God." Jesus replied, "Blessed are you, Simon son of Jonah, for this was not revealed to you by man, but by my Father in heaven."" (Matthew, 16, 13-18, NIV)

James and John discussed Jesus' statement.

"It is strange that some of our followers think he is an ancient prophet, who has been dead for many years, but they don't understand his message," James said.

He looked at John and waited for him to respond.

"I have been with Jesus for a while and it is hard for me to understand all the miraculous things that he says and does," John said. "Understanding Jesus is a matter of faith. It takes great faith and many prayers."

"It took us a while to understand," Peter said. "In time, they will understand."

"It is important that they know who Jesus is," John said.

James looked at Peter and asked, "Are we going to Jerusalem for the feast? I would like to spend some time in the wilderness on our way south."

"Yes, we will go to Jerusalem," Peter said. "I am sure they have forgotten us and the problem with the money changers."

"James, do you remember John the Baptist, telling us about the wilderness?" John asked. "He loved the wilderness, and he loved the shepherds who lived in the pasture. I think I could learn to like the wilderness. We will enjoy our journey for a few days before we arrive in Jerusalem."

"The wilderness is a spiritual place," James said. "I have always liked pastures and the sea. I am glad father was a fisherman and not a shepherd. I prefer to eat fish. I don't really like lamb."

As the twelve disciples walked along the Sea of Galilee, they marveled at the beautiful shore. The sun shone brightly, and it was difficult to look at its reflection on the water. The disciples discussed which one of them was the greatest. It was a challenge to see who had performed the greatest number of good deeds.

"I think Peter is the greatest," Matthew said. "He answered Jesus' question correctly."

"No, I think it is James," Peter said. "James studied to be a Rabbi. He knows more than we do."

"I think it is John," James said. "Jesus likes him best."

They hadn't noticed that Jesus had joined them. He was not amused with their game. He looked directly at them and rebuked them.

Peter was startled by Jesus' manner and became concerned.

Jesus knowing their thoughts took a little child and had him stand beside him. Then he said to them, "Whoever welcomes this little child in my name welcomes me; and whoever welcomes me welcomes the one who sent me. For he who is least among you all – he is the greatest." ^{(Luke,} 9, 47 & 48, NIV)

The disciples became worried.

"We can have great faith," Matthew said. "That is the purpose of baptism."

"After we are baptized, we use religion to point us to God," James said. "Our faith is maintained as we communicate with God in prayer. That is why we should pray every day."

"Prayer is an important religious tool," John said. "It provides us with a direct link to God. He is never too busy to listen for us."

"You tell your stories, and you perform miracles," James said. "You have told the twelve of us the secrets of God."

They walked to the shore of the sea and knelt. John stared across the great sea.

They arrived in Jerusalem just in time to celebrate the religious holidays. The city was noisy and crowded. Roman soldiers were posted at each street corner. People walked shoulder to shoulder along the streets. Women clung to their children and made their way to the temple. The disciples broke into small groups. James and John continued to talk about their good fortune of being with Jesus.

John looked at James and grabbed his hand.

"Are you going to show me around Jerusalem?" he asked.

"Yes, John," James said. "Follow me. First, I want to show you the walls. The first wall has encircled the city for about one hundred and fifty years. The second wall was built by Herod. The city had grown, so the second wall became necessary."

"Did he build anything else?" he asked.

"Yes, he had many things built," he said. "He rebuilt the temple, and he built a palace and a fortress. He was always having something built. He made Jerusalem into a great city."

They walked through the gates and looked back at the walls. John removed a pebble from his sandal.

"I like the aqueduct," he said. "It is very impressive. The people and animals must use a lot of water."

As they continued their tour, James asked John about Jesus' message. He knew he listened, but he wanted to make certain John understood the important points Jesus had stressed.

"Did you hear Jesus teach in the temple?" James asked. "He taught a great lesson."

John stopped walking and put his bag on the ground. He sorted through his belongings, trying to find something. James noted a puzzled look on his face.

"Yes, I heard him," he said. "I heard many people murmuring about how he could know so much without being taught by the local teachers."

"They should have faith," James said. "Everyone wants to see a miracle."

John continued to sort through his belongings.

"They are still refusing to acknowledge him," John said. "Great faith can bring miracles, but miracles may not bring great faith."

"Why did you throw your clothing all over the ground?" James asked. "Whatever you are looking for, I am sure you will find it."

John looked at James.

"Did you pay our tribute money?" he asked. "I don't have any money."

James was surprised about John's concern.

"Put your clothes back in your pack. I paid our shekel," he said. "Father gave me plenty of money. I paid for both of us. He expects me to take care of you."

"Thank you for paying my tribute," John said.

He picked up his clothes and repacked his bag.

"I was looking for a coin that father gave to me," he said. "It was my lucky coin."

James decided to have a little fun at John's expense.

"You lost the coin father gave you?" James exclaimed. "You lost our lucky coin?"

John didn't look at James.

"Now, I know how mother felt when she lost a coin out of her headband," John said.

He thought for a moment.

"I really liked Jesus' criticism of the Pharisees concerning the women. I didn't see anyone cast any stones."

"They were not sinless," James said. "No one, except Jesus, is sinless."

"He certainly is like a beacon, shining in our lives," John said. "The longer I know him, the brighter his light becomes."

"God is lighting our path," he said. "He will keep the darkness from us."

"What did Jesus mean when he said, 'Then you will know the truth, and the truth will set you free.'?" (John, 8, 32, NIV) John asked.

"It is a promise of peace," James said. "Understanding God's message will bring you peace."

"It all revolves around faith," John said. "Faith brings freedom, and freedom brings peace."

"Did Peter tell you about the problems Pilate had in Galilee?" John asked.

"No, I haven't talked with Peter recently," James said. "What did he tell you?"

"Pontius Pilate had a group of Galileans murdered," he said. "They were preparing a service to honor God. While they were preparing to make sacrifices to God, he murdered them."

"He murdered them while they were worshiping?" James asked. "Everyone should be safe when they are worshiping."

"They had no chance," John said. "He claimed they were speaking against the taxes that Pilate planned to use to build a new, larger, more expensive, water system for Jerusalem."

"Jerusalem is growing," he said. "I am certain the city needs more water."

"A group of men who worked on the aqueduct was killed when a tower fell on them," he said. "The Romans seem to have problems with the faithful. If they could blame something on us, I am sure Pilate would kill us. We need to be very careful."

The disciples departed Jerusalem and walked north. When evening came, they built a fire and relaxed. They discussed the need for many more churches. Finally, seventy followers were commissioned and sent out to start new churches. Their message was well received, and many churches were formed. Those commissioned had followed him, and they had studied with Jesus for many months. They prayerfully started their new ministry.

James and John stayed with Jesus constantly. They rarely visited home.

The disciples taught along the Jordan River, but many of the converted lived in Jerusalem.

The disciples planned a stop in Tiberias.

"John, I saw you talking with Jesus," James said. "What were you talking about? What are we going to do next?"

"He suggested we stop at Tiberias," he said. "He wants to make God's message available to the soldiers."

"They have soldiers in almost every town on the west bank of the sea and the river," James said. "I think they are worried about being invaded by the pagans from the east. We live on the frontier of the empire."

"I have located a large field for our next meeting," John said. "It is not far from the fortification. We should attract a large crowd."

"Did you see all those tents?" he asked. "Some are quite large. This must be a legion of soldiers."

"Yes, I saw them," he said. "Do you remember our host at the wedding in Cana?"

"Paul's father was the host," James said. "I remember Paul said his father is a tent maker. I wonder if he made these tents."

As James and John inspected the tents, a gentleman approached them.

"Hello, John," he said. "I remember you from the wedding in Cana. I am Paul's attendant."

John was surprised to see him.

"I haven't see Paul. Why are you here?" he asked.

"Paul is at home," he said. "I have brought a message to his friend, Jesus. Paul rarely comes to the meetings."

Paul's attendant explained to James and John that Paul didn't want the Rabbis in Jerusalem to know he was a close friend of Jesus.' He also told them that Paul was occasionally assigned to attend Jesus' meetings. He was expected to report to the others Rabbi at the temple about Jesus' popularity.

"What were you both talking about?" Paul's attendant asked.

John looked up and smiled.

"We were talking about the tents," John said. "The fortification uses a lot of tents."

"Yes, it does," he said. "Paul's father's plant made all of them. He sells many tents to the Roman army."

"That is what I told my brother," John said.

"We like to visit the fortifications," James said. "We usually convert a few soldiers."

"You should have a lot of converts," he said. "When you are in Jerusalem you could probably find Paul."

"It is satisfying that so many are being converted," John said. "I hope this new group that was commissioned will work with the soldiers."

Philip joined James and John.

"We are away from home most of the time," Philip said. "The newer followers might not adapt to their new lifestyle."

"Soldiers are away from home most of the time," John said. "They are able to adapt."

"Being away from mother and father is a heavy price," James said. "I am glad you decided to come with me."

"James, do you want to visit with mother and father?" John asked. "I would like to see them."

"I would as well," James said. "But we have a lot of work to do here. This is a great opportunity for us."

"We could take a few days away from work," he said. "I miss mother."

"We can't go home every time you get home sick," he said. "Someday, we will visit with them."

"The soldiers will remain at the fortification," John said. "We may not be close to home for a long time."

"We will always have mother and father with us," James said. "We carry them with us in our hearts. We need to do God's work."

John mumbled at him and pouted.

"I guess you are correct," he said. "I am glad I have you to help me."

"You will be fine," James said. "Say a prayer for mother."

"Our next stop will be in a Samaritan village," John said. "I hope we are welcome."

After the disciples spent a few days at the fortification, they departed and entered into Samaria.

"Just keep going," a Samaritan said to the group. "Jerusalem is farther south. We don't have time for Jewish people who think they are better than us. You don't have to pass through Samaria to get to Jerusalem. You can go through Perea."

"Jesus, I am sorry they didn't welcome you," John said. "Do you want us to do anything?"

Jesus looked at John and tried to comfort him. He agreed to travel through Perea. Jesus and John decided to pray. They stopped and knelt on the ground. After a moment of silence, Jesus blessed the Samaritans.

"The Samaritans are our neighbor, and you taught us that we must always remember who our neighbor is," John said. "Many of the people of Samaria are faithful to the Jewish religion."

The disciples started to walk east.

"I have read about a town called Heshbon," James said. "It is an old town that has a strong link to the faithful. We can rest there for a while. I am certain we will be safe."

They traveled to Heshbon. It was a day's walk east of the Jordan River. They taught Jesus' message to those in Perea. That evening, they went outside the town to rest. They stopped and built a large fire. The flickering of the flames affected the disciples in a manner similar to the stars twinkling on the sea. They rested and spoke about their upcoming trip to Jerusalem. It became clear that this would probably be their last trip to Jerusalem as a group. The Jewish faithful strongly persecuted the followers of the Christian Way. Jesus decided it was time for them to continue their trip.

Heading toward the Salt Sea, they crossed the Jordan River near the town of Jericho. John pointed out the crumbled wall which lay next to the new wall. When they looked for water, John saw a blind man. He thought about his friend who had been blind. He and James went to Jesus.

"Did he or his parent's sin?" John asked. "Someone must have sinned."

"He isn't blind because he or his parents sinned," James said.

John looked at James.

"I am sure Jesus will heal him," James said. "I hope the Pharisees don't learn we are healing people on the Sabbath. They were upset the last time. They seem to be very tightly bound by the laws, but they don't understand love."

The three of them knelt and prayed with the blind man. His sight returned. He stood and ran toward the synagogue.

The other disciples joined Jesus. They discussed the importance of being a good Shepherd.

"Helping the less fortunate is a good thing," John said. "When we are given an opportunity to help, we should be ready and willing."

The sky seemed to clear. It became a beautiful shade of blue. John stared intently at a cloud. He thought about what Jesus had taught them concerning how sheep knew their shepherds. The shepherds often allowed the gate to be open when they fed the sheep in their stalls. The sheep remained with their shepherds. Most shepherds carried a crook that allowed them to rescue any lamb that faced danger. They showed concern about the safety of their flock, but they cared for each sheep individually. He looked at his brother.

"I guess our crook is Jesus' message," John said. "People will know us by his message."

James looked at John and smiled. He hugged him.

A small, short man named Zacchaeus was on the streets of Jericho, and he was having trouble seeing Jesus.

"Hello, Jesus," Zacchaeus said. "Sometimes, we of small stature have problems speaking with you."

Jesus introduced him to little John.

"Your height doesn't matter," John said. "Those on their knees see Jesus clearly."

Zacchaeus reveled in Jesus' attention.

"Will you have dinner with me?" Zacchaeus asked. "I would be very pleased. I don't live far."

Jesus inquired about the availability of his inner group to go to dinner at Zacchaeus' house.

"I am too busy," Thomas said. "Take John with you."

"I am glad you are busy doing God's work," John said. "I don't have many meals with Jesus. Brothers need to break bread together."

"He taught us well," Thomas said. "I will kneel and pray for you tonight."

Jesus returned to Zacchaeus and informed him that most of his disciples were very busy, but a few would join with him for dinner.

"Follow me," he said. "It is a short walk."

"It will be good for us to rest," John said.

They walked a few blocks and arrived at Zacchaeus' house. It was a large, nicely kept house surrounded by trees and flowers.

"Come in," he said. "My wife has prepared bread and vegetables for us."

"You are a generous man," John said. "God bless this meal and you to His service."

"You and Jesus have brought honor to me," Zacchaeus said. "Look, Lord! Here and now I give half of my possessions to the poor, and if I have cheated anybody out of anything, I will pay back four times the amount." (Luke, 18, 8, NIV)

Jesus said to him, "Today salvation has come to this house, because this man, too, is a son of Abraham. For the Son of Man came to seek and to save what was lost." (Luke, 18, 9 & 10, NIV)

It was obvious to John that the Lord was with Zacchaeus.

"We thank you for your gifts," he said. "We bless this house and those who live in it."

Their dinner with Zacchaeus was a very spiritual meeting. Before they left, they knelt and prayed together.

"John was correct," Zacchaeus said to Jesus. "When I am on my knees, I do see you much more clearly."

After dinner, Jesus and John returned to the disciples and continued toward Jerusalem. They hadn't traveled very far when a troubled man approached Jesus.

""Teacher, tell my brother to divide the inheritance with me."

Jesus replied, "Man who appointed me a judge or an arbiter between you?" Then he said to them, "Watch out! Be on your guard against all kinds of greed; a man's life does not consist in the abundance of his Possessions." (Luke, 12, 13-15, NIV)

"He should be helping the needy," John said. "He is probably too rich for his well-being."

"I don't think he is interested in helping others," the man said. "He is interested in helping himself."

The man looked at Jesus.

"My father loved both of us," he said. "When we didn't complete our work, he always forgave us. When we returned from the field, he greeted us and gave us a cup of water."

"Our heavenly father will also greet you when you return," John said. "Go to the temple, and you will see your heavenly father."

The man headed toward the temple and became part of the crowd.

John brought a woman to Jesus.

"I know it is the Sabbath," he said. "This woman has been a cripple for many years. Please pray with us."

Jesus laid his hand on her and she was freed of her infirmity.

"Thank you, Lord," she said.

She walked a few steps and knelt before Jesus. Then she straightened her back and looked at him.

"I can stand straight, and I can walk," she said.

"She is healed!" John exclaimed. "I could tell she had great faith."

James motioned to John.

"It is time for us to rest," he said. "Please join me in prayer."

The next morning, the leader of the local synagogue went to Jesus and told those who traveled with Jesus that people shouldn't be healed on a Sabbath. Jesus became upset and called him a hypocrite. He explained that the Jewish leaders worked on the Sabbath.

It wasn't very far to Jerusalem. When they arrived, they went to the temple. James again explained Jerusalem to John.

"John, this is Solomon's Colonnade," he said. "This is a favorite gathering place for the Jewish faithful. They are speaking with Jesus now. This area is crowded due to the Feast of the Tabernacle. It is warm in here, when it is cold outside."

A messenger who was looking for Jesus found John instead. He gave John a message to deliver to Jesus. John found Jesus on his knees, praying.

"Jesus, Mary from Bethany sent you a message," John said. "You remember Mary. She washed your feet, and she dried your feet with her hair. Her message says your friend Lazarus is sick."

When he heard this, Jesus said, "This sickness will not end in death. No, it is for God's glory so that God's Son may be glorified through it." (John, 11, 4, NIV)

"She wants you to come immediately," John said. "She is quite fearful Lazarus is dying. Do you want me to send her a message?"

"Our friend Lazarus has fallen asleep; but I am going there to wake him up." (John, 11, 11, NIV)

John was surprised by Jesus' actions, but he wasn't worried. He knew Jesus had a reason and would eventually discuss his actions with them. He knelt and said a prayer.

Early the next morning, John received another message for Jesus. He exhibited a solemn attitude as he explained to Jesus that Mary's message indicated Lazarus had died.

"We should be with him," John said.

"Let's go to Bethany," Thomas said. "He is our friend."

"We need to be there, before he has been dead three days," John said. "We should go as soon as possible."

"Time is a tool of man," James said. "God is eternal."

It became obvious to John that Jesus' hesitation was very deliberate. He was certain Jesus was going to use his delay tactics to make a point.

"Bethany is not far," James asked. "Should we prepare to travel?"

"Please, Lord," Thomas said. "May we go?"

So then he told them plainly, "Lazarus is dead, and for your sake I am glad I was not there, so that you may believe. But let us go to him." (John, 11, 14, NIV)

They didn't understand, but they stayed with Jesus. They spent many hours that evening on their knees, praying.

The next day, Jesus and several disciples traveled to Bethany. Lazarus had been placed in a tomb. He had been dead four days. They found Lazarus' sister, Martha.

"If you would have been here sooner, he wouldn't have died," Martha said. "We needed you."

Jesus said to her, "Your brother will rise again" ^(John, 11, 23, NIV)

"Before you came to help him, we had to entomb him. He has been dead for four days," she said. "You waited too long."

Jesus said to her, "I am the resurrection and the life. He who believes in me will live, even though he dies, and whoever lives and believes in me will never die. Do you believe this" "Yes, Lord," she told him, "I believe that you are the Christ, the Son of God, who was to come into the world." (John, 11, 25-27, NIV)

Martha and Jesus knelt and prayed.

"I loved my brother," she said. "Please help us."

When they arrived at the tomb it was sealed, "So they took away the stone.

Then Jesus looked up and said, "Father, I thank you that you have heard me. I knew that you always hear me, but I said this for the benefit of the people standing here, that they may believe you sent me." When he had said this, Jesus called in a loud voice, "Lazarus, come out! The dead man came out, his hands and feet wrapped with strips of linen, and a cloth around his face. Jesus said to them, "Take off the grave clothes and let him go." (John, 11, 41-44, NIV)

"He is standing," John said. "He is walking toward us."

"He is alive," Thomas said. "I knew you wouldn't allow him to die."

As he walked toward them, Lazarus removed his grave cloths.

"Give me the clothing you brought for me," Lazarus said. "Thank you, Thomas. Your faith is an example for all of us."

"Your faith has raised you from the dead," John said. "Jesus waited four days because he wanted everyone to understand the power of God."

"I understand, and I am glad you waited," Lazarus said. "It will strengthen the faith of all who hear your story."

"Jesus tells stories so people will believe, but they don't understand," John said. "Miracles and secret knowledge is often required to convince those who are having trouble believing."

"This incident will be an example for all time," Thomas said. "It will bring many people to God."

Jesus spoke to Mary and thanked her for the messages. She hugged Jesus.

The disciples withdrew to the wilderness. It was no longer safe for them to move about freely. The Jewish Rabbis planned to kill Jesus. Jesus had performed too many miracles for them to allow him to continue his great works. No one really understood all of Jesus' messages.

The disciples followed their Jewish tradition and were ceremonially cleansed. The disciples listen to Jesus speak.

"I think Jesus just predicted his death," James said.

James looked at John.

"Before he goes to Jerusalem to die, he wants us to bring him some small children to bless. Small children remind him of the kingdom."

John looked at Jesus.

"Jesus, your brother Jude is here," he said. "He was in Jerusalem, and he was going home to Nazareth. He heard you were in the wilderness. He wants you to bless his child, Menahem."

Then little children were brought to Jesus for him to place his hands on them and pray for them. But the disciples rebuked those who brought them. Jesus said, "Let the little children come to me, and do not hinder them, for the kingdom of heaven belongs to such as these. When he had placed his hand on them, he went from there." (Matthew, 19, 13-15, NIV)

Eventually, his brother found Jesus. Jude told him all the current news about their family. They talked for a long time. Jesus wanted to know everything concerning his earthly family.

The children were given a special measure of the spirit of God. Many of the children remembered their day with Jesus their entire lives, and several lost their lives while helping to disseminate Jesus' message.

CHAPTER 11

JOHN STANDS WATCH

Traveling to Jerusalem, Jesus knew that he would soon be killed. Although he tried to explain to his disciples and his followers that his death was an important part of his ministry, many didn't believe him. The crowd that followed him prepared the way to enter Jerusalem. Jesus rode the donkey that Peter had obtained for him. The street was covered with palm fronds. John walked next to the donkey.

"It is Sunday, and we are finally going into Jerusalem," John said. "When it is crowded with people for the feast, the city is full of life. I saw some of these people last week when we were with Lazarus."

"The people who glorify Jesus in this manner will make it very difficult for him," James said. "The Pharisees are likely to react to the crowd's overt expression and endorsement. They might have him killed."

James was concerned for Jesus. He and John walked shoulder to shoulder, so they wouldn't be separated.

The next morning, Jesus talked briefly with the disciples. Then he went to the temple. The disciples stayed behind to plan their day. Soon, they became aware of a disturbance in the distance. John nudged James.

"Jesus is with the money changers," he said. "The Pharisees will surely have us arrested this time."

"Stay with me," James said. "The crowd is very large, and our best bet is to become a part of it."

There were so many people around Jesus that the Pharisees didn't act immediately. They weren't sure what to do about the crowd. They seemed confused about what was happening.

Later, when the disciples joined Jesus, the Pharisees confronted him.

"By what authority do you perform these acts?" the chief priest asked. "You have caused quite a disturbance."

John answered the Pharisees' question for Jesus. Jesus listened as John spoke.

"He is with us," John said. "We didn't like the surcharge. Everything is fine now. We are moving along."

"Surcharge?" the Rabbi asked. "I will look into it."

The disciples departed. John looked at James.

"I couldn't help but notice how they adorned the temple with beautiful stones. How long have they been here?" John asked. "They certainly have done a nice job getting ready for the feast."

"When they built the temple, it was not this fancy," James said. "They added many of the ornaments later."

The disciples stayed north of Jerusalem. On Tuesday morning, they entered the city.

"Did you hear the story that Jesus told?" John asked. "He expounded about the Jewish leaders."

"No, I didn't," James said. "He should be careful."

"He said the crowd should watch out for men who walked around the marketplace in flowing robes," he said. "He also said they make lengthy prayers for show."

"It is almost like he is tempting the Pharisees," James said. "I am worried for his safety and for ours."

"Let's go and watch people put their money in the temple treasury," John said. "I saw a man deposit a handful of gold coins."

"That woman put in two small bronze coins," James said. "That was a lot of money for her. She gave out of poverty."

Peter, James, Andrew, and John asked Jesus about God's kingdom. They wanted to know when it would come to earth. John told Philip what Jesus said.

"He said that many people would deliver his message, but many wouldn't tell the truth," John said. "We must be on our guard. We will be persecuted."

"We are persecuted now," Philip said. "He is talking about present time."

"I don't think so," he said. "He said no one knows. I can't tell you most of what he told us. It is a secret."

"Several of us have been with him for three years," James said. "We all saw him perform miracles. We all saw him heal many people."

"That doesn't mean we will all remember exactly the same thing," Philip said. "It doesn't mean we will all say the same thing."

"My brother is writing what Jesus says," John said. "We will have his notes to refresh our memories."

"Thomas, Jesus' brother, is also writing about his lessons," Philip said. "He has followed Jesus for many years."

"He might think of Jesus differently than I," John said. "I hope I have a chance to read what he has written."

"It is one story," James said. "We will all remember the most significant days. We won't remember all those days walking in the dust or in the rain."

The chief priest tried to find a method to get rid of Jesus, but the large number of followers intimidated him.

Then the Pharisees went out and laid plans to trap him in his words. They sent their disciples to him along with the Herodians. "Teacher," they said. "We know you are a man of integrity and that you teach the way of God in accordance with the truth. You aren't swayed by men, because you pay no attention to who they are. Tell us then, what is your opinion? Is it right to pay taxes to Caesar or not?" But Jesus, knowing their evil intent, said, "You hypocrites, why are you trying to trap me? Show me the coin used for paying the tax." They brought him a denarius, and he asked them, whose portrait is this? And whose inscription?" "Caesar's," they replied. Then he said to them, "Give to Caesar what is Caesar's and to God what is God's." When they heard this, they were amazed. So they left him and went away. (Matthew, 22, 15-22, NIV)

When Judas heard that the Pharisees couldn't trick Jesus, he saw a way to profit. He approached them and offered to betray Jesus. They agreed upon a sum of money. Judas would have to find a time when the crowd was not present. John and James walked through the crowd.

"James, I saw our family. They will spend Wednesday with us," John said. "It has been a while since we have seen them. Mother will bring food in a basket, and we can sit under the olive trees on the hill."

The remainder of the day passed quickly. Jesus and the disciples prayed in the temple. Then Jesus taught a lesson on the street corner. James and John were excited about seeing their parents. They only slept for a few hours.

John and James went to an olive grove, located on the other side of the Kidron Valley, and waited for their family. Soon, John saw his mother and ran to her.

"How have you boys been doing?" she asked. "Later in the week I think I would like to meet your teacher."

"Hello, father," John said. "I understand you have several grandchildren."

"Yes, we have been greatly blessed," Zebedee said. "We have two grandchildren with us. The very young are at home with the attendants. Hezekiah is keeping us all busy. The wheel and hub business has become quite large."

"I guess everyone now has a carriage," John said. "It is the way of the future."

"I think we are working on two boats most of the time," he said. "If you need a job, I am hiring. Sit down and have some cheese and water with us."

Zebedee stared at John and James and flashed a large smile.

"John and I are always planning for the next day," James said. "The people who are following us seem to like the 'One God for All' messages. I think the gentiles and women especially like that message."

"Look at all the food that mother has prepared for us," John said. "My mouth is watering."

They enjoyed their day together. After James and John returned to the disciples, the sun sunk below the horizon.

The next day was Passover. The disciples were very busy. Zebedee's family would spend most of the day at the temple. Jesus was with his disciples.

"Jesus, are we all going to have the Passover meal together?" John asked. "It has been a great day."

"I am not referring to all of you; I know those I have chosen. But this is to fulfill the scriptures: He who shares my bread has lifted up his heel against me. I am telling you now before it happen, so that when it does happen you will believe that I am He. I tell you the truth, whoever accepts anyone I send accepts me; and whoever accepts me accepts the one who sent me." After he had said this, Jesus was troubled in spirit and testified, "I tell you the truth, one of you is going to betray me." (John, 13, 18-21, NIV)

"I can't believe one of us will betray him," John said to James. "I hope he is wrong."

James looked at John.

"He wants you and me to go into town," James said. "We are to find a place to meet."

They walked a short distance.

"Hello, sir," John said. "Do you have a guest room for our teacher?"

He motioned for them to follow him up the stairs. John inspected the room. That evening, Jesus met with his twelve disciples. They shared a Passover meal. It was the fourteenth of Nisan. They all ate bread and drank wine from the cup.

Peter asked John to inquire of Jesus who was going to betray him.

Jesus answered, "It is the one to who I will give this piece of bread when I have dipped it in the dish." Then, dipping the piece of bread, he gave it to Judas Iscariot, son of Simon. As soon as Judas took the bread, Satan entered into him. "What you are about to do, do quickly," Jesus told him, but no one at the meal understood why Jesus said this to him. (John, 13, 26-28, NIV)

John looked at Jesus.

"Let's sing a hymn," he said. "It is a joyous method of honoring God."

After they sang, John asked James about the next day.

"I think we are going to meet in the olive grove," James said. "It is the place where we met with mother and father."

"That is a beautiful grove," John said. "The trees are quite old."

The next day, Jesus and his disciples walked to the Mount of Olives. Peter and Jesus talked.

"I will never deny knowing you," Peter said. "I am your friend. I would die for you."

Then Jesus answered, "Will you really lay down your life for me? I tell you the truth, before the rooster crows, you will disown me three times." (John, 13, 38, NIV)

"I love you more than life," he said. "No one can make me deny you."

Then Jesus went with his disciples to a place called Gethsemane, and he said to them, "Sit here while I go over there and pray." He took Peter and the two sons of Zebedee along with him, and he began to be sorrowful and troubled. Then he said to them, "My soul is overwhelmed with sorrow to the point of death. Stay here and keep watch with me." Going a little farther, he fell with his face to the ground and prayed. "My father, if it is possible, may this cup be taken from me. Yet not as I will, but as you will." Then he returned to his disciples and found them sleeping. "Could you men not keep watch with me, for one hour?" he asked Peter. "Watch and pray so that you will not fall into temptation. The spirit is willing, but the body is weak." He went away a second time and prayed. "My father, if it is not possible for this cup to be taken away unless I drink it, may your will be done." When he came back, he again found them sleeping, because their eyes were heavy. So he left them and went away once more and prayed the third time, saying the same thing. Then he returned to the disciples and said to them. "Are you still sleeping and resting? Look, the hour is near, and the Son of Man is betrayed into the hands of sinners. Rise, let us go! Here comes my betrayer." (John, 26, 36-46, NIV)

Judas came to the meeting place leading a group of soldiers. The soldiers arrested Jesus and took him away. He looked at Peter, James and John. They felt very poorly because they failed to honor Jesus' request to keep watch. The disciples were willing to fight the soldiers, but Jesus instructed John and the others to be at peace.

Jesus was taken to Annas, the father-in-law of Caiaphas, the high priest. The disciples watched from across the courtyard.

"Where is Peter?" John asked. "I don't see him."

"They didn't allow him in the courtyard," James said. "They didn't know him."

"I will go and find him," John said. "He should be here with us."

Annas asked Jesus a few questions. He didn't like Jesus' answers. He sent him to the high priest. Peter was recognized by a servant of the high priest. He denied being a disciple of Jesus.

Calaphas explained that Jesus was a problem for the Romans.

The Jews led Jesus from Caiaphas' grand residence toward the palace. The Jews didn't enter the palace.

"Come with me, and we will determine how they are charging him," John said.

"Pilate will probably have a few questions for him," James said. "I really don't think Pilate will be interested in him. He can release one prisoner during Passover. He will release Jesus."

James was convinced that Pilate would not kill Jesus. Pilate considered the Jews' problem with Jesus to be an interfaith disagreement, not a confrontation that required the action of the Roman government. Pilate told the Jews to judge Jesus. They responded that they didn't have the right to execute anyone. Pilate asked Jesus a few questions. He was startled by Jesus' answers. He interpreted Jesus' answer to his questions to be that Jesus considered himself a king.

It was Friday, and Jesus was scheduled to be crucified. James and John remained distant from the site. They were afraid they would be arrested as followers of Jesus. They could tell by the attitude of the crowd what was happening.

"John, did you hear that?" James asked. "The crowd chanted that they wanted Barabbas to be released. Pilate set him free."

"They have convinced Pilate that Jesus is saying he is king," John said. "Pilate sentenced him to be crucified."

Many of the disciples were frightened and fled. When Jesus was crucified, the sky darkened, and only a few remained with him. John found Mary, Jesus' mother, and stayed with her.

"Mary, come and stand with me," John said. "You can bring the other women. I have met Mary of Magdala, and of course I know Peter's wife. The other disciples have gone underground to be safe. I will take care of you."

"I am so glad you are here with us," Mary said. "You won't have to take care of me. Paul's family has been caring for us for quite a while. I am shaken, but I will be fine. I will remain with you and the church for a few days."

"With the help of Nicodemus, Joseph of Arimathea is taking care of the burial," John said. "They have wrapped Jesus' body and placed spices with it. My mother helped anoint the body. Then they placed it in Joseph's garden tomb."

"I want to visit the tomb," Mary said. "Maybe we can visit Jesus in a few days."

"The Romans have sealed the tomb with a large stone, and they placed guards at the tomb," John said. "Pilate remembered that Jesus predicted he would rise after three days."

That evening, James and John met at their appointed location. They were exhausted and slept soundly. John awoke first and found a few pieces of fruit to eat. James finally woke.

"Good morning, John," he said. "Have you heard any news about Jesus?"

"I have, but you better stay seated," John said. "I have been talking with Mary, his mother, and Mary Magdalene."

"I am sure Jesus' mother is very concerned," James said. "What did they tell you?"

"They said they went to the tomb, and the tomb was empty," he continued.

"There was a violent earthquake, for an angel of the Lord can down from heaven and, going to the tomb, rolled back the stone and sat on it." (Matthew, 28, 2, NIV)

They saw an angel, and that the stone had been rolled away from the grave," James said. "Tell me more."

"The guards were so afraid of him that they shook and became like dead men. So the women hurried away from the tomb, afraid yet filled with joy, and ran to tell his disciples." (Matthew, 28, 4 & 8, NIV)

"They should have come to us," James said. "I would have helped them."

"I found Peter. He was still in shock," John said. "He told me he talked to a large cross, and then he talked to Jesus."

"Peter said he had talked with a cross?" James asked. "He must have been in shock."

"I tried to calm him, but he ran to tell the other disciples," he said. "If he doesn't calm down, they will not believe him."

"The guards at the tomb are going to have a lot of explaining to do," he said. "Pilate isn't going to be happy."

James took John by the hand. He saw tears in John's eyes.

"Let's take a walk," he said. "A walk always comforts me."

"We could walk to Emmaus," John said. "It is not that far. I think it would help me."

As they walked, John saw Jesus and spoke to James, "Do you see who that is? It is Jesus. I hope he will take time to speak, and maybe eat with us."

After they ate their lunch, they returned to Jerusalem. They found the other disciples and told them what they had seen on their walk to Emmaus. Thomas, Jesus' brother, was a little doubtful. But it wouldn't be long, before he would see Jesus. When they were in the upper room praying, Jesus appeared to all of them and instructed them to go to Galilee.

Then the eleven disciples went to Galilee, to the mountain where Jesus had told them to go. When they saw him, they worshiped him, but some doubted.

Then Jesus came to them and said, "All authority in heaven and on earth has been given to me. Therefore go and make disciples of all nations, baptizing them in the name of the Father and of the Son and of the Holy Spirit, and teaching them to obey everything I have commanded you. And surely I am with you always, to the very end of the age." (Matthew, 28, 11 – 20, NIV)

After they departed the mountain, John and James walked.

"James, I think we should go home for a while," John said. "I would like to talk with our family. We can walk along the Sea of Galilee."

"Yes, I think that would be a good idea," James said. "We need to reflect."

They started walking north to Bethsaida.

"This new village is Tiberias," John says. "I remember when it was just a fortification. The Romans are building everywhere. I am glad Peter decided to come with us."

"I am glad you decided to walk through Tiberias," James said. "I love walking along the sea. We will all have some decisions to make. Peter, I will see you in a week."

Peter stayed in Capernaum. John and James went to Bethsaida.

It was evening when they arrived at their home. They could see the candles flickering in the living area.

"Hello, mother," John said. "We have come home for a week. We hope to visit with all of you. How are you and father?"

"We are fine," she said. "How are you?"

She walked to her sons and kissed them.

"James and I are still trying to sort things out," he said. "We need some time to relax and think."

"Have you been able to adjust to your time in Jerusalem?" John asked. "It was good to see you in Jerusalem. When you anointed Jesus' body, I was especially proud of you. You would have really liked him. Hello, Hezekiah, come in."

Hezekiah entered the living area and was seated with them.

"How are you and James?" he asked. "Things at home are going very well. You will have to visit with us and your sister. You will be able to learn to know your nephews and nieces. They are the joy of our lives. If you feel like working on a boat, we could arrange it for you."

He looked at John and smiled. John rubbed his hands together.

"No, thanks," he said. "James and I have a lot of planning to do tomorrow."

"Have you decided what you are going to do now that Jesus is dead?" Zebedee asked. "You are always welcome here with us in Bethsaida."

John stared at the floor.

"I guess we have decided," he said. "James, Jesus' brother, is going to remain in Jerusalem where he will work with Peter, James, and me to continue telling Jesus' message."

"It will take a while to determine who else will remain with us," he said. "We are very hopeful."

"After everything settles, I am going to go on a mission." John said. "I am not exactly sure where. It is important everyone hears Jesus' message."

Jesus had left this earth and ascended into heaven. The disciples rested. Then they returned to Jerusalem to make certain that Jesus' message survived. James, the brother of Jesus, worked closely with Peter, James, and John.

CHAPTER 12

JOHN IN JERUSALEM

After Jesus' ascension, considerable turmoil existed within the church in Jerusalem. The disciples hid and tried to decide how they could comply with Jesus' instructions. James, Jesus' brother, remained in Jerusalem. He stayed with the disciples attempting to learn what they knew about Jesus. Times were very difficult for those who followed Jesus. They had heard Jesus' commission, but they feared for their lives. Roman soldiers, two by two, marched throughout the city. The disciples felt it was necessary to meet with Jesus' followers at secret locations. As time passed, the disciples served a small loaf of bread and a cup of wine to everyone who attended their secret services. They did this in remembrance of their last supper with Jesus. After a while, the presence of Roman soldiers decreased. The church and the followers of Jesus became significantly bolder.

During one of their meetings, the disciples discussed different plans concerning how they would spread the work of God.

"I think our commission is straight forward," John said. "We were told to take the church to all nations, the world. Now that Jesus' resurrection has pierced the dark cloud over us like a great light, we must spread his message."

"John, we don't understand what was meant by 'the world.' " James said. "We are Jewish, and I think we should take Jesus' message first to the Jewish nation."

"I agree with you, but those who were our friends in Jerusalem will try and kill us if we take any more members from them," Peter said.

"That is a real problem," John said. "I think we would be safe in the areas away from Jerusalem."

The three leaders of the church in Jerusalem were Peter, James the brother of John, and John. Jesus' brother James rapidly became part of the inner circle, as did Jesus' other brother, Thomas. However, Thomas was not satisfied being an administrator and decided to take Jesus' message to India. Each of the other disciples taught Jesus' message in an area around Jerusalem. The church grew slowly and cautiously over the next few years. After the disciples started to formulate church policies and practices, they ventured farther from Jerusalem.

The moon was bright and the stars shone brightly, so James and his brother John decided to take a walk along the streets of Jerusalem. The night was cool and eerie. Every strange noise they heard caused them concern, and they constantly looked over their shoulder.

"James, stay here in Jerusalem. I will go to Samaria and spread Jesus' word," John said. "As you know, we have a friend in Sychar and a group of members of the Way meet in the town close to the inn."

"I remember staying in the stable at that inn," James said. "I think the innkeeper's name was Abraham."

"Samaria will be my home for a while," he said. "I will return to Jerusalem on a regular basis and visit you."

"We need to bring the church together. I will establish contact with our brothers in God in Antioch," James said.

"Antioch?" he said. "Why?"

"I think Antioch is far enough from Jerusalem that we would be safe there," he said. "Be careful, and I look forward to your return."

"Can you inform me of a good place to obtain supplies?" John asked. "I need really good prices."

"Getting supplies can be a problem," James said. "We don't know who we can trust."

"Let's try to find a follower of Jesus who is in the retail business," John said. "Maybe, we can negotiate good prices."

At the next clandestine meeting of The Way, mission supplies were the major topic of discussion.

"We have found a friend of The Way, James said. "She and her husband have a small shop and have agreed to provide supplies for our missions."

"Does she offer good prices?" John asked. "We have a very limited budget."

"Visit with her, and tell her you knew Jesus," he said. "She will help you."

John went to the shop and explained who he was. She smiled at him and told him to return to his friends.

The next day, he went to Peter.

"I have a package for you," Peter said. "I can't believe what it cost."

"Take them back to her," John said. "People will comfort and feed me."

"At least you have what you need," Peter said. "We paid for the supplies."

John loaded with food and filled with the Holy Spirit headed to Mount Gerizim. His shoulders ached under his load. John's first stop was in Bethel. It was important that he got off to a good start. He brushed the dust from his clothes and went to the synagogue.

"Hello, my name is John," he said. "I would like an opportunity to teach you about Jesus. He is our gate to heaven."

"Come in, John," she said. "My name is Theoca. You are welcome to worship with us, but we already have a teacher."

"Has he been here a long time?" John asked. "I might know him."

"Yes, he has," she said. "Being this close to Jerusalem, we have had some problems with those who teach about Jesus. We have become very careful."

"I can understand that," John said. "Those of us that were with Jesus everyday didn't always agree on what he said."

"Before you will be allowed to teach, you will have to be here a long time," she said. "A few false prophets have been here."

"So, it has started already," he said. "Jesus warned us about false prophets, and that we would be persecuted."

"We try to study carefully and use Jesus' original words whenever possible," she said. "We especially like a few of the scrolls we have obtained."

"He didn't write much," John said. "His brother was always writing. He recorded many of Jesus' one-liners."

"A few people meet in a home to study," she said. "I think they might be studying your Jesus. I will introduce you to them."

They walked several blocks across town and knocked on the door of a small house.

"Hello, please come in and join our group," he said. "My name is Joel. We understand that you are teaching about Jesus."

"Yes," John said. "When I tell his stories, I try to be accurate."

"Some of us have heard Jesus speak," he said. "We would be glad to hear your comments. Have you ever met Jesus?"

"Yes, I knew Jesus quite well," he said. "I traveled with him for three years. Before that, I traveled with John the Baptist."

"Did you record his messages?" he asked. "Do you have any scrolls for us?"

"No, my brother, James, recorded his messages," he said. "He stayed in Jerusalem. He and a few others are trying to organize Jesus' followers."

"Being with Jesus must have been great," Joel said. "Most of us work here in Bethel. After we heard about Jesus, we visited Galilee and listened to him. You must have been with him when we visited."

"Yes, I am certain my brother and I were with him," he said. "I was quite busy feeding people, baptizing people, and preparing for the next day's lesson. I would be glad to tell you some of Jesus' stories."

"You can tell one or two to me," Joel said. "Then, I will recommend you to our members."

"Jesus told a great number of stories to make a point," John said. "I'm not as good at storytelling. It seems to take me longer, and I always use more words. Story telling is an art, and like other arts, you must practice."

John spent the day with Joel and told him several of Jesus' stories. Joel trusted John and recommended him to the congregation. John stayed in Bethel for six months. The church grew rapidly. When he felt he wasn't needed any longer, he moved on to Shiloh.

The reception in Shiloh was very much the same as that in Bethel.

"Hello, John," he said. "Welcome to Shiloh. One of the members of the Way visited us from Bethel. We knew you would be heading our way."

"So, you know about me," he said. "I guess I don't have to convince you I knew Jesus."

"We want you to tell us about Jesus, and we expect you to tell us some of his stories," he said. "My name is Judah. You may stay with me."

"It is nice to meet you," John said. "One of Jesus' favorite lessons was about a shepherd. He lost one of his sheep and spent days looking for the one sheep. The point Jesus made was that each of us is important to God, and we are part of his flock."

"That is a very interesting story," Judah said. "Jesus loved everyone."

"I have many stories," he said. "God has a lot to teach us."

"Would you be concerned if we make notes about the lessons?" he asked. "That way we will keep them accurate and learn them as Jesus told them. Fortunately, we have a member who is very good at writing Greek."

"Yes, that is fine with me," he said. "I will try to tell you stories that Jesus only told to his disciples. It will be good for me to try to remember all of them."

After a few months passed, John explained to the members that he had promised his brother that he would regularly visit the central church in Jerusalem, and it was past time for his visit.

"You should stay with us a little longer," Judah said. "We need your guidance. We want to be accurate in what we teach."

"I want to see my brother," John said. "I need to be updated about our church in Jerusalem."

"I guess the teacher who was at Bethel could come and stay with us," Judah said. "We could try to ensure his stories are truthful."

"The people of Bethel told me that he was a false prophet," John said. "He will mislead you."

"You have told us the truth," he said. "We would make certain that he told the truth as well."

"Do you have someone who is willing to learn how to teach?" John asked. "I could train him."

"I will work with you," Judah said. "You can teach me."

John stayed, in Shiloh, another three months. Judah was a quick learner, and he enjoyed telling others about Jesus. It was time for John to depart.

"We are sorry that you must go to Jerusalem," Judah said. "We understand you want to see your brother."

"I have been away longer than a year," he said. "I promised him that I would come back and visit with him and the central church."

"If you are ever in this area, please stop and teach us a lesson," he said. "We now have several scrolls of the lessons you have taught us. We will do our best to teach the lessons accurately."

After John's eight month stay in Shiloh, he returned to Jerusalem. He planned to visit with his brother. He learned that the church in Jerusalem converted pagans. He was pleasantly surprised to be greeted by his brother. James wanted to discuss John's missions.

"They probably had many visitors," James said. "Did they allow you to teach?"

"I was able to help grow the churches that were already established. I also formed new churches," John said. "I taught several of the faithful about baptism. I need to rest for a few days. It is good to be with you and the other disciples."

James hung his head and looked at the floor.

"I have some disturbing news to tell you," he said. "One of our first acts was to elect seven men to take care of the daily food distribution to the poor."

"Why did you need to do that?" he asked. "The poor appreciated the food."

"It seems the Greek speaking Jewish people thought they were not being treated fairly."

"I hope you picked some who I know," John said. "I have many good and dear friends."

"One of the seven we chose was Stephen," he said. "He was a man full of faith and of the Holy Spirit. He debated with the Jewish Rabbis everywhere he went."

"I know Stephen," he said. "He is a good man."

"They couldn't refute his story, so they told untrue tales about him. The

Sanhedrin cast him out, and he was stoned to death," he said. "Stephen's death caused a lot of fear and concern."

Tears flowed from John's eyes.

"I will miss Stephen greatly," he said. "They are still trying to stop our efforts. I hoped the persecution had decreased."

"I think it is getting worse," James said. "We are being very careful."

"I understand that Philip, one of our deacons, is in Samaria, do you know where he is located," John asked.

"I think he is near the Great Sea, but I haven't heard from him," he said.

John lived with his brother in Jerusalem over a year. He worked his brother, Peter, James, Jesus' brother, and the other disciples. Finally, he decided he would return to Samaria. Peter asked him if he would like a traveling companion. They agreed to be missionaries to Caesarea. They prepared for the journey and planned to depart after two weeks. John and Peter knew each other but had never worked together as missionaries.

"Before we go to Caesarea, we should spend time together, in Jerusalem, for a couple of weeks," John said. "We can gather some supplies, and we can say our goodbyes to friends and relatives."

"That is a good idea," Peter said. "Let's go for a walk. I want you to meet a lame man I know. Maybe, we can heal him."

Now a man crippled from birth was being carried to the temple gate called Beautiful, where he was put every day to beg from those going into the temple courts. When he saw Peter and John about to enter, he asked them for money. Peter looked straight at him, as did John. Then Peter said, "Look at us!" So the man gave them his attention, expecting to get something from them. Then Peter said, "Silver or gold I do not have, but what I have I give you. In the name of Jesus Christ of Nazareth, walk." Taking him by the right hand, he helped him up, and instantly the man's feet and ankles became strong. He jumped to his feet and began to walk. Then he went with them into the temple courts, walking and jumping, and praising God." (Acts, 3, 2-9, NIV)

The local Jewish Rabbis were concerned about Peter and John's success and popularity. They were detained and questioned about what they had accomplished. John responded that they had healed a lame man in the name of Jesus, the Christ, and that many had witnessed the event. They were strongly rebuked by the Rabbis but were released.

James informed John that supplies were available at a greatly reduced price. The shop owner, who had been helping the Way, was almost giving them to James. They gathered their supplies and headed to Caesarea.

"John, I think we should go to Caesarea by way of Joppa," Peter said. "Walking from Joppa along the sea will be great. It will remind us of our sea."

"You know I love the sea," John said. "Remember when you came to see me, and our boat repair business was adjacent to the sea? I am certain we will enjoy the walk."

"We can probably find some fishermen to teach about Jesus," he said. "They make good converts. They don't expect a great deal and are accustomed to hard work."

He smiled, and he looked directly at John. They enjoyed a good laugh.

On their way to the sea, they stopped and taught a few lesson in Emmaus.

After they reached the sea, they walked north.

"Peter, did you see that?" John asked. "It was large fish. It was so big; I wouldn't fit into his mouth. I guess we better pray, and we had better make sure we are doing what God wants us to do on our journey."

Peter quickly turned and looked out at the sea. He didn't see any ripples in the water.

"I didn't see anything," he said. "It sounds like a fish story to me. You and your brother always liked to tell fish stories."

Peter made a few gestures with his hands and smiled.

"Why don't we relax for a day and fish?" John asked. "I will show you how to catch fish."

"I want to keep traveling north," Peter said. "I don't think you could show me very much."

"I can catch a larger fish than you can catch, if I don't, I will clean the fish and cook dinner," he said.

John had gained Peter's attention.

"I really want to go north," he said. "After we have been in Caesarea for a while, we can fish."

John looked at Peter.

"Don't you know how to make a fire?" he asked.

"You really want me to show you how to fish?" Peter asked. "You can start the fire now."

John opened up his pack and under his clothing he found a small fishing net he had packed. Peter looked at the net and frowned.

"You didn't tell me you had a fish net," Peter said. "I was going to make a spear from a piece of wood."

John held the net up and laughed.

"Fishermen are always prepared," John said. "Watch closely at my technique."

Peter sat on a rock and watched John fish. After a few moments, John netted a medium sized fish.

"Here is my fish," John said. "It is the best size for eating. I'll allow you a little time, and then you can start the fire."

"I can eat more than that," Peter said. "Are you finished?"

"Yes, it is your turn," John said. "Good luck."

Peter took off his clothing, and he waded out into the sea. He stood very quietly for a few moments. Then he quickly stuck his hand into the water and pulled out a large fish.

"It is a good thing you caught that fish," Peter said. "My fish might have eaten him for dinner. I'll take a nap while you prepare dinner."

Peter walked back to John and placed the large fish at his feet.

"That net is so small you can't catch real fish," Peter said. "After I am full, you can have a piece of my fish. I am sure you will still be hungry after you have eaten your fish."

John was quiet. Reluctantly, he built a fire, cleaned, and cooked the fish. Peter woke up about the time the fish was ready. He rubbed his hands together and sniffed the air. The odor of fish cooking always pleased him.

"Nice job, John," Peter said. "If you ever want fishing lessons, I will help you."

The next morning was sunny, but cool. When they reached Joppa, they visited the synagogue. They didn't receive a welcome. They were politely told that the Jesus believers met on the other side of town. They looked for a church.

"Hello, gentlemen," Able said. "You look like you could use a drink of water."

"That would be nice," Peter said. "Do you know where we can find a church?"

"We have one large church and a few smaller churches," he said. "The larger one is about two blocks from here."

"I guess we can find it," Peter said.

"I am a member," he said. "I will take you to it."

"That's great," John said. "That water was just what I needed."

As they walked the two blocks, Peter explained who they were, and that they wanted to teach Jesus' message. As soon as they arrived, Able introduced them to Jonah, the teacher at the church.

"Hello, come in," Jonah said. "So you both knew Jesus? I heard him several times. What did you say your names were? I have trouble remembering names."

"I am Peter," he said. "This is my good friend, John. We both traveled with Jesus. We could teach a lesson to your members."

"Teach a lesson to me," he said. "Then I will introduce you to the members."

John and Peter stayed in Joppa for a few weeks and then continued north.

The next town they visited was Apollonia. They stayed one week and enjoyed the hospitality of a church that had been formed by Philip. They each taught a lesson and then headed to Caesarea.

"Apollonia is a very interesting seaport," John said. "I heard a lot of stories of strange people. I am glad Philip started the church."

"I am certain we will like Caesarea," Peter said. "I am looking forward to finding my friend."

Peter had a funny look on his face. He scratched his forehead.

"I have listened to my father talk of Caesarea," John said. "Herod, the Great, spent a lot of money building the city about fifty years ago. Most of the buildings are quite new."

"I didn't know that, but I did see many new buildings," Peter said.

"The harbor was improved so that large ships can use it," John said. "It is the Roman center of administration for the province of Judea. The ships load grain, and then they sail to Rome. The city is very important to the Romans. I am looking forward to our visit."

Peter yawned and said, "I hope my friend, a Roman centurion, still lives there."

"I hope he feeds us a good meal," John said. "I am hungry."

"If we can find him, I am certain he will feed us and escort us around town," Peter said. "It is possible that he started a church in his home. If he started a church, we can help him increase its size."

"What did you say his name is?" John asked. "I want to address your friend properly. It sounds like a good place to start."

"His name is Cornelius," he said. "You will like him. He is a good person."

"Cornelius," John said. "I will remember that."

"I am glad the people of Samaria are accepting the word of Jesus," Peter said. "Our friend Philip, the lecturer, built a house there. I think the house is being used as a church."

"It must be a large house," he said. "It doesn't take many people to fill a house."

"He is not using the house," he said. "He is on a journey to Ethiopia." John looked at Peter.

"This isn't a ship story; do you see that large ship in the distance?" he asked.

"No, I don't see it yet," he said. "Before I will be able to see it, it will probably have to get closer to us."

"I didn't know you had problems seeing," John said.

"I can see what is important," Peter said. "Why is that ship important?"

"The ship is probably on its way to Caesarea," he said. "We must be getting close."

They continued to walk along the coast. The gentle sea breeze energized them. They breathed the crisp sea air and walked at a brisk pace.

Finally, they arrived in Caesarea. They approached a house and knocked on the door.

"Hello, is this where Philip lived?" John asked. "We are looking for a church."

"Yes, come in," Cornelius said. "We are using this house as a church."

"I have Peter with me," he said. "I guess you know him."

Cornelius embraced Peter. They exchanged greetings and talked about the church.

"You can help us baptize our converts," he said. "I want you to baptize me. I have been waiting for a disciple and friend of Jesus' to come to Caesarea. Now, we have two. This is a great occasion for us."

"That is the reason we are here," he said. "We hope to convert and baptize many people. It would be an honor for us to work with your church and serve with you."

"I think you will like our members," Cornelius said. "They are mostly working people."

"I would like to meet them," Peter said. "We might even help you teach."

"Can you tell us about Caesarea?" John asked. "It isn't an old city, is it?"

"No, it is not old," he said. "It was built by Herod, the Great, only fifty years ago. It has a great harbor. It is large, like the harbor at Athens. Ships visit every day."

"I think my father was here," John said. "He repaired boats, not large ships."

"We have mostly large ships," he said. "We also have a good library at the university."

"I would enjoy seeing the university," John said. "My brother, James, studied in Jerusalem."

"I am here as a veteran of the Roman military," Cornelius said. "The town was built for us as a colony. Now, it is a Roman administrative center."

"I guess many veterans live in Caesarea," he said.

"Yes, we do," he said. "Tomorrow I will show you a monument to Pontius Pilate. I hope you will like it here."

"Why build a monument to Pontius Pilate?" John asked. "Did he ever do anything good worth remembering?"

"He was here for a while, and he must have been popular. You still hear people talk about him," Cornelius said.

Peter and John both liked Caesarea. They were successful in converting pagans and baptized many people. They converted so many pagans that a new church was started. Before long, several new churches were established. The older churches grew very rapidly. They stayed in the area of Caesarea for two years and made many friends. Eventually, John decided that they should return to Jerusalem. He wanted to see James, and he wanted to learn about the central church. He missed his brother and began to worry about him. Peter agreed to return to Jerusalem.

Whenever an opportunity arose while traveling, they would stop and teach lessons. They increased their pace, as they reached the streets on the outskirts of Jerusalem. They knew the streets very well. They went to a church and found James. They exchanged greetings. John talked with James about visiting their parents.

"Allow me to talk with Peter. Maybe Jesus' brother, James, will look after the church, while we all go home for a visit," James said. "I think he would like to manage things."

James agreed to maintain the church, while Peter, John, and James visited with their parents.

They started the long walk home. When they reached Capernaum, Peter was home. He spent his time with his family. His brother Andrew taught in the local synagogue. James and John continued to Bethsaida. The warm sea breeze blew gently in their faces. When they saw their home, they started running.

"Hello, mother," John said. "I have missed you."

"Welcome home, boys," Salome said. "Are you hungry?"

She hugged John, as tears rolled down her face.

"James and I sure would like one of your special meals," he said. "It's a long walk from Jerusalem. How have you and father been doing with the business?"

"We are fine," she says. "Hezekiah is totally responsible for all of the businesses. Occasionally, your father will purchase a boat. Then it is someone else's job to get it home and repaired."

"That hasn't changed," James said. "Usually, it was me."

"Have a seat at the table," she said. "I will have a meal prepared for you. It is getting hard for us to get around. We are quite old."

"Yes, I can imagine," he said. "Some days James and I feel old. That sounds just like father, purchase a boat, have it repaired, sell a boat, and find another one."

"I will visit with Hezekiah and Chava tomorrow," James said. "Tonight, I am going to enjoy dinner and sleep in my bed. It is so good to be home with you."

John stood up and stretched his arms over his head and sighed. The time went by very rapidly. Zebedee and Salome realized that James and John were both doing very well, and they enjoyed their missionary work. It was a fun week for everyone. The brothers inspected the boat that was being repaired and offered many suggestions but stayed away from the tools.

After a week, the two brothers slipped out of sight, like a boat in the wind. They left their home and started for Peter's house. Peter joined them, and they continued their journey back to Jerusalem. Peter told James he had taught John how to fish. James enjoyed the story. John quickened his pace and led the way.

Seeing the Roman soldiers on the streets reminded them that they were back in Jerusalem. Jesus' brother James greeted them. He seemed concerned.

"I have a situation for you to oversee tomorrow," he said. "Get some rest."

The next morning after breakfast, James and John found Jesus' brother.

"We are happy to be back, what do you want to discuss?" John asked.

"A man, Paul, is coming to see us," he said. "He tells an interesting story."

"I think I have heard of him," John's brother said. "He is a Rabbi and a member of the Sanhedrin in Jerusalem."

"That is what he used to be," James said. "He claims to have been converted."

"I wonder what he wants." John's brother said. "I think we met him when we were with Jesus in Galilee. Do you remember him?"

"I know of him," John said. "We met him at his sister's wedding."

"The same Paul, whose father provided everything for the wedding?" James asked. "I remember him."

"His sister is very nice," John said. "I talked with her at the wedding."

"He probably is interested in what we are doing," James said. "Thomas and my sister, Salome, are also here."

"Hello, John," Thomas said. "We want to talk with you. We came from Nazareth to tell you that Paul is a good man."

John scratched his head and said, "I remember you. You traveled with Jesus."

Paul walked forward and addressed the group.

"I have met many of you. A few of you are my good friends," he said. I want you to allow me to become a member of the inner circle of the church."

"I thought you were a high level Rabbi," John said. "It is good to see you."

"Please, listen to me," Paul said. "I was on my way to Damascus when Jesus spoke to me. I now know I placed too much emphasis on the law, and I should have been emphasizing love."

"You spoke with Jesus after he was resurrected?" John asked. "You must have been a very good friend of his. What did he tell you?"

"I taught briefly in Damascus, but they tried to kill me," he said. "If you give me a chance, I will do a good job for Jesus."

"You talked with Jesus after he was resurrected?" John asked again. "I want to know what he said to you."

"It is my job to take his message to the world," he said. "He asked me not to reveal the details of what he told me."

John stared at Paul. He began to believe him.

"Jesus often told people not to talk about what he did and what he said," John said. "He told me the same thing."

"I plan to be in the area north and west of Antioch," Paul said. "It will take me a while to build my foundation in Antioch."

"Why Antioch?" he asked. "Why not start in Jerusalem?"

"There are several Christians in an active church in Antioch," he said. "I am comfortable working with them."

"We are familiar with the church in Antioch," Peter said. "We all have friends in that area."

"We will meet as a group to discuss your request," James said. "Please, give us some time. Return tomorrow."

Not everyone was thrilled with the idea of allowing a former Rabbi, of the religion that was persecuting them, into their inner circle. Not all those present at the first meeting returned with John to greet Paul at the second meeting.

"Paul, we are pleased to welcome you to our church," John said. "My brother and Jesus' brother gave me the privilege of informing you."

"I won't disappoint you," he said. "If you want to know what I am doing, just send me a message."

"You must be very careful during your travels," John said. "Please keep in touch with us. We will all pray for you. We understand how much Jesus loved you."

After a few years, Paul returned to Jerusalem to see, James, Jesus' brother, Peter, James, John's brother, and John. They were surprised to see Paul. When they saw him, they hugged and kissed one another.

"I don't forecast my travels," he said. "I don't want to cause my family any harm."

"I remember," John said. "You have family in Jerusalem."

"Yes, I do," Paul said. "I want you to meet my sister. You haven't seen her since her wedding. It will have to be a secret meeting. She attends the synagogue."

John's face seemed to glow. He smiled at Paul.

"She runs a large retail outlet," Paul said. "She has been providing supplies for our missions for a long time. We agreed to secretly give you free supplies for future missionary trips."

"Have her come to see me," John said. "Is tomorrow satisfactory?"

After the meeting, Yona's shop became the only source of supplies for missionary trips.

As time passed, the Jewish religion sporadically used the Roman local rulers to enforce persecution of the Christians. In year forty-four, John's brother James was martyred by Herod Agrippa the Roman ruler. The Jewish Rabbis in Jerusalem were aware of increased persecution of Christians and focused Agrippa's attention on James. As John watched, Agrippa ordered James to be beheaded. John had to be taken home. He was heart-broken, despondent, and he was spending many hours each day praying for guidance. It was a severe blow to John. James' death dampened his spirits and caused him great grief. People, who were once James' friends, had him killed.

After several months, John wanted to talk with the other disciples. The church in Jerusalem needed a new leader.

"James, now that my brother is dead, you will have to manage the church in Jerusalem," John said. "I am a missionary and need to travel."

"We must not allow your brother's death to stop the growth of our churches," James said. "I will do what I can."

"I am very upset with the local Jewish Rabbi," John said. "They should not have had my brother killed. They need to have their memory refreshed about sin and punishment."

"I understand why you are so upset," James said. Maybe traveling will make you feel better,"

"I need to get away," John said. "Jerusalem reminds me of my brother."

"I think Peter will help me when he returns." James said. "My brother Jesus would be pleased with me. I am sure he often wondered about me."

They heard a man approach.

"Hello, John," Peter said. "It is good to see you. My wife and I just returned from a long mission in Bethsaida."

"Welcome home," James said. "The central church needs help."

"The churches in Galilee are strong and growing," he said. "We were sad to hear about your brother."

"It has been very difficult for me," John said. "I loved my brother very much. Our old friends shouldn't have had him killed."

"They knew he was your brother," Peter said. "They have killed many who they consider revolutionary."

"The Pharisees get the Romans to do their executions for them, but the

Romans won't always be their friend," John said. "Sometimes, it is difficult to practice love, but I am sure love is the correct answer."

"Yes it is," Peter said. "I, myself, had a problem or two. I know your faith is strong, and I am certain you will remember your brother."

"I am going on another mission in Samaria," John said. "I will be going to the Jezeel Valley."

"Good luck," he said. "I will pray for you."

"When I return, I will come see you," John said. "James is doing fine with the church. He could probably use your help. If you need someone to write Greek for you, I am certain John Mark will work with you. I think he enjoys writing much more than being a missionary."

"Have a safe trip," Peter said. "We will be seeing you. I will contact John Mark. We all should have learned how to write Greek."

John stayed several years in the region of the Carmel Ridge. It was a beautiful area, situated along a trade route that connected Egypt and Assyria. It was far above the sea and a very sacred place. John thought he would be able to find someone who would discuss Elijah with him. He wanted to know about Elijah's mountainside summer residence. He was persistent about taking the words of Jesus to everyone he came in contact with. He thought of his brother every day.

CHAPTER 13

FROM JAMES' DEATH TO TITUS

In an effort to please the Jews, during the year forty-four, Herod Agrippa, the King of Judea, had John's brother, James, put to death. John prayed about James' death for several hours each day. He was despondent and remained aloof. He tried to understand good and evil. Herod Agrippa's uncle was banished and he gained his territory. He continued to demonstrate a severe lack of financial responsibility and proved to be a troublesome administrator. After he had James killed, Herod Agrippa died strangely and unexpectedly. John remained in Sychar for a while, and then went to Bucolon Pola. That area was on the trade between Egypt and Assyria and was located far enough from Jerusalem to be safe.

John and his scribe, Nathan, were seated on the porch of their home near Mount Carmel.

"The famine is very difficult for those in Jerusalem," Nathan said. "Peter has sent a request to The Way for help."

"The church in Antioch is doing well," John said. "They should be able to help."

"I am sure the faithful in Antioch will help," he said. "Many of them lived in Jerusalem for years."

"I am glad I decided to leave Jerusalem," John said. "I enjoy living in towns near a sea."

Nathan looked at John.

"Jerusalem seems to have more than its share of problems," he said. "The Jewish temple's income has been greatly reduced because many members have joined The Way."

"As a result of its success, The Way must operate clandestinely," John said. "They never seem to have enough food or clothing for all the members."

"Each church in Jerusalem is seeking a sister church, in a successful location, to help them survive," Nathan said. "The Way's problems seem to be getting worse."

Nathan stood and walked a few steps.

"I plan to remain here for a while," John said. "I like our house, and I like this area."

"I, too, like the area," he said. "I have always liked living by the sea."

"We will meet a lot of people and have many opportunities to convert them to The Way," he said.

John looked at Nathan, hoping to see a sign of agreement.

"I will collect my writing materials and be ready to write whatever you desire," Nathan said."

"I want you to translate many of Jesus' stories into teaching lessons," John said. "They will be more straightforward, but they will be longer."

"I can help with that," Nathan said. "Tell me what you want me to write."

"I am sure we will need many blank scrolls," he said. "I hope our members will understand the meanings and remember the stories. I want to emphasize the meanings."

"Are you sure you want to change Jesus' words?" he asked. "Some people might have heard Jesus."

"I have heard him many times," John said. "Jesus didn't always tell his stories in exactly the same manner, but he delivered a consistent message. The message was the important idea."

Nathan realized John became defensive concerning his approach to his lessons.

"It is fine with me," he said. "I enjoy writing in Greek. I am sure that will keep us busy for a long time."

John and Nathan spent most of their time creating new scrolls. John would think and speak, and Nathan would write. After several weeks, John decided they needed to rest.

"Maybe next week, we will spend a few days in Caesarea," John said. "I know they have a few churches."

"I hope we have nice weather," Nathan said. "The walk will do us good."

"We can see what they are doing to attract people who live by the sea," he said. "They also attract many who make a living and must travel on the highway."

John understood Nathan was saying the area was similar to Bucolon Pola.

"That is two really different groups of people, but a good Jesus story can attract anyone" Nathan said.

"Everyone needs a foundation built on faith," John said. "Once the foundation is built, you need to maintain it."

"I always like going to Caesarea," Nathan said. "It is much larger and has more to offer. We will have to be careful not to draw too much attention."

"Yes," he said. "I only intend to spend a few days."

They started towards Caesarea. The area near the town was cooled by the sea breeze. It was a pleasant walk, and they soon arrived.

"Being close to a larger town has its advantages," Nathan said. "What is that building?"

He pointed at a large stone building.

"It is a building used to store grain," John said. "Many farmers, in this area, sell their grain to the Romans. They bring it here to be shipped to Rome."

Nathan pondered John's statement for a moment and then smiled.

"They could use some of the grain in Jerusalem," he said. "They could send it to Jerusalem."

"No, they can't do that," John said. "Once you promise your grain to Rome, you are bound by your agreement."

The smile on Nathan's face turned into a frown.

"That is too bad," he said. "The Way could distribute it to the poor and needy."

John decided to change the subject.

"Nathan, I had a dream last night," he said. "You know I have been doing a lot of praying."

"Yes," he said. "I have noticed."

"I think God is trying to answer my prayers," John said. "I have been asking for understanding concerning evil. Why is our world so evil?"

"What did God tell you?" Nathan asked. "I've never given it much thought. Maybe, it is because of Adam?"

John was surprised by Nathans's comment.

"He said the world is evil because man is greedy," he said. "It will remain evil until God convinces mankind to resist."

"We resist evil," he said. "You teach people to be good."

"That is not enough," he said. "He told me it is more evil to denounce the Messiah than to be a pagan. Pagans don't know about the Messiah."

"I am glad I believe Jesus' message," Nathan looked at John and said. "You must continue to teach."

When they arrived in Caesarea, John recognized many of the buildings and streets. As they walked a stranger approached them.

"Hello, I think I know you from Jerusalem," the stranger said. "Did you live in Jerusalem?"

John looked at the stranger. He didn't recognize him.

"Yes, I have lived in Jerusalem," John said. "I moved a few years ago."

"I also moved," he said. "I spend most of my time as a crew member on a sailing ship."

"You must spend most of your time at sea," he said. "Is Caesarea your home port?"

"Yes, it is," he said. "The government always wants something delivered to Rome, and when we leave Rome, there is always something to bring back. I really don't understand the process, but I like the work."

"It sounds like a good steady job," John said. "Not everyone has a steady job."

"It is fine for me," he said. "I love the sea."

The man said goodbye and departed.

The encounter scared John. If the sailor could recognize him, so could others. He knew he had to do something. He pulled his fingers through his uniquely styled beard.

"Nathan, that was close," he said. "For a while, I thought he might cause us some trouble. I might alter my appearance."

"That is probably a good idea," Nathan said. "You are a popular man."

"I could change the style of my beard, and I could purchase a different style of head cover," he said.

"You could shave your beard completely off," Nathan said. "Then I won't know you."

"No, it took me a long time to grow a beard," he said. "We are good friends."

"Making new friends can be enjoyable," Nathan said. "You don't have to follow all the old Jewish laws."

"Without a beard, I look like a child," John said. "I will trim it."

"That would change your appearance quite a bit," he said. "People would have to really take a close look at you to recognize you. Are you ready to start home?"

"I want to visit a clothing shop," he said. "You can help me chose a new head cover."

"That will be fun," he said. "I can trim your beard."

"After we return home, you can do that," he said. "I hate to trim my beard."

"I think you should do it," Nathan said. "Your beard is somewhat unique."

"That is one of the things, I like about it," John said. "It is a little different."

"You will be better off with a common style beard," he said. "I could make it look like my beard."

John looked at Nathan and shook his head.

"We will start back soon," John said. "I have seen what I wanted to see."

"Did you learn anything at the church?" Nathan asked. "It seemed a little different to me."

"Maybe, we can use some of their ideas at the church I have been attending," he said. "I wasn't thrilled with their ideas about eternity."

"Did you see the new coins?" Nathan asked. "We have a new emperor."

"No, I didn't notice them," he said. "What happened to Claudius?"

"They are saying his wife might have killed him," he said. "The new emperor is named Nero. I haven't heard much good about him."

"Nero," John said. "I don't know of him. He is probably a pagan. If you hear anything about him, be certain to tell me."

"I also heard that they had a few fires in Rome." Nathan said.

"I wonder if Nero will violently persecute non-pagans." John asked. "I have noticed some emperors use The Way to deflect concern from real problems."

"One of these years, they are going to have a very large fire," he said. "They need more distance between buildings. Building wider streets would help."

"They destroy a small building and construct one twice as large on the same site," John said. "Nero can always blame his problems on someone else."

"If I hear anything I will tell you," Nathan said. "Fire scares me. I like living where I can leave in a hurry if I need to."

They started back to Bucolon Polo. They walked by the grain storage building.

"Seeing that building makes me sad," Nathan said. "Many of our friends in Jerusalem are probably going without food."

"Let's stop and say a prayer for them," John said. "God is good at answering prayer."

They stopped and knelt. John stared at the blue sky above the building. After they prayed, they continued their journey.

"Did you dream last night?" Nathan asked. "What did God tell you?"

"I am still receiving visions," John said. "I am having trouble interrupting them. I need to do more praying."

They returned to their safe haven. Safety makes one more productive.

"I am planning on attending a different church on the next Sabbath," John said. "It is fine for you to go with me."

"I will go with you," he said. "Most teachers sound the same to me."

The next Sabbath, they attended a newly formed church. The members were young, and Nathan liked the church very much.

"I understand the church is not growing very rapidly," John said. "We will see what we can learn."

"I believe the fact that the teacher is so young, it is keeping older people from joining," Nathan said. "Perhaps you can talk to him and give him some encouragement. It might help him to gain confidence."

"I think I will speak with him," John said. "I have heard about a letter Paul recently wrote to young Timothy in Ephesus. He was facing a similar problem in a relatively small, new church."

"Who told you about Paul?" he asked. "Did Peter send a message to you?"

"Yes, Peter is keeping me up to date," he said. "Paul's letter gave Timothy courage. Paul reminded him that many older members had laid their hands on him when he became a teacher."

"I am certain you can help him," Nathan said. "Being young is usually only a problem for the inexperienced."

John was able to help the young teacher. The teacher was very thankful and offered to allow them to pick some fresh figs from the tree at his house.

"I will get us some figs," Nathan said. "You can start home."

"You shouldn't take his figs," John said. "We don't need them."

"Maybe, you haven't checked lately," he said. "We need almost everything."

"It was nice of him to offer figs to us," he said. "Come with me."

"No," Nathan said. "If we don't take any figs, it might hurt his feelings."

"Sometimes, I don't understand you," John said. "I'll see you at home."

After talking with the teacher for a while, Nathan picked a small bag of figs and walked home.

A few days later, Nathan was in the square when he heard some men discussing Paul. He was surprised to learn that Paul was in the area. He returned home.

"John, did you know Paul is in Caesarea?" Nathan asked. "He is being held a prisoner. They don't know what to do with him. He is claiming to be a Roman citizen and is demanding a Roman trial."

"No, I didn't hear that," John said. "That will keep them busy for a while."

"I understand he is allowed to have visitors," he said. "Do you want to visit him?"

"No," he said. "I don't think visiting him would be a good idea."

"We haven't done anything wrong, why don't you want to visit him?" he asked.

"He is a Roman citizen," John said. "I hope he is being treated fairly. If we visit Caesarea again, we will have to be especially cautious."

Not long after Paul was imprisoned, John and Nathan moved to another small town on the Great Sea. They were careful to avoid spending long periods of time in the Caesarea area. They continued to be successful. The emperor Nero spent a lot of money building theaters in many cities, and he took part in athletic events. Nero's mother was a great granddaughter of Augustus, and she was very important to Nero's rule. As time passed, Nero and his mother had a serious misunderstanding. The fact that Rome was so busy with itself was a great benefit to John. Areas away from Rome weren't being watched closely, and The Way was able to grow. The town of Nebo was on the sea, but it didn't have a port. The water was too shallow for larger ships. The local fishermen enjoyed a good business. They were able to fish and sell what they caught. John and Nathan enjoyed Nebo, and they lived there for several years.

The weather was warm, and the breeze kept the temperature pleasant. John and Nathan decided to relax for a day. They walked to the sea and sat on a rock to watch the sea birds. The sea reminded John of home.

"Nathan, did you see the bird swallow that fish?" John asked.

"That is not unusual for sea birds," he said. "They hunt by flying just above the water, and then they dive and catch fish. They eat them later."

"Where do they store the fish they catch?" he asked.

"I don't know," Nathan said. "I guess they put them inside."

"Nathan, do you know where the Nile River starts?" John asked. "The Nile is a very long river."

"First you want to know where the bird keeps the fish he catches," he said. "Now you want to know about the Nile. I think it is time for you to go back to work."

"Today is my day off," John said. "Do you know about the Nile?"

"No, I really never thought about it," Nathan said. "It must start somewhere south of Alexandria."

"That is how Nero is spending our tax money," John said. "He is having some of his troops travel to find where the Nile starts. Obviously, we pay too much tax."

"As long as they are trying to determine where the Nile starts, they are not looking for us," Nathan said. "That is a good thing."

"I guess every major city has a theater," he said. "I should be happy. When he is busy, he was not persecuting Christians."

After the sun became was low in the sky, John and Nathan walked home. They sat on the porch.

"I have a few of Jesus' stories ready for you," Nathan said. "They are now in discussion form. I hope I have written them the way you want."

John held out his hand.

"Let me see them," he said.

Nathan handed him a scroll. John read it very carefully.

"These scrolls are great teaching aids. After looking at the other writings, I might remember some stories Jesus told that are not being taught."

"You wanted to know when I heard something new," Nathan said. "There was a great fire in Rome."

"That doesn't surprise me," he said. "I knew it would happen someday. They are always experiencing fires."

"The people are very unhappy with Nero," he said. "They are holding him responsible for the fires. Many are afraid to live in Rome or the other large cities and are moving to the countryside."

"In a way, he is responsible," John said.

"I also heard that Nero is expelling people from Rome," Nathan said. "He is being particularly difficult with those who believe in one God. He wants everyone to attend Jupiter's temple."

"It sounds like he wants to rid Rome of all the Jews and Christians," John said. "He is difficult to understand."

"The Romans collect a fee from everyone who enters the temple," he said. "Some days it is quite crowded."

"I am sure they collect a lot of money at the temple," he said. "They collect tax whenever it is possible."

"Taxes are a growing problem," Nathan said. "It is a problem for us and for the government."

"Thank you for informing me about the situation in Rome," John said. "Unfortunately, that will make life difficult for my friends, Peter and Paul."

"If they are in Rome, they might have a problem," Nathan said. "Paul moves around more than us."

"I think Peter told me that Paul is back in Rome," he said. "He was in Spain for a while."

"He was in Spain?" he asked. "Did he have much success there?"

"Peter's message indicated they were very successful," John said. "I believe Peter was worried about Luke and himself."

"I also heard that a new military division is situated along the Jordan River," he said. "I don't trust Nero."

"I think the Jewish people in Jerusalem are getting really upset with Roman control," he said. "They would like to be free from Rome."

"If Nero is worried about One God believers, I'm afraid that Jerusalem will be his next target," Nathan said. "If they hope to drive the Jewish people out of Jerusalem, the Roman military will need help."

"Maybe we should go to Jerusalem," John said. "The Way might be in trouble."

"I agree," Nathan said. "I am ready to move on."

They mapped their journey to Jerusalem.

"I think it is closer if we go by way of Sychar," John said. "I visited that area with Jesus."

"That is fine," Nathan said. "It will take several days to get there."

"I don't think we will find any caravans going from Caesarea to Sychar," he said. "We will be alone most of the time."

They walked until sun down and found a tree to sleep under. The sky was black and dotted with stars. The night was so quiet; John thought he could hear his internal parts working. When the morning sun rose, John tried to waken Nathan.

"Get up, Nathan," he said. "We have dried fruit to eat for breakfast."

Nathan didn't answer. John wasn't able to awaken him. He knelt and prayed for him. Soon, Nathan awoke.

"I was really sleeping," he said. "How long have you been awake?"

"I have been awake for a while," John said. "I was worried about you."

"Why?" he asked. "I feel fine."

"I couldn't wake you," he said. "I thought you might be sick."

"No although, I do feel a little weak," he answered. "We can get an early start."

"We can't get an early start," John said. "It is already mid-day."

"Mid-day? I guess I was in a deep sleep," he said. "I am ready to walk for a while."

"Here, eat a piece of fruit," John said. "I have water for us."

Due to the late start, they didn't walk nearly as far as they had planned.

The next day, however, they walked all day. It was early evening before they arrived at the inn.

"Abraham is going to allow us to sleep in the stable," John said. "He gave me some food. Here, eat a root."

He handed a few vegetables to Nathan.

"Thank you," Nathan said. "I am sorry for delaying us."

"We will reach Jerusalem in two days," he said. "We will leave early in the morning."

Nathan hesitated, and then looked at John.

"I'm not going to Jerusalem," Nathan said. "I know you want to see your brother, and you should go. I have a friend who lives in Samaria. I am going to visit him."

"Why aren't you going to Jerusalem?" John asked. "They need us."

"They don't need me," he said. "Do you remember when I was sick yesterday? It felt like I was outside of my body, looking at it."

"Yes, I remember," John said. "But what do you mean/"

"I think I was dead," Nathan said. "I was afraid to tell you."

"What makes you think you were dead?"

"God talked to me," Nathan said. "He told me if I go to Jerusalem, I will be killed."

John didn't know what to say. He thought for a moment.

"There are worse things than dying for good causes," he said. "I am going to Jerusalem. You are welcome to come with me."

"I am going to Samaria," Nathan said. "I believe I was saved so that I can help those in Samaria."

"The Way in Jerusalem needs our help," John said. "Come with me to Jerusalem."

"I am sure they can use help," Nathan said. "God be with you. I will keep you in my prayers."

"You could tell me more about what God told you," John said. "It might make a good story for a lesson."

"If you stay with me, I will tell you," Nathan said. "You could go to Jerusalem in a few months."

"I am worried about my friends who are there," John said. "I really don't know how many remain. Many have gone."

"Some might be in Samaria," Nathan said. "We could look for them."

"I wish you great success," John said. "I have packed all the scrolls you have written for me. I am going to have to find someone to write and carry scrolls."

Two days later, John arrived in Jerusalem and was able to locate the underground church.

"I have just returned from a mission in Caesarea," he said. "Where is everyone?"

"My name is James. We are hiding from the Jewish nation," he said. "I think things are going to be bad."

James didn't recognize John because of his new beard.

"What have they been doing?" John asked.

"The Jewish nation is planning to revolt against the Roman empire," he said. "Almost every day, we hear people talking about it. Most people are afraid and are storing up food."

"I'm afraid the Roman army is too large for them to engage," John said. "They wouldn't stand a chance."

"They have their members on edge about the Roman taxes," James said. "I think the Romans know they are planning a revolution."

"I am sure the leaders of the army know what is being talked about on the street," he said.

"They probably know exactly what is going on," he said. "I see soldiers on every corner."

"If the Roman army knew the configuration of the streets of Jerusalem, the Jewish people wouldn't stand a chance," John said. "They shouldn't have had my brother killed."

"They have had a lot of good people killed," James said. "What they need to know is about the water supplies and the underground tunnels. If the Romans controlled the water, it would only be a matter of time."

"I think I am going to have a new purpose for a few years," John said. "Doing good deeds can take many forms."

John was correct; Jerusalem was a target of Nero's. However, Nero didn't live long enough to see the final results of the revolution. John was also correct about the Roman military machine needing help.

CHAPTER 14

FROM TITUS TO ROME

Over the course of the thirty years after Jesus was killed, John completed several missionary journeys. When he wasn't on a mission, he lived primarily in Jerusalem. The Jewish nation had planned a revolution against Roman control. The activities in Jerusalem became volatile. The Roman government was aware of the planned revolution, and the empire had sent a major army legion to the area. Emperor Nero assigned Vespasian and his son, Titus, to Judah. They planned to lead the Roman military against the revolution. Once victory was decided, the Roman army would occupy the city. King Agrippa and Berenice fled Jerusalem to Galilee, where they surrendered to the Romans.

As the sun slipped below the horizon, the soldiers set up camp and rested. Vespasian and Titus sat in a large tent located at their temporary military fortification.

"Titus, the empire is not in a hurry," Vespasian said. "This revolution isn't really new. The administrators of the Roman government and the Jewish people have been at odds over religion and taxation for a long time."

"We have been enforcing their desires for many years," Titus said. "They should understand our protection and building programs cost money."

"They are only interested in how much money they have in their treasury," he said. "They discount the roads and aqueducts."

Titus relaxed and removed his boots.

"It is time we teach them a lesson," he said. "They have made a grave mistake this time."

"This could be a good opportunity for us," Vespasian said. "Our sixty thousand soldiers are strong and ready to fight."

"We are doing fine in Galilee," Titus said. "I have obtained some information from Berenice. She seems like a nice woman."

"You should be careful," he said. "The last time you said a woman was nice, it ended in divorce."

"Don't worry. I learned my lesson," he said. "I don't envision me getting married any time soon."

"Plans and actions are not always the same," Vespasian said. "Take your time. Don't be in such a hurry."

"We could use more current information about Jerusalem," Titus said. "Before we go into Jerusalem, I plan to occupy several cities. I want to be prepared."

"The more we know about the streets and buildings, the easier capturing Jerusalem will be," Vespasian said. "The underground there is full of tunnels."

Titus stood and walked toward his father.

"The other day when I traveled in Galilee, I met a man named John," Titus said. "He was teaching a lesson about Jesus to a large crowd of people, do you know of John?"

"I have heard of him," Vespasian said. "I don't think he is a friend of the Jewish leaders."

"He severed ties with them," Titus said. "They had his brother killed."

"He might be a good person to know," Vespasian said. "And I am sure he is familiar with Jerusalem."

He looked at Titus and smiled.

"I thought the same," Titus said. "The next time I see him, I will make it a point to talk with him."

"Make sure we can trust him," he said. "Ask some of your friends if they know of him."

"He can probably tell me all about Jerusalem," he said. "You have a good evening. I think I will go and visit with Berenice."

"You are better off with John," he said. "I am sure that he wants revenge for his brother's death."

Titus smiled at his father.

"Good night, father," he said.

"Good night, son. I will see you tomorrow."

The smoke from the campfires filled the air, and an occasional ember rose into the night sky. Titus pushed back the tent flap and cautiously walked into the night.

As the months passed, Vespasian and Titus prepared to capture the town of Yodfat. Nero sent orders to them to increase their war efforts. In preparation, they collected all the facts about Yodfat that they could obtain.

"We need to find some additional information about Yodfat," Vespasian said. "Do you know anyone from that area?"

"I have been talking with John. He gave me all the information we will need," Titus said. "You were correct about him. He is a very knowledgeable person."

"You should cultivate a friendship with him," he said. "He might be looking for a friend in the Roman army."

"I will protect him," Titus said. "The best plan is to lay siege on the town. After about three weeks, the people will become restless. After forty days, they will deplete their supply of food."

"I am pleased we have a plan," Vespasian said. "I will inform Emperor Nero that our troops are in place."

Vespasian gave specific instructions to his scribe.

John returned to Jerusalem and visited with the disciples. Most of the members of the church, including the disciples, were very careful not to draw attention to their activities. They feared additional persecution from the leaders of the Jewish religion. The disciples held their lessons in a barn.

"Hello, John," James said. "It looks like the Jewish nation is in trouble. Soon, the Roman Army is going to defeat our enemies."

"It is just a matter of time," John said. "They shouldn't have taken my brother to the Romans and had him murdered."

"Everyone seems to be able to convince the Romans to do their dirty work for them," James said. "Now, it looks like the Roman soldiers are going to destroy Jerusalem."

John looked at James, and they smiled.

"You have to be careful who you convince to kill your enemy," he said. "They might kill you."

"Someday, they might consider you an enemy," James said. "Have you talked with Titus recently?"

"Yes, I saw him the other day," John said. "He and his father's troops are at Yodfat. I gave them some information that will help them."

"It is a little strange working with the Romans," James said. "Do you think we can trust them?"

"I really don't feel like I am dealing with the Romans," John said. "I am dealing with Titus, and he just happens to be a Roman."

"Titus just happens to be a very important Roman," he said. "How well do you know him?"

"Did you know he has a Jewish girlfriend?" John asked. "I believe I can trust him."

"In a few years, they will probably be here in Jerusalem," he said. "He might be a good person to know."

"I told him about our friend, Josephus," John said. "When they capture Yodfat, Josephus is going to surrender to Titus."

"Are you sure he is going to surrender?" James asked. "Why would he?"

"Titus will take him prisoner along with several others" he said. "It is important that people know he was captured. Titus will give him special treatment."

"I hope you know what you are doing," James said. "I will do a lot of praying for you."

"I have forgiven," John said. "But I haven't forgotten."

"Stay in touch with Titus," he said. "Keep me informed about the movement of the army."

John stayed with James for several days.

The information John provided to Titus proved to be accurate. After a forty-seven day siege, Vespasian and Titus's legion captured Yodfat. They killed many of the residents, and many people committed suicide. Josephus surrendered to Vespasian and became a prisoner of war. Many children and women were taken as slaves. Josephus located a guard and asked to be taken to Vespasian. At first the guard refused. After Josephus insisted, he delivered him to Vespasian.

"I am looking for Vespasian," he said. "I am Josephus. I know John. He told me you might want to talk with me."

"I am Vespasian," he said. "Why would I want to talk with you? I can't recall anyone named John."

"He told me you were interested in Jerusalem," he asked. "As a historian, I am very familiar with the city. When you go to Jerusalem, I could probably be very useful to you."

Vespasian hesitated and then explained that his son had met with John. Then he took control of their meeting.

Vespasian looked directly at Josephus and said, "You are my prisoner. You will be given material to write and draw. I need a map of Jerusalem. Also, I want a drawing of the Temple area."

"I can do that," Josephus said. "Say hello to John for me."

He took the drawing material and sat at a table.

By the year sixty-nine, the entire coast and the northern areas of Judea were occupied by Roman soldiers and under the control of Vespasian. It was, however, a very difficult year in Rome. Nero had committed suicide leaving the government very unsettled. After a series of emperors, Vespasian was named the fourth emperor of that year. After he gave command of the Judean military forces to Titus, he returned to Rome.

"Titus, you will have to capture Jerusalem on your own," Vespasian said. "I have been recalled to Rome. They have named me emperor. Make me proud of you."

Titus looked at his father in disbelief.

"You can't leave," he said. "I need your direction. I depend on your counsel every day."

"I am emperor," Vespasian said. "I may never get another chance like this. I must return to Rome."

Conflicted by disbelief Titus continued to stare at his father.

"I guess I understand," he said. "You can count of me. It has been a difficult time in Rome. Are you certain you will be safe?"

"Yes, I believe the hostile element is gone," he said. "I will be safe in Rome. I hope to be emperor for many years."

"We all hope you are emperor for many years," Titus said. "I will take care of Jerusalem for you."

"I will take care of Rome for you," Vespasian said. "Remember, your father is now emperor. I want no problems with your women."

"I don't have any problems with women," he said. But dealing with the Jews in Jerusalem could be a problem."

"Keep John with you," he said. "He has given you good counsel. We might be able to use him in Rome."

He bid his son farewell and started his journey to Rome.

John and James heard the news about Vespasian. They were concerned about any possible change in military strategy. They remained careful as they moved around the city.

"I think Titus is coming to Jerusalem," John said. "I will visit with him."

"His father is in Rome," James said. "He is now in control of the Roman army."

"I will ask Titus if he plans to make many changes," he said. "He will be straight forward with me."

"Knowing the son of an emperor could be beneficial," James said. "Determine his plans with regards to Jerusalem."

"Titus could be the next emperor," John said. "Knowing an emperor might be an even better thing."

"I think he has an older brother," he said. "His brother is in Rome with his father."

"I have never heard him talk about an older brother," John said. "He must not be a warrior."

"He might not be a warrior," he said. "He will most likely be the next emperor."

"I understand Josephus is working with Titus," John said. "I will see you in about a month. We probably need to make plans to vacate Jerusalem."

"Be careful, John," James said. "I will expect you back in a month. I will meet with our church and tell them what we have planned."

"Don't tell them my identity," John said. "This must be kept from the Jewish nation."

"Our members need to scatter before Titus gets to Jerusalem," James said. "Near the end of his time as emperor, Nero had most of the Christians and Jewish people in Rome killed."

"I hope he didn't kill our friends in Rome," John said. "When Nero became emperor, they went underground."

"I am afraid they have disappeared," James said. "We haven't heard from them in several months."

"Nero is no longer a threat," he said. "Tell our followers to stay distant from the temple area."

"I want to give our friends time to escape," James said. "I think many of them will go to Antioch. Antioch has become very important to The Way."

It wasn't difficult to locate the temporary headquarters of the Roman military. When the army moved, the people became concerned. After three days, John found Titus.

"We are doing well," he said. "I am sure you know my father is now emperor. I am commander of the army in Judah. Come in and be seated. I have a prisoner you might like to meet."

"Hello, John," Josephus said. "Remember me? I have drawn Titus a map of Jerusalem and the temple areas. Take a look at them, and tell us if anything has changed."

Josephus handed the maps to John. He looked them over for a few moments. He didn't know of any major changes and returned the maps to Titus.

"The main thing that is happening with the Jewish nation is they are fighting a civil war," John said. "They can't agree with each other. It is probably a good time to invade Jerusalem."

"Have you checked the map?" Josephus asked. "Titus needs to know as much as we can tell him."

"Yes, I see you have drawn all three walls," he said. "I recommend that you allow any Jewish person, who wants to enter Jerusalem, to do so. Don't allow anyone to leave. Eventually, their water and food will be depleted."

"That is a good idea," Titus said. "At the proper time, we will secure the gates."

"The Jews have dug a few more tunnels," John said. "I will have Josephus add them to the map. Many people could be trapped in the tunnels."

"John, you will have to join Josephus as a prisoner," Titus said. "That way I will be able to protect you."

"I don't need protection. My people will protect me," he said. "We have learned to be very careful."

"You will be taken to Rome with me," he said. "I will send a messenger to James and explain you are safe."

"Is this necessary?" John asked. "What does my being a prisoner involve?"

"Everyone will know you are my prisoner," he said. "While you are in my custody, you will be safe."

"I see," he said. "It is for our benefit."

"I will also tell James to secure the Christian church and have them leave Jerusalem," Titus said. "I need you as an advisor. Josephus can do the writing."

Mentally, John had not prepared to be a prisoner. He knew it would be necessary eventually, but he refused to plan for the circumstance. Now that he was a prisoner, he spent all his time with Titus.

"I really wanted to see our followers one more time," John said.

"No, you can't leave camp," he said. "We are preparing the army to move. It is imperative that you stay with us."

"When he hears from you, I am sure James will have Jesus' followers leave Jerusalem," John said. "I hope James has completed the evacuation plans, and they are not harmed."

Titus sent a messenger directly to James. The messenger was ordered to speak with no other person and to report back to Titus.

Titus' troops were joined by two additional legions of Roman military troops. Jerusalem refused to surrender, and the city was plundered. Hundreds of people trying to escape through the tunnels were trapped and killed. The great temple was burned to the ground. Titus ordered his troops to sift through the rubble. Most of the gold and jewels became property of the army and was taken to Rome. Josephus and John now understood why they must be taken to Rome. The weather turned cold, and Titus didn't want to sail during the cold, inclement weather.

"Josephus, cold weather brings high seas," John said. "When spring arrives, the seas will return to normal."

"Waiting until spring is fine with me," he said. "I like calm seas."

"This time of year, we often endure strong storms," John said. "I am sure Titus will have his troops busy in Jerusalem for many months."

"I understand Titus is doing some traveling with Berenice," Josephus said. "I wonder where they are planning to go."

"I think they are planning to keep each other warm," John said. "Living in a large palace and soaking in a hot bath sounds enticing."

"It sure is cold," he said. "Maybe we can go somewhere warmer."

John and Josephus lived in a tent at the military fortification outside of Jerusalem. It was safe, almost warm, and dry. John saw Titus approach.

"Titus, I know we are your prisoners," he said. "This winter, we would like to spend some time in Antioch. Is that satisfactory with you? We can find a house and be dry and warm."

Titus laughed.

"You don't want to sail the rough sea?" he asked. "I don't like rough seas any more than you."

"If you allow us to go to Antioch, we will join you before you get to Rome," John said. "I want to show Josephus around Antioch."

Titus walked to his carriage. John noticed Berenice seated inside it. He gave her a smile. Titus spoke with Berenice for a moment and returned to John.

"You have been helpful to me," he said. "You may go to Antioch, but I want to know where you will be staying."

"We will be staying at the large church," John said. "You can trust me. The people at the church know me."

"Don't disappoint me," Titus said. "Before we head to Rome, Berenice and I will stop at the church in Antioch that you spoke of. I will expect to see you in a few months."

Titus climbed into the carriage and departed.

John thought about Antioch and their situation. He turned to Josephus.

"While we are in Antioch, we must be careful what we say," he said. "Explaining our situation could be tricky."

"I am looking forward to living in a house," Josephus said. "Let's get going."

Josephus and John walked to Antioch. Josephus wasn't nearly as practiced a walker as John. He was accustomed to riding in carriages. They walked slowly, and they made many stops. Josephus' feet became blistered and ached.

"When we get to Antioch, one of the first things I want to show you is the circus," John said. "It is surrounded by the Orontes River."

"Completely surrounded?" Josephus asked. "Did the Romans build a bridge?"

"The circus, Palladium, and stadium were all built on an island by the Romans," he said. "They are located in the northwest part of town, and you can visit them by crossing a bridge."

"Antioch is important for both the Jewish and Christian religions," Josephus said. "I have met many Jewish people from Antioch."

"It certainly is important to The Way," John said. "After Jerusalem was determined unsafe, Antioch became the home of Christianity. Paul organized many mission trips that started in Antioch. His brother doesn't live far from there."

"I believe he was from Tarsus," Josephus said. "I know of him."

When they arrived in Antioch, they were exhausted. John wanted to find the church and rest. As they headed toward the church, he continued to describe the city.

"The older part of the town is Greek," he said. "The Greeks built the Agora as their town center and market. I always enjoy a visit to the market."

"This is quite a river," Josephus said. "I am looking forward to seeing the remainder of the town."

"The circus is there," John said. "It is where the Romans hold chariot races."

"What is that?" Josephus asked. "It is a large complex."

"That is the amphitheater," he said. "When we are in Rome, we will see larger examples of most of these buildings."

"Do you think I will be safe in Rome?" Josephus asked. "I am somewhat concerned."

"Titus will make sure we are safe," John said. "We will stay in this section of town for a while. I will introduce you to some of my friends."

"Are they all Christians?" he asked.

"Yes, many of them were pagans," he said. "And many of them were Jews."

John knew Judah's son lived at the church and would provide housing. John was once assigned, on a temporary basis, to study in Antioch. When they found the church, they went inside and prayed.

John looked at Josephus and said. "I would like you to meet Menahem. Joseph was his grandfather."

"Josephus is the Latin form of Joseph, did you realize that?" Josephus asked

"No," he said. "Joseph was Jesus and Judah's father. Judah was Menahem's father."

"I have read about Judah," he said. "I have heard of Menahem."

"Judah was an important part of our church for many years," John said.

"Hello, Josephus," Menahem said. "I have heard of you. You write Jewish history."

"Yes," he said. "It is very nice to meet you. John is showing me around Antioch."

"I am sure John will do an excellent job," he said. "Welcome to our town. If you have time, please come and worship with us."

"I am tired," John said. "Menahem has found us a house where we can stay for a while."

"I look forward to not sleeping in a tent," Josephus said. "I know a tent is much better than being outside, but I still prefer a house."

"Our hosts are a nice Christian family. I don't think they will try to prevail on you," he said. "We all have goodness in common."

Josephus and John stayed in Antioch for several months. They became familiar with the entire town and especially enjoyed the Forum, the Roman public meeting place, and market.

Soon, Titus and Berenice arrived. The four of them traveled to the coast, where they would sail to Rome. They traveled to Rome with great fanfare. They were treated as Great War heroes. When they arrived, Vespasian met them.

"Welcome to Rome. We have many surprises for you, who do you have with you?" he asked.

"Hello, father," Titus said. "This is Berenice. You remember her from our time together in Syria."

Vespasian abruptly pulled his son aside. A deep wrinkle appeared on Vespasian's forehead.

"Do you remember what I told you about women?" he snapped. "Keep her out of sight. Hide her, or get rid of her. If you don't, I will."

Titus tried to deflect his attention.

"This is Josephus and John. They are my advisors," he said. "Without them, it would have taken much longer to destroy and capture Jerusalem."

John recognized Vespasian and hoped he would be glad to see him.

Vespasian looked at John.

"I know John and Josephus," he said. "I have talked with them."

"They have been advising me," Titus said. "Josephus is a writer, and John is a very good thinker."

"They are captives," he said. "You can keep them as advisors, but they are prisoners."

"Thank you, father," Titus said. "I am sure they will be of great help to me."

"If you would keep them out of sight, whenever possible, I would appreciate it, do you understand?" Vespasian asked, sternly.

He looked at Titus.

"Yes, I know they might not be popular," he said. "They are not pagans."

"It is important for me to be what everyone expects of their emperor," Vespasian said. "I don't need any problems from my son."

"I understand. And I will keep Berenice out of site," Titus said. "I will have Josephus and John as advisors in a special capacity. Thank you for receiving us, father."

"Your brother and I have a great parade planned for you," he said. "Rest and we will celebrate tomorrow."

The next day, Titus, accompanied by Vespasian and Domitian, paraded through the city and greeted the Roman people. Throughout the parade, the treasures of war, including items taken from the great temple in Jerusalem, were displayed to the people. It was a joyous time for the Romans. They were pleased with their military and their victory.

The following day, Vespasian went to see his son.

"In a short while, we will go to the Forum to watch the execution of your more troublesome prisoners," Vespasian said. "I plan to show you the marble tablet we had erected at the entrance to the Forum. I had it placed there in your honor."

"It is good to be home with you," Titus said. "Domitian and I will share your duties with you."

"It is nice to have both of you with me," he said. "Domitian has already been helping me."

"You can count on me and my advisors as well," Titus said.

Rome had grown, and its influence was felt throughout the world. It was a relatively peaceful time. After reigning for many years, Vespasian died in the year seventy-nine. It was expected that the emperor's oldest son would reign as next emperor. However, because Titus was embraced as a war hero, he was named emperor. His brother wasn't a hero, and the senate didn't know much about him. Domitian felt slighted, but he remained loyal to Rome. Titus went about trying to assuage his brother's apprehension.

"I have sent Josephus back to Jerusalem," Titus said. "Our future is good."

"Will he be safe?" Domitian asked. "He is a traitor."

"He will be safe," he said. "The Jews think I captured him."

"That is why he was your prisoner!" Domitian exclaimed. "I understand."

"My dear friend and advisor, John, will remain with us. He will work for you and me," Titus said. "I will have to find him a new scribe."

"I am very sad over father's death," Domitian said. "It is fine that you were named emperor. I will work with you in any capacity."

Titus sensed his brother was upset. He hoped he and his family could adjust to his not being named emperor. Many situations at the palace were awkward for the brothers and their families. Domitian's wife was particularly distraught.

In the year seventy-nine, Mount Vesuvius erupted and many people were killed. Entire towns were obliterated. Panic overcame the people of the area around Vesuvius.

"Let's see what John can do to make us appear as a concerned government," Domitian said. "This is a serious situation."

"I think I will take John to visit the area," Titus said. "As emperor, I must do something to help these people."

"I am sure they need help," Domitian said.

Titus told his aids to prepare to visit Pompeii. When the emperor moved, a great number of people were required. The carriages and guards were ready. Titus informed John of his plans.

"It will be an honor to go with you," John said. "I am sure we will be able to bring help to many people. Naples would be a good place to visit first."

"I will want to visit Pompeii," Titus said. "Keep track of the damages. After we determine the extent of the destruction, we will inform the treasury how much money will be required to provide relief."

They weren't able to see downtown Pompeii, because everything was covered with volcanic ash. They stayed several miles north of Naples. After dinner, Titus and John discussed the destruction.

"I have never seen anything like this," John said. "The volcanic ash is very deep. Most of the buildings are completely buried."

"It is a catastrophe," Titus said. "Many of the people didn't escape."

"You can't do anything until the ash cools," John said. "It will take months."

"I will order some of the troops to stay here and erect temporary shelters," he said. "We have many extra tents."

"You can provide help for those who were not killed," he said. "They will have to be relocated."

"I will send my sergeant to find them homes," he said. "They will also need food."

"Give families money, and hold them accountable," John said. "The next few days are critical for them."

"I will have my doctor stay with them," Titus said. "I need to return to Rome."

A short time passed when a large fire broke out in Rome. Again, Titus, with John's advice, provided a significant relief effort. Domitian was very quiet about the money being spent on relief. The relief efforts proved to be very popular. When Titus was seen in public, large crowds would gather and chant their approval of his actions. Domitian became discouraged. He found ways to assist his brother concerning other matters.

"Titus, the Coliseum is finished," Domitian said. "We should celebrate. It has taken ten years to finish the project. We can celebrate and honor father at the same time."

"That is a good idea," Titus said. "I will have John plan a celebration."

"You will probably have to have a pagan plan some of the games," he said. "John can help plan other events."

"Domitian, we will both help inaugurate the games," Titus said. "We will make sure they are special and continue for a long time. At the end of the games, I will dedicate the amphitheater."

Two months later, Titus informed John that they were going to visit Naples. After they had determined what had been accomplished with the money provided by the relief effort, Titus planned to address the senate.

"I am certain the people of Rome would be interested in additional relief plans," the sergeant said. "I will interview those who received relief. I will require them to explain how the government helped their families."

"You can plan for a longer trip," Titus said. "I will tell my brother to remain in Rome. I want him available to make the daily decisions."

Titus was now seen as a great political hero. The people in Rome gave him great acclaim, and he received even greater acclaim from those living south of Rome. Domitian faded from political focus.

Later in the day, John saw Domitian approaching.

"John, I want you to stay close to my brother during your trip," Domitian said. "If you have any problems, send a messenger to me."

John agreed.

"It will be nice to be away from Rome," Titus said. "Tomorrow, we will travel most of the day, and then we will stop overnight and have a good dinner. The next morning, we will get an early start."

The entourage traveled at a good pace. Those who couldn't maintain the pace joined the encampment at the end of the day.

"We are covering a great distance every day," John said. "Maybe, we need to rest longer this evening."

"Yes, we are doing well," Titus said. "Tonight, I am going to have the cook prepare me a special meal. My brother had some food packaged especially for me."

"Are you sure about the meal?" John asked. "While we traveled, it probably became very warm. Smell it before you eat it. You have to be careful about what you eat."

"I am not afraid," he said. "Domitian made sure I had a special meal. I will have someone get fresh food for you."

"If I were you, I would have a guard taste the food first," he said. "Make sure it is not spoiled."

"Someone always tastes my food first," he said. "That is not necessary today. My brother didn't send any extra food."

Before the food was served to Titus, John took a small sample of each food item and fed it to Titus' horse.

"I will taste it for you," John said. "Then you can eat it."

"Stay away from my food," Titus said. "Domitian didn't send enough food for me to share it with you."

"I think I would throw that old food away," he said. "Eat fresh vegetables with me."

"You worry too much," he said. "The meal will be great. Domitian even marked my portion, so no one else would take it from me. It is nice to have a caring brother."

After the meal, Titus became very ill. He doubled over in pain. His speech was very low. He was gasping for air.

"I am not feeling well," he said. "I am sick, and I am sad. My horse died. How do you feel?"

"I feel fine," John said. "I didn't eat the food that was brought from Rome. I ate fresh vegetables."

"I should have listened to you," he said. "I am really sick. I ache all over."

"Should I get the doctor?" John asked. "I see him at the other tent."

"Yes, get the doctor for me," Titus said. "Please hurry."

John brought the doctor to Titus. The doctor bent over him and listened.

"This isn't good," the doctor said. "Did someone sample his food before he ate it?"

"No, he ate a special meal," John said. "Domitian had it prepared. He had the food sent with his cook."

"It must have been very special," he said. "I wish he could expel it."

After a short time, Titus sweated one moment and shivered the next. He finally went to sleep. In the morning, John wasn't able to wake him. He went to the doctor's tent.

"I can't wake Titus," John said. "I am afraid he is really sick."

They went to Titus' tent.

"I will check him," the doctor said. "Let me see if he is breathing."

John watched the doctor very carefully.

"Is he breathing?" he asked. "He isn't moving."

"He is dead," the doctor said. "It might have been the food."

John sent a messenger to Domitian.

Domitian
Emperor of the Roman Empire

May your God bless you.
Your brother, Titus, died.
The doctor thinks he ate bad food.
I will bring his body back to Rome.
We should be there in three days.

John
Prisoner of the Empire

"Domitian, I have a message for you," the guard said. "John sent it to you."

"A message from John," he said. "Read it to me."

"It says your brother died," the messenger said. "The other evening, after he ate his dinner, he got sick."

Domitian became the next emperor and quickly proclaimed Titus a deity. He also had the marble removed at the Forum and had the Arch of Titus built. He didn't want anyone to think he was involved with his brother's death. John knew the truth. Domitian went to see John and explained the new power structure.

"John, you are safe with me," he said. "As long as I am emperor and can protect you, I will keep you with me."

"Thank you," John said. "I think I can help you make good decisions."

"My brother told me how valuable you were to him. You have been a great help to both of us since father's death," he said. "I plan to keep you with me for a long time."

John was relieved that Domitian allowed him to remain an advisor. He was also very concerned. He knew Domitian had killed Titus. John couldn't trust him and maintained a constant vigil.

"Things will be different around here," Domitian said. "I will now have a real job and real responsibilities."

"Yes, Titus was always busy," John said. "I know his routine quite well."

"I'm not as public a person as my father and brother," he said. "We will be spending a lot of time away from Rome. I will simplify the government to allow this to happen."

"Do you want me to travel with you?" John asked.

"Some of the time," he said. "I will tell you."

Domitian rose and motioned for John to follow him. They walked down the hall of the government building.

"I have a lot of people I want you to meet," he said.

"I already know most of the people who worked with Titus," he said. "Some of them were in Judea with us."

"I am not a Christian," Domitian said. "I follow the basic Roman religion. I am a follower of Jupiter."

He looked at John and laughed.

"I will be glad to meet your friends and relatives," John said. "Are any of them Christians?"

"No, John. This is my wife Domitia," he said. "We have one son. He means everything to me. He is almost a year old."

"It is a pleasure," John said. "He is a beautiful boy."

"Next, I want you to meet my uncle. He raised me most of my life," he said. "My sister and mother died, and my father and brother were fighting wars most of the time."

John was concerned, and he listened very carefully.

"I also want you to meet Nerva. He also helped to raise me," he said. "He is my trusted friend. He will come to you on many occasions with questions from me. I trust his judgment."

"I look forward to working with him," John said.

Domitian made many changes in the government. Eventually, he became quite popular. Nerva was his right-hand man. They went everywhere together. Nerva also spent a lot of time with John. Domitian was not very interested in expanding the empire. He delegated those matters to Nerva.

John was at his table working on government matters for Nerva, when Domitian quickly approached him.

"John, I have bad news," Domitian said. "My son has died."

"I am very sorry for you and your wife," John said. "Maybe I can help her in her grief."

"I am going to exile my wife," he said. "She must have done something to cause my son to die. I think I will send her to Patmos or somewhere like that."

"Why exile her?" he asked. "She needs you."

"I just can't stand to look at her," he said. "She reminds me of my son. I don't understand what she did. We shouldn't have suffered this great loss."

John was shaken and tried hard to find the proper words. He looked at Domitian, and then he took his hand and said a silent prayer. Domitian didn't know what John was doing, but he felt more at peace.

"I am very sad," John said. "Are you sure it was you wife's fault? I wouldn't be too hard on her. I know you love her. Treat her fairly."

Their conversation ended and Domitian walked away. John didn't see him again for many months. He worked with Nerva every day. John didn't know where Domitian went, but he knew Nerva was running the government. It was a very busy time for John.

"Things are changing again," Nerva said. "We are moving to our new palace. Domitian has made arrangements for us to be close to him," he said. "I am going to like being in Rome. Domitian said to tell you that you were correct."

Nerva had a puzzled look on his face.

"What did Domitian mean?" he asked.

"I will have to see Domitian," John said. "He usually doesn't say anything when someone is correct."

John sat working in his new office, and when Domitia appeared, he was quite surprised to see her.

"Hello, John," Domitia said. "I am back from Patmos. It wasn't too bad, but the new palace is much better. I plan to be here for a long time."

She smiled and looked John directly in his eyes and said, "Thank you."

The next few years were quite eventful. Nerva departed the palace and fought several minor wars. He collected many honors and medals. Emperor Domitian seemed happy even though he didn't have another son. He focused on building. He restored the temple that honored Jupiter and had many new buildings constructed in Rome. If he wasn't building something, he was at the games honoring the winners.

One day, John saw Domitian and took the opportunity to speak with him.

"Domitian, I have an idea," he said. "I think we should have some public banquets. They helped your father retain his popularity."

"That sounds like a good idea," he said. "Have you seen my new buildings?"

"I have seen some of them," he said. "They are beautiful."

"I love the games and races," he said. "Oh, I guess you won't like the games."

"No, I don't like persecuting anyone," John said. "We are all children of God."

"We are just having fun," he said. "Everyone thinks I am collecting too many taxes. I keep telling them that I am building new roads and buildings."

After several years passed, Domitian established a governmental pattern that provided relative peace and prosperity. However, the situation in Rome was not to his liking. Many people were finding fault with his taxation and spending habits.

"John, I am receiving criticism because you are a Christian," Domitian said. "It is getting harder for me to justify having you as an advisor."

The next day, John saw Nerva at work. He was certain Nerva knew what was going to happen. They discussed the situation. Nerva explained that John being a Christian wasn't the real problem. The people were really upset about the taxes they were forced to pay. Domitian blamed the problems on his advisors, and he was going to have to make some changes. He said if things got much worse, John might be in danger.

"I don't know how much longer we can justify having you with us," Nerva said. "I know you are a great advisor, and we all trust you. The people are very dissatisfied. If anything happens, you will be able to count on me."

John knew it was just a matter of time. He made plans.

After a week, John saw Domitian approaching his work area.

"John, your usefulness is over," he said. "I must banish you."

"What did I do wrong?" John asked. "I have done everything you asked."

"You are a Christian," Domitian said. "I shouldn't have a Christian advisor."

"I am a Christian," he said. "I will always be a Christian."

"I must exile you to Patmos. I don't have a choice," he said. "You will be safe and sustained. You must remain there until I die."

"That is where you sent your wife," John said. "She seems to have survived."

"Things are out of my control. I want you to understand that you did a fine job for me," he said. "The emperor has to be responsive to the people. I can't always understand what the people want of me, but I do know I want to be emperor for many more years."

Domitian collected so many taxes; the people became dissatisfied with him. He felt obligated to make some changes in the government. Because he wasn't willing to sacrifice Nerva, he dismissed John. He hoped John's exile would quiet the turmoil. John was pleased that he was still alive. He decided he could endure exile. He had been told stories about Patmos.

"I understand your situation," John said. "I will need a scribe. I have a few things I want to write. If you want my help, you can send Nerva to me. I will pack and be ready to sail."

Domitian was constantly bothered by the astrological signs and was having great difficulty sleeping. Lack of peaceful sleep was a common problem among pagans. He became restless and difficult to be around. He became paranoid of dying. He thought everyone was trying to kill him. When he reviewed Roman history, it gave him a clear picture of how unpopular emperors had been eliminated. He was especially fearful of John. Domitian only lived a few more years before he was assassinated.

CHAPTER 15

JOHN IN EXILE

In a political move to reduce the dissatisfaction over taxation and the people's concern about his Christian advisor, Domitian agreed to exile John to the island of Patmos. Many Roman citizens had asked why a Christian was so important to the emperor. They insisted that everyone worship the emperor. Because of his wife's exile, Domitian knew that Patmos was a beautiful island not far from Ephesus. Abraham was familiar with the idea of one God, so Nerva had him assign to be John's scribe. He was granted considerable freedom and allowed to write. Exile stimulated John to write in a symbolic manner. Based on his dreams, John and his scribe stayed busy writing his book concerning his revelation.

A few days before they sailed, Nerva introduced Abraham to John.

"I have been assigned the duty of being your scribe," Abraham said. "I have agreed to care for you as long as you need me."

"We will be on Patmos," John said. "I'm not looking forward to being in exile, but I am excited about having time to write."

"Do you know anything about the island?" he asked.

"I understand it is an island with beautiful views of the sea," he said. "I hope we are able to locate a suitable place to keep warm and dry."

Abraham looked at John.

"I have seen you around the palace, but I have never met you," Abraham said. "Our first endeavor will be to arrive on Patmos. I believe they have made plans for our care. I have been given writing supplies."

John and Abraham were taken to the port.

"The ship that is taking us to Patmos doesn't look very large," John said. "I hope the sea is calm."

Many ships were docked in the harbor, some loading and some unloading. Several had delivered prisoners to Rome. Other prisoners had been assigned duties of labor that would benefit the empire. Their guards took them to the ramp leading to the ship.

"I see Roman guards on the ship," Abraham said. "This is probably our ship. I will put your pack onboard. I will see you in a few moments."

"The name of the ship is Maximus. I like that name," John said. "Where are you going? We need to get aboard."

"I am going to talk to the captain," he said. "I will be back."

"Find out how many days we will be at sea," he said.

Abraham found the captain and talked with him, and then he returned to John.

"The captain wouldn't discuss the trip with me," Abraham said. I also hope the sea is calm. I have never traveled by ship."

Abraham had talked to the captain about this being his first trip on a ship. The captain said he would be fine. He knew they were friends of Nerva. Soon the ropes were cast off, and the ship moved.

"We are underway," John said. "I wonder how far from land we will venture?"

"I have been able to see land all of my life," Abraham said.

"I can sense when we are on the open sea," John said. "The breeze is generally quite stiff. I will be glad when we arrive at Patmos."

"Seeing land helps me feel better," Abraham said. "When I go below the main deck, I get sick to my stomach."

After a few days, the ship sailed close to some islands. Abraham and John were allowed to stand on the main deck.

"Are you better?" John asked. "We have been near islands for a while."

"I see a large piece of land," Abraham said. "It looks like we are headed straight to it. Do you think that is where we are going?"

"He is sailing directly at it," John said. "I guess we will know in a few moments."

"Ahoy," the captain said. "This is Patmos. My job was to deliver you safely to Patmos."

"Thank you, sir," John said. "We will be here for a while."

Abraham scrutinized the small path up the very steep hill.

"I will climb the hill," Abraham said. "After I find a place for us to live, I will be back for your pack. You can look around a little."

"I will be here," he said. "I might start up the hill."

John looked at the hill and scratched his head. He knew getting to the top would be a difficult task.

After a while, Abraham returned. He found John located in a shady spot next to a bush. John started up the steep, high hill. When he climbed halfway, he could see for miles across the beautiful blue sea. He enjoyed the many shades of blue and wondered how far he would be able to see when he reached the top of the hill.

"I found a small cave where we can live," Abraham said. "It will provide a lot of shelter from the wind and weather."

"I will eventually make it to the top," John said.

"I will take your pack," he said. "Follow me, I will lead the way. It is almost straight up, but it is not far."

John waved at Abraham.

"Abraham, wait," he said. "I have to rest. I want to look at the sea."

"The sea certainly is beautiful," Abraham said. "Have a seat."

"You may go ahead," John said. "I will wait here for you."

"I will be back," he said. "Just relax for a few moments. I am a few years younger than you, sir."

John rested and enjoyed the view. When Abraham returned, John immediately stood up.

"I am ready to go," he said. "I think I can make it now. I love the sea."

"I am glad you regained your strength," Abraham said. "It isn't far."

After a few moments, they reached the top of the hill. Abraham showed John the cave.

"This should be fine," he said.

They entered the cave.

"It is dark and cold in here," he said. "We need to maintain a fire for light and heat."

"I will gather some twigs," Abraham said. "I don't see many large trees."

"It isn't the palace," John said. "After it is heated and lighted, it will be fine."

John looked at Abraham and smiled.

Abraham made another trip down the hill. He returned with a large pack.

"They provided supplies for us," Abraham said. "Once a month, they will deliver additional supplies."

"I'll find some berries to eat," he said.

"I will just stay here and rest," John said. "I think I will take a nap."

When Abraham returned, John was asleep. Eventually he woke up, and Abraham told him about the island.

"I took a long walk," he said. "The island isn't as large as it looked from the ship. I only found a few trees."

"No trees?" John asked. "I wanted a fire."

"We can burn the dry grasses and shrubs," he said. "The island is rocky and covered with small plants."

"What is that stuff you are burning?" John asked. "It smells good – it is sort of sweet."

"I don't know," he said. "The island is covered with it. It will provide light and heat for us."

During the next few days, Abraham arranged their living area. After he gathered a large pile of dry grasses, he unpacked the supplies.

"I have everything organized for us," Abraham said. "When you are ready, you can start telling me what to write."

"I am getting accustomed to the smell of the burning grass," John said. "I could learn to like it."

He looked at Abraham and smiled.

As the months passed, John and Abraham grew accustomed to the cloud of smoke that filled the cave. They didn't realize that their senses had become altered, and John's writing had become very metaphorical. They remained warm and stayed busy writing. The cave wasn't a palace, but they had everything they needed. They had arranged a few flat rocks, and Abraham used them as a desk.

"Abraham, I am receiving a revelation," John said. "It is telling me about the end of time. The last many years have been difficult for me. I believe I am again in tune with the Holy Spirit."

"You feel in tune with The Holy Spirit?" Abraham asked. "I am not a very religious person. What does feeling in tune with the Holy Spirit mean?"

"Sometimes, I feel like Ezekiel must have felt," he said. "Make sure you keep careful records of my visions. I prefer they be written in Greek. Being spiritual is a good feeling."

"I will be glad to record them for you," he said. "I will of course be thinking in Arabic, but I will do my best to write in Greek."

"I thought you could write Greek," John said. "I wonder why Nerva sent you."

"I can write Greek," he said. "Some of my relatives were Jewish. That is why they sent me with you."

"I am glad they sent you," he said. "Maybe someday, the people in Ephesus and the other six churches in the surrounding area will read my material. We might even live in Ephesus."

"We aren't far from there," Abraham said. "Ephesus was the next stop for the ship that brought to Patmos."

"People need to know God will soon overcome the demonic forces of our world," John said. "I am going to interpret my visions in a highly symbolic manner. That will allow them to be interpreted in several different ways. It will give my stories an eternal aspect. People will read what I say and you write for a long time."

They stayed busy for many weeks. John received visions, and Abraham recorded them.

One morning after breakfast, Abraham went outside. He noticed John staring at the sea. It was a beautiful day, the sky was light blue, and it was filled with puffy white clouds. In contrast, the sea was a very dark blue.

"I could stand here and look at the sea all day," John said. "God must have created the sea so man could enjoy its beauty."

"Would you like to go for a walk?" Abraham asked. "It is a beautiful morning. You haven't seen most of the island."

"Have you already walked the entire island?" John asked.

"I haven't seen the far end of the island. Also, I haven't seen a Roman soldier for more than a week."

"Where did you see a Roman soldier?" John asked.

"I found a place on the other end of the island where Roman soldiers are keeping close watch over a few prisoners," he said. "They are making the prisoners work in the mines. We need to stay away from them. I don't want to end up working in a mine"

"I didn't know Patmos had mines," John said. "There seem to be many things I don't know about this island."

A few days later, a Roman soldier appeared at the entrance of their cave. He introduced himself and explained that he was responsible for all the prisoners on the island. He knew of John and Abraham's situation and of their favor concerning the emperor. He explained that when they visited his complex, they would be provided with fresh goat's milk. He asked if they needed anything else, and then he invited them to visit the mines.

"I would love to see the mines," John said. "I have never been in a mine. How deep are they?"

"Some of the mines are very old and have become quite deep," he said. "We haven't had many workers since Nero died."

John looked at Abraham, and they smiled.

"Tomorrow morning, we will expect you," the soldier said. "Does that fit your schedule?"

"My scribe says we will fit it into our schedule," John said, jokingly.

"I will be waiting for you," he said. "Just ask for Nero. I know it is quite a name. I am no relation."

The next morning, John and Abraham walked to the other end of the island. As they walked, Abraham asked John why he was so interested in the mines. John explained that when he was in Rome, ships arrived loaded with copper bars and, sometimes, slabs of marble. He wanted to see if he could identify anything. He also said he liked some of the shiny rocks. When they reached the mines, they were confronted by a soldier. They asked for Nero. In a few moments, Nero appeared and gave them two cups of goat's milk. Then he conducted a tour.

"What is it that you are mining?" John asked. "Is it copper?"

"Yes, it is," Nero said. "We take the soil and burn it, and metal flows from the soil. We send the metal to Rome."

"It takes less space to transport metal," he said. It is also much easier."

"They seem to be happy with what they are receiving," he said. "We work the prisoners very hard, but we treat them fairly."

"Do you find other metals?" John asked. "Have you found any gold or silver?"

"Not yet," Nero said. "Occasionally, we find a shiny stone. If you want one, I will give you one."

"I see the fire," John said. "It is an interesting operation."

"How large are the bars?" Abraham asked. "Most of them appear quite small."

"We make small bars, so we can easily carry them," he said. "We carefully dig a hole in the soil and pour it full of metal."

A Roman guard approached Nero and handed him a sack. He poured the contents into his hand and showed it to John and Abraham.

"These are the stones we have found today," he said. "Here, take this large red one. I don't think we have found a use for the red ones."

"Thank you," John said. "I will keep it as a memento. Do you send the stones back to Rome?"

"No," he said. "They don't want them. I give them to the ship's captain, and he sells them to the craftsmen in Ephesus. I have given a few to favored prisoners. The emperor's wife liked the clear blue stones."

After their tour ended, they slowly walked back to the cave. As John repeatedly tossed his red rock into the air, a ray of sun shone through the stone and a rainbow was visible on the ground.

The next morning, they arose early.

"Abraham, get a parchment," John said. "You might want to take some notes."

John began telling him is latest vision. Abraham stayed busy trying to write down every word.

"Let's take a walk," he said. "Did you write down everything I told you about my vision? We can discuss it while we walk."

"I got most of it," Abraham said. "There were a lot of sevens. I remember you said stars are symbolic of angels, and lamp stands are symbolic of churches."

"That's right. I will not tolerate the worshipping of emperors any longer," John said. "My vision reveals that Rome will be destroyed at the end of time, along with everything else."

"I don't understand what you mean by 'the end of time'?" Abraham asked. "When is that?"

"I don't know," John said. "I do know that we must all be ready for judgment. Do you practice emperor worship?"

"No, I don't," he said. "Caligula was the only emperor I remember trying to force the Jewish people to worship emperors. I was mostly exempt from emperor worship. Did they force you to worship emperors?"

"No, I never worshiped anyone except God," John said. "Nero persecuted the Christians not because of emperor worship, but because he wanted to blame the great fire on them."

"He sought to blame anyone for his problems," Abraham said. "He did kill a lot of Christians."

"When Titus took me to Rome, he and his father were indifferent to emperor worship," John said. "Emperor Domitian is a different story. He knows I was a special friend of Jesus, so he never bothered me."

"You were a close friend of Jesus?" he asked. "No wonder you have so many visions."

"It was the people who worshipped Domitian. They couldn't understand why he had a Christian advisor," John said. "He had to exile me. He continually faced ridicule, so here we are."

Abraham considered everything he had just been told. Past events started to make sense to him.

"I wondered why we are being treated so well," Abraham said. "Now I understand."

"I have known for a long time that I was in trouble," John said. "When

Domitian deified his brother, things started to change. He didn't do anything that wasn't to his benefit."

They sat on a rock, and John stared at the dancing glimmers of sunshine that appeared on the sea. Abraham took notes and enjoyed the sea breeze.

"Name those churches again," he said. "I will remember them this time. I hope you don't mind me saying so, but I like your vision. I think of two distinct time frames, present time and end time."

"Ephesus, Smyrna, Pergamos, Laodicea, Philadelphia, Sardis and Thyatira," John said. "I know some of the bishops in these areas. Menahem is a relative of Jesus, and Onesimus was a friend of Paul's."

"Phila - what did you say?" Abraham asked. "I think I got the other ones."

"Philadelphia, you know, brotherly love," he said. "It means everyone loves their neighbor. It is located just east of Ephesus. All of those churches are close to us."

"I got it," he said. "Philadelphia means brotherly love. I guess there are quite a few churches. Many of them are a result of Paul and his disciples work. I think we are coming to the end of the island. Do you want to rest for a while? We can sit and enjoy the sea."

"That sounds good to me," John said. "I am always surprised at how beautiful and blue the sea appears. I like the wind. It keeps the bugs away from us. We are lucky to be exiled in such a lovely place."

Abraham noticed a ship on the horizon. He watched the ship for a few moments and realized it was headed to Patmos.

"I see a ship," Abraham said. "It is time for them to bring us supplies."

"Are we out of supplies?" John asked.

"We still have a few supplies," he said. "I don't want us to run out."

"They won't allow that," he said. "They keep an eye on us."

"When we get back home, I'll check where they have been leaving the supplies," Abraham said. "I think they bring prisoners to the mines on a regular basis. I wonder if any prisoners ever leave this island. They must carry a large amount of supplies to feed the soldiers and the prisoners."

"It is kind of Emperor Domitian to keep sending supplies to us," John said. "On my way back to the cave, I will gather more weeds. You go ahead and check on the supplies."

When John returned to the cave, Abraham had arranged all their supplies.

"John, we got more than just supplies," he said. "I have a message from Domitian. It is for you. He probably wants to know how we are doing."

"Give me the message," he said. "I will read it and then we can discuss it."

John took the message.

"He is checking to make sure we receive everything he sends to us," John said. "He is worried about the senate."

"I will write him a message," Abraham said. "I'll thank him for the supplies. I want to keep him happy."

"He has a strange relationship with some parts of the government," John said. "I think many of them like Nerva better than Domitian. Some people still suspect him of killing his brother."

"We got another supply of candles," he said. "We were about out of candles. We use many candles."

"You need a lot of light to write," he said. "I can talk in the dark, but it is hard for you to write in the dark."

John looked at Abraham and laughed. Abraham held one hand over his eyes and held a scroll in the other hand.

"I can see by the fire, but I prefer the candles," he said. "Candles make it much easier to write. We also received a large supply of food. Before the next delivery of supplies, the weather might become significantly worse. We will probably receive fewer deliveries of supplies during the poor weather."

It was a cold winter. A chilly sea breeze constantly blew across the island. In an effort to stay warm, John and Abraham burned many piles of grass. When spring arrived, they became excited. The weather turned warm, and the island turned green. The warm sea breeze allowed them to spend most of their time outside. They stood near the top of the cliff and looked toward the sea. They scanned the horizon.

"I see a large ship," Abraham said. "They usually send our supplies on a smaller ship. I am going to the edge of the cliff and watch. Do you want to go to the rim with me?"

"No, I will stay here," John said. "Don't go too quickly; be careful."

"It is a very large ship that is being escorted by several smaller ships," Abraham said. "It looks like they are putting a small boat over the side. Someone important must be coming to visit the island."

John walked to Abraham and looked at the ships.

"That large ship can't get close to shore," John said. "Probably just more supplies for us."

"The large ship might be bringing prisoners," Abraham said. "They can use them in the mines."

"I think someone is coming to see us," John said. "It looks like a military escort. It might be Nerva. Do you know him?"

"Not really but he introduced me to you," he said. "I have only heard you talk of him. They are coming up the hill."

Eventually, the group of six Roman soldiers reached the top of the hill. They stopped and rested. After they caught their breath, they approached John.

"Hello, John," Nerva said. "It has been too long since I have seen you. It is good to be with you. Who do you have with you?"

"This is my friend and scribe, Abraham," he said. "You assigned him to me. He has been a great help. I didn't think I would ever see you again. How are things in Rome?"

"Things are a little better," Nerva said. "Domitian was executed, and I was named emperor. I am here to tell you that you are free."

John fell to his knees.

"I am free?" he said. "Domitian said I was to be exiled for as long as he lived. I never wished he would die."

Nerva looked at John and then pointed to the fleet of ships.

"One of these small ships will take you wherever you desire," he said. "Captain Judge has a bag of gold coins for you. I am going to visit the mines and deliver a load of prisoners to them. A lot of the prisoners were enemies of Domitian. I must say goodbye. Before I can return to Rome, I have many missions I have to accomplish."

"Emperor, before you depart, I would like to ask a question," John said. "Can I take Abraham with me?"

"Yes, he is yours," he said. "I forgot he was with you. I should have known you would request a scribe. We will probably never meet again. I hope your God will continue to bless you."

He waved at John and thanked him for his help and advice.

Five of the soldiers returned to the large ship. One soldier remained with John and Abraham. He had been assigned the duty of escorting them to their ship, and he was to ensure all their belongings were secured.

"Come on, Abraham," John said. "You heard the man. We are free. Pack our bags and take them to the small ship. Be careful with my scrolls. From now on, we will have to purchase scrolls."

"Yes, sir," Abraham said. "It is hard to believe they are setting us free. I will get our materials while you start down the hill. I guess we are going to Ephesus."

An hour later, their packs had been transported to the ship. It was time for them to say goodbye to Patmos. John, now an older man, exhibited a childish grin as and they boarded the ship. He took a solemn look at the hill and waved at the grass.

They were greeted by the ship's captain.

"Hello, my name is Captain Judge," he said. "You must be John. I was just told there would be two of you."

"We are glad to see you," John said. "For the last two years, we have been on this island."

"We have quarters for you and for your attendant," he said. "Allow me to help you to your cabin."

"I can make it," John said. "I am just a little old. When I was younger, I handled the ramps and ladders with ease."

"I will have a few crew members help your attendant," he said. "It is my duty to deliver you to your port of choice. How do you know Nerva?"

"Thank you, Judge," John said. "Abraham is my scribe. We have been together for many months. After everything is loaded, could we have a hot meal? We haven't had any real food for a long time."

"Yes, I will have the cook talk with you," he said. "We don't have a lot of meat, but I will share some of my meat with you and Abraham. You have known Nerva for a long time, haven't you?"

"Yes, I have," John said. "We lived in the palace and advised the emperors. I worked with Nerva almost every day. The emperor was ridiculed because I am a Christian."

"You lived in the palace and worked with Nerva?" he asked.

"I lived in Rome for about twenty-five years," he said. "I have known the last three emperors quite well. I would like you to take us to Ephesus. Nerva told me you had something for me."

"Yes, I have a sealed bag for you," he said. "It feels like coins. As soon as all your things are stowed, we will sail to Ephesus. My well-being probably depends on you signing these parchments for me."

"Don't forget to remind me to sign them," John said.

"After I deliver you to Ephesus, I will be glad to give them to you," he said. "I am sure you know Nerva much better than I."

John sensed the captain was really interested in the sack of money. He thought he owed the captain an explanation. He opened the bag.

"Yes, it contains gold coins," John said. "I stored everything that I owned and had value. My belongings were placed in the palace, and Nerva took care of them. When I was exiled to Patmos, I didn't need them."

"I see, you stored valuables in the palace while you were in exile," he said. "You are lucky they are being returned to you. You must have had many friends in high positions."

"Domitian provided everything Abraham and I needed for the last two years," he said. "He didn't want to exile me. He felt forced by the political situation. I hope the seas are calm. Abraham and I aren't sailors."

"The seas are calm," he said. "Ephesus is a short trip. I will have you there by the day after tomorrow.

"I am looking forward to seeing Ephesus," John said. "It is a great town."

"Before I return to Rome, I will help you find lodging," he said. "If there is anything you need, give me a call. A mate will be posted to insure you are comfortable. I will take you to your quarters."

They walked to the first cabin.

"These are your quarters," he said. "I will have the cabin next to your cabin cleared."

"These quarters are quite large," John said. "We only need one room. Abraham will sleep in the other bed. Don't disturb those in the other cabin."

"Are you sure one cabin is satisfactory?" he asked. "Here is Abraham and your packs. I will have the crew put them in your cabin. Your food will be here soon."

"Abraham, you are in here with me," John said. "I would like you to stay with me in Ephesus. We will find a place to live. I will teach, and you will write. I am sure you will like Ephesus."

"Have you ever been there?" Abraham asked.

"Yes, I was there for a short while many years ago," he said. "It had a great library and university. Paul lived there for many years. Jesus' mother is buried there."

"I would like to see a great library," he said. "Are we going to remain in Ephesus a long time?"

"Yes, I hope I can stay there the remainder of my life," John said. "I am getting too old to keep moving around. Captain Judge gave me enough money to last quite a while."

"I will stay with you," Abraham said. "I don't have any plans of leaving you. When they assigned me to you, it was for life. I promised to be your scribe, and I promised to help you as long as you needed me."

"Have a seat," he said. "They are going to bring us some meat for dinner. We haven't had any meat for a long time. I can smell it cooking."

John sniffed the air and rubbed his hands together. His face glowed.

"I hope my body will eat meat," Abraham said. "It has been a long time! I hope it is lamb."

"Ahoy," Judge said. "We are about to sail."

Just as promised, the trip lasted only a few days, and the seas were calm. After they arrived in Ephesus, Captain Judge secured John and Abraham a place at the inn. John signed the release parchment, and the ship headed to Rome. John and Abraham were safe and they were in Ephesus.

CHAPTER 16

JOHN IN EPHESUS

While exiled on Patmos, John thought of Ephesus many times. It was like a heavenly dream that kept him from realizing the desolation of the island. Now, he was finally in Ephesus and brought with him his visions of heaven. During his first few days, he planned to walk the streets of his new city. Then he would be a tour guide for his scribe, Abraham. After they were comfortably located in a home, they joined one of the churches that Paul had started. Paul lived in Ephesus about fifty years earlier. It had been a long, two years on Patmos, but the memories of the island diminished every day. Many things had changed over those two years, but John's new freedom was his latest blessing. The Roman Empire had a new emperor, Nerva, and John and Abraham were free to live as they could afford.

Before the captain of the ship departed, he secured them a room at an inn.

"Abraham, we have talked about Ephesus, and now we are here," John said. "We will rest today. Tomorrow, we will go to the baths on Curetes Street."

"A public bath?" Abraham asked. "I think I will learn to like this city."

"The Romans built many buildings in this town," he said. "However, I will show you a few old buildings that were built by the Greeks. Before the Romans, the Greeks occupied this area."

"I knew it was an old city," he said. "This seems to be a good location for trade."

"Ephesus is located on major trade routes. It has been an important city for hundreds of years," John said. "It is very important to the Romans."

They decided not to sleep at the inn. Instead, their first night in Ephesus was spent under a tree in a public park. When they arose, they decided they needed to find a house. Abraham showed his leg to John, and he found many bugs on it. They went to the public baths.

"The hot mineral bath is great," Abraham said. "The salt water on the ship just didn't feel good. Everything is fine, I have checked. Cerinthus isn't in Ephesus."

Abraham smiled and waited for John's response. John didn't respond; he just looked at Abraham. Cerinthus was a heretic. Abraham was familiar with him, because he and John had discussed his distortions of Jesus' message.

They walked to an area close to the water. Eventually, they located a house.

"We are lucky to find a place to live near the harbor," John said. "It is on the west side of town and convenient to the market."

"I like visiting the harbor," Abraham said. "This is a fine location." "Ephesus is a good size city, small enough that we can get around and large enough to have everything we need," John said. "I am tired. I will see you tomorrow."

When John heard the sounds of sailors unloading a ship the next morning, he became a little restless. He woke Abraham to discuss their day.

"In the morning, the sound of the harbor is interesting," John said. "I like the sound of dock labors loading the ships. Also, I like the cool breeze that blows across the sea."

Abraham was still sleepy.

"What did you say?" he asked.

"Good morning, Abraham," John said. "The first thing I want to do is walk up to the river."

"I am still sleeping," he said. "Walk to where?"

"The harbor is very active this morning," he said. "If you look, you will find ships from many different countries. The largest ships have to unload and have their goods brought in by barges."

"Delivered by barges," he said. "Why is that necessary?"

"Silt has filled the waterway," he said as he pointed toward the docks. "Smyrna has a deep harbor. If Ephesus doesn't keep this harbor clear, those ships will go to Smyrna."

"Where is Smyrna?" he asked. "I have heard of it. How far from Ephesus is Smyrna?"

"It is north of Ephesus," John said. "I am not certain about the distance. Because of their harbor, Smyrna is growing rapidly. Someday, we will visit Smyrna. Paul started a church there several years ago."

After they watched the ships being unloaded for a few hours, they returned home for lunch. John was sorry he mentioned Smyrna; he didn't want Abraham to think he was dissatisfied with Ephesus. He felt good, so he decided to take another walk.

"We have seen the harbor," he said. "Let's walk the other direction. Ephesus is the place to be, and I am glad we are here. Come on, follow me, and we will head east. It is not far to the markets."

Abraham agreed he needed to know where the markets were located. It was necessary to purchase fresh fruit and vegetables almost every day. Abraham convinced John they needed to relax and enjoy another hot bath. This time he planned to clean his clothes. The last time, he didn't understand why John had cleaned his clothes. When Abraham put his clothes back on, he was again covered with bugs. They walked to the baths.

"That really feels good," Abraham said. "I remember when we were on Patmos, and you were writing. You said something about Ephesus. Do you remember what you said?"

"Yes, I wrote that the people were not as prayerful as they used to be," John said. "They need to return to their former state."

"It seems we get passive with age. Some lose their passion," Abraham said. "Most who live in Ephesus seem to be doing quite well."

"It looks that way," John said. "Someday, I will teach at a church, and I will remind them of their great place in the kingdom of God. I am sure many of the people don't remember. It will be a good lesson for them."

"That should get their attention," Abraham said. "I am sure they will understand."

"We can't stand still. We must keep moving forward," John said. "If we don't, we will be passed by."

"We don't stand still much. We are always walking," he said. "I am glad we both like to walk."

John splashed water toward Abraham.

"This warm water feels good," he said. "If they keep the water this warm, I might stay here all day."

"You won't hear me complain," Abraham said. "I am glad we live close to the baths."

"It is nice to have a little money and not much we have to accomplish," John said. "Before we go home, we will go by the market and purchase some produce."

"We've had a good day," Abraham said. "I want to walk a different street on our way home."

"Tomorrow, we will find a church," John said. "I am certain there is one close to the house. I have heard several of our neighbors talking."

They returned home, and John ate some fresh fruit, and then they sat outside until the sun disappeared.

The next morning, they arose early and looked for a church. They hadn't traveled far, before they located one and heard a voice.

"Welcome," he said. "My name is Ezekiel. We meet for a short time almost every day."

John greeted Ezekiel. Ezekiel motioned for them to enter.

"We study our scrolls several times a week," Ezekiel said. "I have a scroll that is a copy of one written by Mark."

John looked at Abraham, and he smiled. Abraham was busy looking at the scroll.

"I have read some of Mark's writings," John said. "This is my friend, Abraham. We are new in Ephesus. We were told we would be able to find a church. May I read your scroll?"

"Not unless you can read Greek," he said. "John Mark made his final copies in Greek."

"We both read Greek," he said. "Abraham even writes Greek. Did Paul start this church?"

"No, we didn't know Paul," he said. "This church was started by a disciple of his. He is getting quite old, but still tells us stories of Paul and his friends, Mary and Salome."

"I would enjoy talking with someone who knew Paul," John said. "I remember Paul."

"I think the disciple's mother took him to church when he was young," Ezekiel said. "Did you know Paul?"

"I met him a long time ago," John said. "He and I were both in Jerusalem. He was a very interesting fellow."

"I think you will like our teacher," he said. "Our teacher knows many of the stories that Jesus told. We study a different story each week. The meaning of the story is not always obvious to us."

Abraham and John had found a church close to their home. It was a friendly group of people, and they welcomed new members. John didn't say much, but he listened carefully. They attended the church on a regular basis. When John wasn't reading, he told his story to Abraham. They enjoyed their freedom, and they enjoyed being in Ephesus. They took time away from reading and writing and walked throughout the town.

During one of their walks, Abraham stared at the old city wall.

"The wall you are looking at was built to provide some protection for this town," John said. "They had determined how to stop unwanted ships from coming up the river."

"They must have had a great military presence," Abraham said. "How did they stop the ships? Did they sink them?"

"No, they would throw torches on them," he said. "They tried to set them on fire, and they captured the sailors who abandoned their ships."

Abraham forehead became wrinkled.

"I am sure that would stop them," he said. "Sailors are always frightened by a fire aboard ship. Fire could cause a serious disaster."

"The wall encircles the town," he said. "The town became so crowded they were required to construct Diana's temple outside the wall."

"A temple to Diana," he said. "I would like to see it."

"It will be a long walk for me," John said. "You may have to help me. I will need to walk very slowly."

"I will help you,' he said. "When you get tired, we can rest."

"You can check on the exact location of the temple," he said. "Almost anyone you ask will know where the temple is located. Ask the next person who passes us."

"I will look at my parchment," Abraham said. "Have you seen the temple?"

"Yes, a long time ago," John said. "I also want to show you where Mary, the mother of Jesus, is buried. She and Salome spent a few years here, when Paul was busy starting churches."

Abraham reached in his bag and took out a parchment showing the buildings of Ephesus. He held the parchment close to John's eyes.

"Yesterday, I found a building guide at the market. I was certain it would be useful," he said. "The temple is northeast of town. We will have to go through the Magnesian Gate, and then turn north."

"I forgot about the gates," John said. "We will have to find the closest gate."

"The parchment shows three gymnasiums in town. One of them is located at the Magnesian Gate," he said. "We will be able to find it."

"That is a nice parchment," John said. "I am glad you purchased it. I am sure we will use it almost every day."

"We have all day, so we don't need to hurry," Abraham said. "Did you know it was called the temple to Artemis, the Greek God?"

"We can stop at the market," he said. "As we walk, we can eat a few fresh figs."

"We can stop anywhere at any time," he said. "We don't have anything we have to accomplish."

"I would like to stop and rest when we reach the gate," John said. "I am always interested in the construction techniques used to build the city walls."

After a short rest and a few figs, John and Abraham continued their walk to the temple. John was very interested in the buildings and decided to draw a picture of the temple. He secured a parchment from Abraham.

"The other group of buildings must be the university," Abraham said. "I think I will also visit the campus."

"That large building is very interesting," John said. "I want to spend more time. I think I will draw a picture of each of the buildings."

"They are quite impressive," he said. "I have plenty of parchment. You can draw as many pictures as you desire."

"You don't have to be able to write Greek to draw pictures," John said. "Take your time and enjoy visiting the university campus."

Abraham looked at him and laughed.

Abraham removed a pebble from his sandal and then walked to the university. He learned from a student that Paul lectured in the Hall at Tyrannus. As he looked around, he was approached by an old man.

"If you want the job writing Greek, you should see the professor," he said.

After a short interview, Abraham obtained a job writing Greek for one of the professors. He was scheduled to work three half-days per week. He returned to John and found him resting in the park. He was certain John would be delighted with his good fortune.

Abraham exhibited a large grin when he approached John.

"The university was very interesting," he said. "I have a job working three half-days per week writing Greek."

John immediately jumped up and stared at Abraham.

"What!" John exclaimed. "You have what?"

"I was given a job," Abraham said. "I wasn't looking for one, but a job found me."

"Why did you do that?" John asked. "You write Greek for me. I didn't know you wanted a different job. I hope you still have time for me."

"I was in the hall, and they thought I came for a job," he said. "I wrote some Greek as one of the professor spoke, and he hired me. I start tomorrow."

"What about me?" he asked. "I need you to write for me."

John gave Abraham a stern look, and then he started to walk. Abraham was shocked at John's attitude about his new job. It was a long walk home, and they talked constantly.

"It is only three half-days per week," Abraham said. "I will have plenty of time for you. Lately, you haven't told me any stories. I thought we could use a little extra money."

"When do you have to be at the university?" John asked. "I will have to adjust my schedule."

The next morning, Abraham went to work at the university, and John went to the morning service at the church.

"Hello, John," Ezekiel said. "We are studying Jesus' message. Did you ever hear Jesus lecture?"

This presented a good opportunity for John to describe some of his past experiences. He was eager to share that he was a friend of Jesus.

"Yes, I did," he said. "I spend some time with John the Baptist, and then I spent about three years with Jesus."

A large smile appeared on Ezekiel's face. He turned toward John.

"You spent three years with Jesus?" he questioned.

"My brother and I knew him quite well," he said. "I remember you saying you had a scroll that was a copy of what Mark said. I hope Mark correctly recorded what Peter said."

"We enjoy the scroll," Ezekiel said. "It is one of our favorites."

"I was one of the original apostles," John said. "I was a lot younger then."

"You are the John that Mark listed?" he asked. "I didn't know that you knew Jesus. Would you be willing to teach us about him?"

John didn't want to appear too interested, so he hesitated for a few moments.

"I am busy writing," he said. "I might be able to find time to teach."

"A few of us have been considering starting another church," he said. "We walk a long way to attend this church."

"I live close to this church," John said. "It is convenient for me. Walking can be difficult."

"We were thinking of starting a church near the city wall on the other side of town," he said. "Maybe you could teach there."

"That would be a long walk for me," he said. "I can walk, but I'm not very steady."

"I could bring my friends to see you," he said. "They would want to hear you teach."

"I will talk to them," he said. "I will teach at your next meeting. I'll find a good lesson."

"We will be there," Ezekiel said. "That is a good time for us."

"I will require help moving," John said. "My scribe Abraham is now working part-time at the university. I am sure he would be willing to move."

John went home and reviewed one of his lessons concerning Jesus being divine.

The next time they were together, he taught his lesson.

"John, we enjoyed your lesson," Ezekiel said. "We never understood Jesus' divinity."

"Many people overlook his divinity," he said. "It is an important part of Jesus' being."

"We will discuss our plans and give you our decision in a few days," he said. "It is important that everything is well thought out and that the church is secure before we ask you to join us."

"I will be at home," he said. "This is a good opportunity for me to pray and rest."

Abraham worried about John being absent for such a long time. When John returned home, he explained he had attended church.

After two days Ezekiel visited with John, he and his friends had decided to start a new church located in the east end of town. They wanted John to join them.

"One of our members will provide you and Abraham with a small house," Ezekiel said. "He owns several small houses."

John looked upward and said a silent prayer. After he had prayed, he stroked his uniquely shaped beard and looked at Ezekiel.

"Good," he said. "I will appreciate being close to the church."

"The house is very close to the church," he said. "We will expect you to lead our worship twice a week. We look forward to hearing Jesus' message."

"I will talk with Abraham," he said. "I will tell you when we are able to move. It will have to be a day that he doesn't work."

When Abraham returned home that evening, John explained that they were moving.

"Abraham, I think you will like the location," John said. "They are going to provide a house."

"I don't want to move," he asked. "I thought you liked it here near the harbor."

"The new church is close to the gate on the other side of town," he said. "It would be a much shorter distance for you to walk to the university."

Abraham thought about all the time he spent walking to work. He agreed that being near the gate would be a better location. John explained he had a new job, and they could use the money. He looked straight at Abraham to discern if he had recognized the phrase, 'we could use the money'. Abraham didn't say anything, but he exhibited a large smile.

"The church is only a block from the Magnesian Gate," John said. "This should work well for both of us. On the days you are not at the university, you can write my lesson for me."

John, Abraham, and the new church settled into a new routine. Everything progressed nicely for the new church. Abraham helped John and turned down a full-time job at the university. Ezekiel decided to visit with John. They sat on the porch and watched people enter the town.

"John, we are very pleased with your lessons," Ezekiel said. "I want you to meet with my friend, Thomas. When we started this church, he was a great help. You should come and spend time visiting with me. We could have a cup of tea."

"That would be nice," John said. "I would enjoy learning to know him."

"I have known Thomas for a long time," Ezekiel said. "Long ago, he and I traveled to Galilee to listen to Jesus speak."

"You have heard Jesus," John said. "You both are lucky men."

"We want you to write down all your travels with Jesus," Ezekiel said. "We will keep it with the other scrolls we have accumulated. There is something about the way you teach. You make Jesus seem so divine."

John carefully thought about Ezekiel's proposal. He wasn't certain he was prepared to start such a great project.

"That will be a lot of work," he said. "I will have to think about it. We already have three versions of Jesus' travels. I know they aren't exactly the same. I have studied them carefully. I will get back to you."

When Abraham returned home that evening, John discussed the church's proposal. Abraham was concerned about the volume of work being too much for John, but he liked the idea, because he was familiar with some of John's stories concerning Jesus. John was certain he could teach and recall his travels with Jesus. He was more concerned about Abraham having the time to record his story. They talked most of the day.

The next day, John spoke with Ezekiel.

"Ezekiel, I have talked to Abraham," John said. "We don't think we have time to write about my travels with Jesus. Abraham is working at the university. It would be very time consuming for him."

"That is too bad," he said. "We were counting on Abraham writing your story."

"I am old, and Abraham is busy," he said.

"I will see what I can do. I will talk with Thomas," Ezekiel said. "We will look forward to your lesson for this week."

Ezekiel talked with Thomas and a few other church members. If they convinced Abraham to work with John full-time, most of the conflicts would be eliminated. They decided to talk with John and Abraham when they were together about the matter. When they saw Abraham on his way home from the university, they approached him.

"Abraham, we want to talk with you and John," Ezekiel said. "Thomas and I represent the church."

"What do you want to talk with us about?" he asked. "I am on my way home,"

"We want to offer you a full-time job, writing about John's travels with Jesus," he said. "Are you interested?"

"You know I have a job at the university," he said. "You will have to talk with John."

They were somewhat surprised with Abraham's devotion to John. They advised Abraham that they would speak with John. After John's next lesson, they approached him.

"John, we have talked with Abraham," he said. "We want you to dedicate some time to having Abraham write about your travels with Jesus."

"I don't know if Abraham will quit the university," he said. "He was lucky to get that job, and he likes it. Maybe he could do both. I will talk with him."

Ezekiel was frustrated. He wasn't able to speak to both Abraham and John at the same time, and he didn't want to lose John as their teacher. John spoke with Abraham.

"Abraham how would you like a full-time job working for the church?" he asked. "They want you to spend all of your time writing about my travels with Jesus."

"You know I am happy at the university," he said. "I really don't want to quit. The professors depend on me."

"Maybe, you could do both jobs," John said. "That depends on how hard you want to work."

"I don't mind working diligently," Abraham said.

"I probably will have a lot to say," he said.

The next time Ezekiel saw John, he asked him if he and Abraham had made a decision about writing a record of his travels with Jesus.

"I think he is the correct person for both of our needs," Ezekiel said.

"If it is fine with Abraham, it is fine with me," John said. "I think I could add a lot to what I have read. I would like access to all the church's scrolls."

"That is not a problem," he said. "You can read them anytime you desire."

"I want to provide more details for you about Jesus," he said. "I don't want to repeat the stories you have already studied."

"That sounds good," he said. "I will tell Thomas."

"I still want to teach a lesson each week," he said. "I think this is a good challenge."

"I am sure Abraham can do it," Ezekiel said. "We will work with him."

"Do you know who is teaching at the church in Smyrna?" John asked. "Abraham and I talked about Smyrna."

"I believe they have a new bishop," he said. "Onesimus died a few years ago. I believe their new bishop is Menahem."

"I am sorry to hear Onesimus died," John said. "He was a good bishop. I will say a prayer for him."

"Menahem was at Antioch for a while," Ezekiel said. "I believe Menahem is the son of Jesus' brother."

"He was very young when Jesus was killed," John said. "I remember meeting his father."

"Menahem has been one of the faithful for a long time," he said. "Smyrna has a very large, older, beautiful church. It also has a few newer churches."

Abraham had two jobs that he was excited about, and John enjoyed remembering his time with Jesus. While John and Abraham sat at a table in their home, Abraham looked directly at John.

"John, I like the way you started your story," Abraham said. "Sometimes people don't understand how powerful 'The Word' can be. This should provide us many new lessons."

"I want it to be a new perspective," John said. "They didn't hire me to repeat what has been written. More volume isn't always better."

"I am sure your stories about Jesus will help the church continue to grow," Abraham said. "I hope we have a place large enough for us to meet."

"Thomas will make sure we have a large building," he said. "You don't have to worry about that."

"When we have a day off, I would like to visit the theater and Mount Pion again," Abraham said. "I enjoyed just sitting on the grass at Mount Pion and looking at the sky."

"I think I am ready for a day off," John said. "Maybe the day after tomorrow will be a nice day for a walk. The Arcadian Way is a good place to walk."

"I was sure I could do both of these jobs," Abraham said. "Occasionally, I can take a day off from working at the university."

Abraham and John looked forward to having a leisurely day walking around Ephesus. They slept late and then slowly arose. John was stiff and stretched his legs. Abraham finally spoke to him.

"Come on," he said. "I am going to treat you to some fresh figs at the Agora. We will pass the market on our walk today."

"I don't know if I can make it," John said. "I am not feeling well today. I don't think I can eat anything."

"You will be fine," Abraham said. "I will wait for a few moments."

"I have been working too hard," John said. "I am getting old. I get tired just thinking about all the good times I have enjoyed. You don't need to wait for me. I think you should go by yourself."

"I would like you to go with me, but I understand if you don't feel up to it" Abraham said. "When I return from the market, maybe you will feel better."

"You can bring me a few fresh dates," he said. "If I feel better, we can eat breakfast together."

The market was the source of daily news for many people. Everyone shopped and spent time talking with their neighbors. Abraham enjoyed shopping at the market and then started a short walk. He was somewhat concerned about John, so he went home. He found John seated in his favorite chair asleep. John heard Abraham. He sat down, and they talked.

"Did you find any good fruit?" John asked. "Did you learn anything at the market today?"

"I have some dates for you," Abraham said. "Everyone at the market was talking about the death of your friend Nerva."

"Nerva died?" John asked. "He was a good friend. I wonder what happen to him. Emperors have to be very careful."

"He was emperor for only a short time," he said. "There has been a peaceful transition of power."

Abraham saw a wrinkle appear on John's forehead.

"That is too bad," John said. "I liked Nerva. He really needed some help."

"He probably missed you," Abraham said. "You were a great advisor to several of the emperors."

"He was uninformed about finances, but he could handle the military like Titus," he said. "Who replaced him?'

"Trajan has replaced him," he said. "The senate convinced Nerva to adopted Trajan as an heir."

John exhibited a puzzled expression.

"He adopted Trajan?" he said. "I wonder what they told Nerva that convinced him to adopt Trajan."

"Trajan is a young and popular general," he said. "He might be able to keep the senate happy for a while. I guess we will have to get used to some new faces on our coins."

John continued his ministry, and Abraham continued writing. His writings impressed many other writers. John included many instances not recorded by the other disciples that traveled with Jesus. The church in Ephesus spread the word that their teacher was the oldest disciple of Jesus. John received many visitors, from throughout the empire, who wanted to talk with a companion of Jesus.'

"I am looking for John, the disciple who traveled with Jesus. Am I at the correct location?" Ignatius asked.

"Yes, you are at the correct place," Abraham said. "Come in. What would you like to discuss with John? I am his scribe."

"I am from Antioch," he said. "Peter appointed me as priest in Antioch. I knew the same people John knew."

"I am sure he would like to talk with you," he said. "Have a seat."

Abraham went to John and told him Ignatius wanted to visit with him. John agreed to speak with him after he prayed. Abraham gave John's message to Ignatius. While he waited, Ignatius told Abraham a story.

"When I was a child, Jesus held me in his arms and blessed me," Ignatius said. "I have been teaching about Jesus since I was a young man."

"You were greatly blessed," Abraham said. "Jesus laid his hands on you. Many people saw Jesus, but very few have touched him."

"I wanted to talk to John about Jesus," he said. "I know they knew each other. You might be interested in the fact that I have written several lessons."

Abraham asked John if he was ready to talk with Ignatius. He explained that Ignatius was also an author and interested in Jesus. He took Ignatius to John. They exchanged greeting.

"Abraham explained that you also knew Jesus. Come in. We can share our recollections."

"I have been teaching about Jesus for several years," Ignatius said. "I have heard many people talk about you and Jesus. They say that you were his favorite apostle."

"Jesus did love me. We were friends," John said. "Jesus loved everyone he encountered, and he still loves all of us. I am blessed to have spent a few years with him."

"I wish I could have traveled with him," Ignatius said. "I was too young. Have you ever heard of Polycarp?"

"I have heard the name Polycarp, but I don't know him," John said. "Is he a friend of yours?"

"Yes, we authored a few things while we were both in Philippi," he said. "I will send him a message and inform him that you are here. I am sure he will visit with you."

"I am glad you came to see me" John said. "The more people I am able to see, the more people who will speak the truth."

"I am going back to Antioch," Ignatius said. "I will tell the faithful in Antioch that I have spoken with you."

John continued to become more popular with those of the early church. Many traveled a long distance to speak with him. Being taught by an apostle of Jesus became very important to those who controlled the early church.

After some time passed, Abraham heard a knock on the door. He greeted the visitor and took him to John.

"John, my beautiful wife is sick," he said. My name is Lycomedes. I am the commander in chief of Ephesus."

"Come in," John said. "What is her problem?"

"I have been told that you could heal her," he said. "Many think she is beyond help. Please look at her."

"If she has faith, she can be healed," John said. "I will go with you to visit her, do you have a carriage?"

"No. It is a short walk," he said. "Follow me."

Abraham gave John his walking stick, and they followed Lycomedes.

After a short time, they arrived at a very large house. John was escorted to a bedroom.

"She is not at all well," John said. "I will hold her by her trembling feet and will pray for her."

As John spoke, her eyes became clear. She looked at John. She didn't know him, but sensed he had made her well. She took his hand and kissed it. She spoke softly with tears in her eyes.

"Thank you," she said. "I don't know you, but I know you possess the power to heal the sick."

Lycomedes bowed to John.

"Thank you," he said. "I knew you could heal her. We want to become members of your church."

"She was healed by God," John said. "Everyone is welcome in our church. We will be glad to have an important man, such as you, worship with us."

The new addition to the church was noted throughout town, and the church began to grow at a very rapid rate. One day, while they were seated at the table in the living area of their home, a visitor appeared.

"John, I have someone who wants to talk with you," Abraham said. "His name is Polycarp."

"Tell him to come in, and I will talk with him," he said. "You can take a rest. I will probably be with Polycarp for a while."

"I came to Ephesus so I could discuss Jesus with you," Polycarp said.

"I thought you might come to see me," he said. "I talked with your friend, Ignatius, and he told me you would probably visit with me."

"I have heard of your church and of your writings," Polycarp said. "I have dedicated my life to teaching. I feel like I am being called. I want to know the truth."

"You are welcome to stay," John said. "We have at least two services a week, and we study Jesus' lessons."

"I plan to stay in Ephesus for a while," he said. "I am very interested in learning directly from you."

"I am busy, writing. You can help Abraham write my memories of traveling with Jesus," he said. "Where is your home?"

"I am from Philippi," he said. "Professor Thomas is my supervisor at the university. I have read several very informative lessons that you wrote."

"I have written many lessons," John said. "I am still writing."

"I stay very busy reading old scrolls," Polycarp said. "When I read a scroll you sent to Smyrna, I wanted to meet you."

"You must do a lot of reading," he said

"I believe you are a great writer, and that the Holy Spirit is with you," he said. "I will plan to study with you each day. I am a young man, and you need to teach young men about Jesus."

"I teach twice a week," he said. "I will talk with you at other times."

"Have you read any material written by Matthew?" Polycarp asked.

"Yes, I have read some of Matthew's writings," he said. "I am certain he read Mark's writings before he began writing."

Polycarp looked at John and smiled.

"Learning directly from a person is much better than studying a scroll," John said. "I have a scribe. He will not bother you. He writes what I say, and when we get home, he transcribes my words and phrases into Greek."

"I have met Abraham," Polycarp said. "I am looking forward to speaking more with him."

"We are happy to have you with us," John said. "You are correct I am an old man, and I should teach a young man about Jesus. Our challenge is different today than when Matthew wrote. He focused his message primarily for those who were familiar with the Jewish religion."

"Jesus is the messiah of the Jewish religion," Polycarp said. "If they will study carefully, they can identify Jesus in the scriptures."

"The church's focus must change," John said. "We need to bring educated, wealthy, Greek speaking people to Jesus. I am writing so both Jews and those who follow Greek philosophy will understand that Jesus is eternal. He is the word. He is Logos."

Polycarp looked at John.

"You must have read material written by Philo," he said. "His writings are great supplements to the scriptures."

"Yes, I have," he said. "I also enjoy reading the wisdom material and the manuscripts of Heraclitus."

"Too many are teaching the wrong message," Polycarp said. "I don't know where they got their ideas. They must have read the wrong scrolls."

"I think I am the last of those who traveled with Jesus," John said. "Most have been killed. I was spared death and given Abraham to care for me."

"I have read material written by and for some of the other original apostles, but you are the only one I have been able to talk with directly," Polycarp said. "It is an honor to be with you."

"You might find some interesting scrolls in our library," John said. "Many of them were written by Paul or about Paul."

"I am looking forward to visiting the library," he said. "I have heard it contains many scrolls."

"Tell the librarian you know me," John said. "He might allow you to read scrolls that aren't made available to the public."

John looked at Polycarp, and he made the sign of a cross in the air.

"I hope they have some of Paul's original dictations," he said. "I am reading and making notes about everything I can find that is original to those who knew Jesus."

"Yes, you will like the library," John said. "It is very impressive."

"I also want to see the university," he said. "It is larger than the university where I work."

"Abraham will take you. He can show you the university and the lecture hall," he said. "Someday, you might deliver some of my lessons to the students."

John gave Polycarp a large smile.

"Long ago, I planned to visit all seven churches that I have written about," John said. "I made it to Smyrna. Someone will have to visit the other churches for me."

Polycarp stayed with John in Ephesus for a long time and helped complete John's writings. Abraham and Polycarp made two copies of the scrolls. After they became good friends and with John's blessings, Polycarp went to Smyrna. He met Menahem and shared his lesson with him. After a long visit with Menahem, he returned to Philippi. Polycarp and John sent messages to each other, and each tried to outdo the other by writing the most accurate and interesting Jesus lesson.

Abraham and John were relaxed at home, when John shared his concerns with him.

"Abraham, it is now obvious to me that I will never go to Thyatira," John said. "Take this scroll I wrote and have a messenger deliver it to them. It is important that they learn the difference between knowledge and wisdom."

John handed a large scroll to Abraham. Abraham packaged it and took it to the military station at the port, so it would travel to Thyatira. When Abraham returned, he questioned John.

"Those in Thyatira believe they will know everything about God by reading and gaining great knowledge," John said. "They are being deceived. They must have great faith."

"Faith is the answer," Abraham said. "Knowledge is good."

"We must stop this heresy," he said. "My message should put an end to Jezebel's wailing from the hill graveyard."

"I hope they will read it," he said. "They need your help."

"I will thunder on with my writings," John said. "My final message is that of Christ's love. We must love one another."

Abraham was concerned by John's manner of speech, but kept it to himself.

"When will they receive the package?" John asked. "Do you have any idea?"

"The military messenger makes a circle around the major cities," Abraham said. "It may take a while for them to receive it. They will respect your message as one from an eagle."

Abraham looked at John and smiled.

"Thank you," John said. "It is important to them, and it is important to me. I would like them to have time to read it before I die."

A year passed, when one day Abraham heard a knock on the door. He took the visitor to John.

"Papias, of Hierapolis, is here to see you," Abraham said. "I believe he is one of those talked about by Polycarp when he visited with you."

"Yes, show him in," John said. "I think Polycarp said Papias was a student of his."

"Hello, John," Papias said. "The first time I came to see you, the boat made me so sick, I wasn't able to speak with you. I am glad to have this chance."

"Come in and have a seat," he said. "Abraham will bring you something to drink."

"I wanted to see you again. This time I walked," Papias said. "I am still working with Polycarp. We are trying to list everything that is original to the twelve apostles, Paul, and those who knew Jesus personally."

"You walked all the way?" he asked. "You didn't sail at all?"

"No, I'm not a sailor," he said. "Polycarp gave me some notes he made when he was here with you. It is an honor to meet you."

"I am impressed," Abraham said. "Philippi is a long walk."

"So you and Polycarp are trying to learn everything you can about

Jesus from those of us who actually knew him," John said. "That is an ambitious undertaking."

"Just locating people to talk with is difficult," Papias said. Many have just disappeared."

"Not many of us are alive," John said. "I think you have a good idea. I will be glad to talk with you. I don't know if I can tell you anything I didn't tell Polycarp."

By this time, Polycarp had expanded his research. He and his fellow professors taught a little and traveled a lot.

"It is nice of you to spend some time with me," Papias said. "I plan to be in Ephesus for a few days. I hope to see you each day during my visit."

"When you tell a Jesus message, accuracy is very important," John said. "Someday, many will read what you are compiling."

"We hope they will," he said. "We want them to get a firm foundation before they teach."

"I have read some of it," he said. "Polycarp and I have written everything that I can remember. I hope you enjoy your stay in Ephesus."

John and Papias spent many hours together that week. John was a great help to Papias and Polycarp in documenting what Jesus did, and what he actually said. "One's memory is changed and may recall different things when aged," John said.

Papias ended his stay in Ephesus and returned to Smyrna. He was tired of walking, so he decided to take a ship to Philippi. He spent a great amount of time bent over the side rail, but he got a good view of the sea.

One day as Abraham helped John, he saw a messenger approach the house.

"I have a message from your friend and student, Polycarp," Abraham said. "He wants to come to see you. He says he would only spend about a week. He will bring a scribe and make copies of everything you have about Jesus."

"Send him a message," he said. "Tell him not to delay very long. I feel weak, but I would enjoy speaking with him."

When Polycarp read John's reply, he immediately made plans to visit him. He sent John another message.

"I have good news," Abraham said. "Polycarp is coming to see you next week. He knows that you are quite weak."

"Can you take me for a short walk?" John asked. "I think I would like to go outside. The weather is quite nice."

"I don't think we can go for a walk today," Abraham said. "The streets are full of people and animals that are being paraded to the games. I don't think it would be safe for you to go outside today."

"People and animals being paraded to the games," he said. "I would like to see that."

"You might be able to sit in the sun in front of the house," he said. "You will have to be careful."

"I will be careful," John said. "Help me find some sun."

"I will go to the market and get us some fresh fruit," he said. "Then we will take our walk. I heard the major games will end in about a week."

The stadium in Ephesus was used a few times per year for major games. The Romans from all around the area came to Ephesus to enjoy the spectacle. The Christians didn't approve of the games, but they were powerless to do anything about them.

While John enjoyed the sun, a young lady approached him.

"I am looking for an older gentleman from Bethsaida," she said. "I thought you might know him."

John was surprised that a young lady was looking for him.

"What is your name?" John asked. "Why are you looking for John?"

"My name is Mary," she said. "My great-grandfather was John's nephew."

"I am John," he said. "Your great-grandfather was Hezekiah's child. Why would you want to see me?"

"I know you traveled with Jesus," she said. "I believe in Jesus, and I came so you could baptize me."

Mary was the last person John baptized. John gave her two scrolls to take with her. One scroll told about his travels with Jesus, and the other scroll was a record of the secrets Jesus told his disciples. John had written the second scroll for Polycarp, but decided to give it to Mary. She thanked John and started her journey home.

Two days after Mary's visit, Polycarp arrived. Abraham took him to John.

"I am not feeling very strong today," John said. "Could you explain to him it will take me a while before I can be ready to talk to him? I am sure he will understand."

Abraham gave Polycarp John's message. Polycarp took a seat and talked with Abraham. As soon as John was prepared, Abraham escorted Polycarp to him.

They exchanged greetings.

"I wanted to talk with you one more time," Polycarp said. "I am very upset that you are so weak. I feel that I should spend as much time with you as possible."

"It is old age," John said. "It is something I have been blessed to receive."

"I have read everything you have written and everything else I can get a copy of. I have talked with Papias," he said. "I am beginning to understand Jesus' message."

"You are a prolific reader," John said. "What I, myself, have written is a voluminous piece of work. It makes me sleepy just thinking about reading it."

"Your writings are a great supplement to what Matthew, John Mark, and Luke wrote," he said. "In many instances, they say the same thing. You must have carefully read their material to have added so many unique instances."

"Yes, their writings are very much the same," John said. "I did try my best to add to what had already been written."

"I like it," Polycarp said. "We didn't need another version. The additional stories are great."

"Someone needed to defend Jesus' divinity," John said. "I hope it will help."

"It is helping," he said. "I have made it available to several priests."

"Everyone seems to know what Moses said a long time ago, but very few know what Jesus said sixty years ago," John said. "We have to be careful to write down Jesus' message accurately for those who follow us."

"I will make sure it will help," Polycarp said. "I will use it with my students. You never know; someday, they might become bishops and use it to teach their students."

"It would be great if the stories could be taught as one body of knowledge," John said. "They are different, but they all tell the same story of Jesus. Maybe, you can teach them as one body of knowledge."

"That is a great idea," Polycarp said. "As long as The Way continues as many small churches, they are limited. If they had one message, they could be one church. The sky would be the only limit."

"Thank you, for coming to see me," John said. "I feel better having talked with you."

"I too feel better," Polycarp said. "My students like your stories."

"I will be with you and your students. I know God will be with all of us," John said. "If you want any of my scrolls, you can have them. Put them to good use. I won't need them."

"It has been great to be with you," he said. "I will miss you."

"I will miss you," he said. "You are a good friend."

"You are the last of a very special group," Polycarp said. "I will take care of your writings, and I will make certain they are preserved for future generations."

"My end is coming," John said. "We don't know about yours."

"You are the best source of information for our future generations," he said. "Goodbye, good friend."

Polycarp returned to Philippi where he and Papias continued their work. A few weeks later, Polycarp received a message from Abraham. The message indicated John had died. Polycarp invited Abraham to come to Philippi, but Abraham decided to stay and serve the church in Ephesus.

ABOUT THE AUTHOR

The author served in the U.S. Navy and then went to college. After graduating with an engineering degree, he enjoyed careers (50 yrs.) as an engineer, businessman, and professor. He is now retired but writes novels. While reading the New Testament for over sixty years and teaching Sunday School Bible classes for twenty years, John Mench Ph.D. has been conflicted by the lack of personality within the testament. He endeavors to add perspective to the message of the testament by creating lives for those who wrote and developed Jesus' message.

Printed in the United States
By Bookmasters